TH

Drago

THE ALARIS CHRONICLES
BOOK I

MIKE SHELTON

The Dragon Orb
Copyright © 2017 by Michael Shelton

ISBN: 0-9971900-7-8
ISBN-13: 978-0-9971900-7-6
Library of Congress Control Number: 2016919677
Greenville, North Carolina

Cover Illustration by Brooke Gillette
http://brookegillette.weebly.com

Map by Robert Altbauer
www.fantasy-map.net

For More information about Mike Shelton and his books
www.MichaelSheltonBooks.com

Acknowledgements

This book is dedicated to my dear mom, Suzi Lewis. She passed away while I was finishing this book. Her influence, love, and encouragement have been a driving force in my writing and in my life. She has always been my number one fan!

As I grow as a writer there are so many people to thank. Of course my wife, Melissa, my children and extended family have always been there for me with tons of encouragement. I cannot say enough about my editors at Precision Editing, my wonderful beta readers, my illustrator and mapmaker. All have worked hard in helping me make my stories come to light.

The Dragon Orb is a work of fiction. Names, characters, places and incidents are the products of my imagination and are used fictitiously. Any resemblance to actual events, locales, or persons, living or dead, is entirely coincidental. I alone take full responsibility for any errors or omissions in this book.

-Mike-

Books by Mike Shelton

WESTERN CONTINENT BOOKS:

Books of the Realm:
The Cremelino Prophecy:
The Path Of Destiny
The Path Of Decisions
The Path Of Peace
The Blade and the Bow (A prequel novella to The Cremelino Prophecy)

Dragon Rider Books:
The Alaris Chronicles:
The Dragon Orb
The Dragon Rider
The Dragon King
Prophecy Of The Dragon (A prequel novella to The Alaris Chronicles)

The Dragon Artifacts:
The Golden Dragon
The Golden Scepter
The Golden Empire

GEMSTONES OF WAYLAND BOOKS:

The TruthSeer Archives:
TruthStone
TruthSpell
TruthSeer
The Stones of Power (A prequel novella to The TruthSeer Archives)

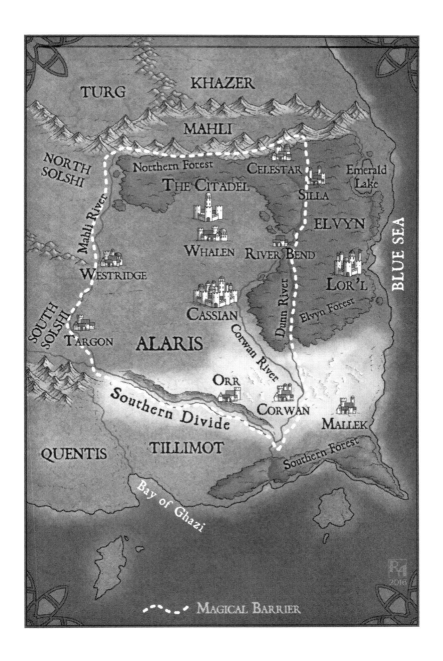

See Color map at www.MichaelSheltonBooks.com

CHAPTER ONE

Allison Stenos, wizard apprentice, walked with guarded steps down the main road leading into the city of Orr. Her shoulder-length black hair, bangs falling over one eye, framed her youthful, pale face. A small smile tugged at her lips as she surveyed the quiet street around her.

Gorn Mahron, her mentor, strode next to her. His hardened, battle-ready body belied his years. Only the graying hair indicated that his age was past what most people would call his prime. However, as a wizard, he could live close to one hundred years. Battle wizards often lived shorter lives, however, due to their dangerous professions.

"Stay alert, Alli," Gorn whispered without turning his head.

"Always, Mentor." She skipped forward a step, as she spun a foot-long knife in her right hand.

"They're here. I can sense them." Gorn peered down a small alley to his right.

The hot desert air stilled, and this usually bustling city, at the southernmost point of the kingdom of Alaris, sat too quiet for the middle of the day. Alli glimpsed a few women peering out of the corners of their windows, pulling their heads back when she glanced their way.

"Why don't these King-men attack in a cooler place?" Alli wiped the sweat from her forehead.

Gorn glanced her way and motioned her over to the side of the street. "I don't think these rebels care about the heat. They only care about disrupting the Chief Judge's government."

Alli nodded, her eyes darting from building to building. She and Gorn were leading a battalion of the Chief Judge's soldiers. They had heard about a group of rebels planning an attack on the governor's mansion in Orr. The King-men, called such for their desire to have a king rather than a system of judges ruling the kingdom, had become more bold lately.

Gorn looked back and signaled for the rest of the battalion to proceed.

Alli and Gorn turned a corner, walking toward the main city square. Two men jumped down from a window, swords in hand, and attacked the two wizards. Dozens of others appeared in the town square and with yells ran toward the wizards and their battalion of men.

With her knife still in one hand, Alli used her other hand to pull her silver sword from the leather scabbard at her waist. She swung purposefully around her in a broad arc, widening the circle of attackers near her. The hot orange sun sat directly behind her, sending out long shadows from the tan stone buildings bordering the town square. The two battle wizards pushed through the attackers, Gorn moving off to Alli's right. They used their physical weapons now, saving their magic for when they would need it the most.

The determined men opposite Alli growled at being beaten back by a mere slip of a teenage girl. Embarrassment and frustration clouded their red faces, and they pushed forward with renewed determination.

With no warning, a young boy ran out of one of the town's buildings, his mother chasing after him. Alli turned toward him, even though she knew she shouldn't fall prey to the distraction. Out of the corner of her eye, she noticed that fighting had erupted in the town square and was spreading down the side streets of Orr. If the boy didn't get back inside, he would not survive.

The men used her distraction with the boy to press home their advantage. Alli grabbed one man's head and pushed him to the ground. Jumping up onto his back, she flipped over another attacker, reaching down to scoop up the boy with a well-toned arm. At the same time, she gathered her magical power and pushed it out from her hand with brutal force. The magic ran along the edge of her polished sword and out the end of the blade in a bright yellow flame.

Holding the boy with her left arm, she held the sword's grip tightly with her right hand and turned in a circle. The flame shot out toward the remaining men in the area. Six men fell instantly, three stumbled and tried to regroup, and two ran off screaming toward a trough of water, trying to put out their burning clothes.

The terrified mother of the boy grabbed him back with a tearful thank you. Alli refocused on the fight. Turning, she saw Gorn a few yards away, shaking his head at her in bewilderment. She shrugged and then plowed into a group of fighting men gathering in the far side of the square. Her battle moves were more a melodic dance than practiced motions. She flowed over the battlefield, barely touching the ground.

Between the thrusts of her sword and the fire flaming from it, she took care of another dozen men.

Eventually, she found herself back to back with her mentor. Extinguishing the flames and returning to her knife and sword, she swatted away a new round of rebels.

"Allison, why did you do that?" Gorn shouted over his shoulder as he fought off a few of the more brave renegades.

"Do what?" Alli jumped up in the air and kicked a large bearded man to the ground.

"Save that little boy. He almost got you killed."

"But he didn't." She turned to her right and parried the blade of a man twice her size. He mistook her size for inexperience, and she jumped into the air while spinning and came around, kicking him hard in the gut. She turned to face her mentor, the sounds of the man, groaning on the ground, fading from her ears.

"We'll talk about this later," Gorn said, wiping the blood from his sword onto a cloth hanging from his belt. "The boy was stupid for leaving the buildings."

Alli needed to concentrate, but she couldn't let this go. "Gorn, most of these people are innocent. They don't deserve to die."

Gorn only grunted. A large, dirty man tried to sneak up behind Alli, but Gorn brought his hand up and released a straight line of fire from his extended fingertips.

"Thanks." Alli smiled sweetly. Her youthful eyes and pale-skinned face stood out in innocent contrast to the bloody battle.

She brushed her dark bangs out of her eyes and took a

deep breath to calm her nerves. The heat of the desert city was affecting her more than had the exertion of the battle.

Gorn grunted again, but this time with less care. Alli knew she infuriated him. Gorn had been in charge of her training since she had left the Citadel a year before, at age fourteen, and she loved him like a grandfather.

No one could beat Alli in hand-to-hand combat or with weapons of any kind. Her powers far exceeded her rank of apprentice, and many men underestimated her and mistook her youth and her slight build as weaknesses. This usually happened to be the last mistake they made. However, she really would like to be treated as a wizard rather than as an apprentice that many thought they could push around.

Alli spied a young man moving on the other side of the courtyard, trying not to be seen. Before she could do anything, she felt the heat of magic shoot out from Gorn's fingers, racing toward the man. Throwing out her own hands, Alli drew on the power of wind and pushed the wizard's flame back. Continuing on, the wind blew into a couple of old crates, knocking them down on top of the man, stopping him in his tracks, while protecting him from the heat of Gorn's magic flame.

"You don't need to kill everyone, Gorn! There are other ways to take a man down."

"But I am a battle wizard, and so will you be someday, Alli. You must learn that, in war, everyone is a potential threat."

"So I shouldn't help *you* out, then?"

"What?" Gorn's eyebrows shot up.

"See you later," Alli said and walked away from Gorn as a man tackled him from behind. She glanced back and grinned at

Gorn, lying on the ground. She knew he could take care of himself.

The captain of the battalion called out for assistance. Alli ran over to where another pocket of fighting had broken out, on the other side of the large town square. She pulled out two knives from the tops of her soft leather boots and threw them at the legs of two men, who were about to take the captain down. They went down instead, holding their thighs and screaming in pain.

The dry wind picked up. Her heightened sense of smell caught the odor of blood and sweat on its hot breeze. This heat washed over her for a moment until she pushed it from her thoughts. She thought instead of the forests farther north, near the magical barrier, where she had grown up. She wished she was there and not on the edge of this forsaken desert.

The people of Orr lived in the middle of the great desert, in the far southern region of Alaris. The Mahli River, running south along the western barrier, here flowed down through the canyons of the great divide toward the southeast, eventually joining the Dunn River to the east. The only water around for miles, the Mahli did little to alleviate the heat. Rumors held that the desert continued for miles south of the barrier, giving way ultimately to more fertile farmlands. But, of course, the barrier of magic around Alaris blocked anyone from confirming the fact.

The ground was hard-packed dirt; the buildings, a dull brown, all made from stone and clay; and the wind blew constantly. The only wood around was used for fires and pieces of furniture and most likely came from the southern end of the

Elvyn Forest, to the east. Generations of desert living had made the skin of those in the southern region darker than that of the people farther north.

Orr was normally a peaceful city, but then someone in town recently invited a group of King-men to disrupt the peace and draw the Chief Judge's main battalion into battle. The dreary wasteland got on Alli's nerves, and she became tired of innocent people getting hurt and dying for no other fact than that they lived where the King-men had decided to attack.

During a brief respite from the fighting, she scanned the town square. Someone needed to end this fight. Looking at Gorn, she realized her mentor would disapprove. But she had been given her powers for a reason, and she would use them now to stop other innocents from dying.

Holding her sword high and straight in the air, she chanted a few words softly. White fire erupted out of the tip. She spun the pommel of the blade vertically in the palm of her hand, and the white-hot light ran out of the sword in a dozen separate tendrils.

"Protect the innocent," she whispered to the flames.

The first man the flames hit fell in a startled heap on the ground. The next group tried to run, but the flames circled around their bodies, holding them tightly, until they, too, collapsed to the ground and gave up their weapons. Even the soldiers in her own company backed away, afraid of standing in the way of the wild wizard's fire.

The fire raced through the crowd and down the dirt lanes, sparing some and taking others, until the tendrils joined again and raced toward one lone man. His long legs carried him into the center of the town square.

"I surrender!" the tall, unshaven man shouted as he threw his bloodied sword down and looked around wildly.

Alli swept her hand back toward herself, and immediately the flame extinguished. The captain and a few others rushed forward to grab the man in the center of the town square, the leader of the attack.

"Where did you learn that?" Gorn moved to her side.

Alli shrugged her shoulders. "It just felt right."

"Felt right? You know the rules. You are only an apprentice," he said. His thick gray eyebrows displayed his displeasure, and his forehead crinkled up in anger.

"It's done, isn't it? No one else needed to die on our side. We gave them enough chances to stop." Alli glared up at Gorn in defiance. "The fight needed to end."

"I don't care," his voice boomed, causing a few soldiers to turn toward the two wizards. "I am the master, and you are the apprentice."

Alli pushed her sword roughly into her scabbard and tried not to clench her fists. Her heart beat fast with anger. Why shouldn't she be allowed to use all her powers in a battle? She was a battle wizard, apprentice rank or not.

"This is only because I'm a young girl. I have trained for over five years at the Citadel and now, at your side, for the past year. Most men are only in training for three or four years, and I am more powerful than wizards at levels one and two—maybe even more powerful than you. You cannot control me forever, Gorn."

"You are only fifteen, Allison!" Gorn shouted in

exasperation. "You are not old enough to be a full wizard—that's simply the way it is."

"My age should not define my rank." She stormed away, leaving Gorn standing alone. She approached the captain and the captured prisoner, pausing to listen to their conversation.

Even while on his knees, the rebel leader was a tall man, his head almost coming up to Alli's chin. Blood dripped down his arms: wounds from the battle.

"Why were you trying to take over the governor's palace?" the captain asked. "What did you do with the southern judge, Azeem?"

"You can't stop it from happening," the man cried out. "We will have a king!"

The captain spat on the ground, his spittle soaking into the dry dirt. "Not this again. The Chief Judge has been lenient so far with this *king* thing, but he can charge you with treason for what you did here today. That would be along with arson, civil unrest, and murder of some of my men. Now, where are the southern judge and the governor?"

"It was not my job to take them; that was for others. I don't know where he is."

"And, what was your job?"

"To disrupt things as much as possible. We need a strong king to hold Alaris together. The Chief Judge is weak. We want someone more powerful, someone who can break through the magic barrier holding us apart from the other kingdoms. We want a king like the other lands have."

His words sounded forced to Alli: memorized lines spewing forth from a small mind.

"What do you know of other lands, renegade?" the captain spat. "The barrier protects us from them, from the wars they would wage against us. Wise men put the barrier in place to save us from the other lands' evils and ambitions. We don't need a king. We have the judges. They have protected us for one hundred fifty years and will continue to do so. Do you deny the right of Chief Judge Daymian Khouri to rule this land?"

All of the captain's remaining men gathered around them.

"The Chief Judges stole the kingship away from the rightful rulers. We need to restore the nobility."

"You realize you now speak treason." The captain motioned for some of his men to lift the prisoner up to his feet. The captain took a step back so as not to appear diminished in size next to the sizable rebel.

The captain turned to Alli. "Battle Wizard Apprentice, what should be his punishment?"

The captain's attention surprised Alli. She wondered if Gorn had put him up to this—another one of his tests for her. Shifting her feet, she pulled the cloth band from her head, wet with the sweat of fighting. Then she leaned over slightly and shook her black hair out, loosening it from the nape of her neck.

"You want my advice?"

The captain nodded his head.

She scanned the buildings and saw some of the townspeople edging out of their doors. At least a few of these families were fatherless after today. And this man in front of her was one of the leaders of the opposition.

"Do you have a family?" Alli asked the rebel. A murmur of surprise rippled from the crowd.

"What does that have to do with anything?" one of the men asked.

The captain hushed him with a raised hand.

"Do you?" she asked again.

"No. Wife died in the desert."

All stood in silence except for the constant rustling of wind around the stone buildings. Alli took two steps toward the rebel leader, putting her hands on her hips, over her leather shirt.

"Then you shall join her today," she said. Having delivered her verdict, she strode away. Her throat was parched. She needed some water.

The captain called two men forward to take the rebel leader out behind one of the buildings for execution.

Alli reached the crude water well. She sat down on its smooth, stone edge and dipped in the bucket that hung from a rope for a drink. The water felt good going over her parched lips. Oh, to be back in the Elvyn Forest or to travel along the Dunn River. She tried to make these memories cool her down.

Taking a deep breath, she closed her eyes momentarily. This blasted heat was infuriating. When she opened them again, a young boy stood in front of her, the same boy she had saved from the battle earlier. He was not more than five or six. His dark hair, peppered with sand, hung in his eyes. Those brown eyes, sitting deep in his darkening face, begged for her attention.

"I want to be a battle wizard like you." The young boy

stood with his chest puffed up.

"Oh, you do, huh?" Alli leaned forward. "Why is that?"

"Cause I want to kill the bad guys." He stomped his foot to emphasize the point.

"It's not all about killing." Alli peered behind the boy and saw Gorn approaching.

"It's not?"

"Oh no, you have to practice a lot, eat healthy, and do what people tell you to do." With this, she glanced up at her mentor and gave him a smile.

"Oh." The boy seemed to be thinking it over. "I don't like it when people tell me what to do."

Alli and Gorn laughed.

"Neither do I." Alli stood up and tussled the boy's hair.

The boy's mother came up to him. "I'm sorry—again. I can't keep track of him: always scampering around."

"That's all right. He told me how he wants to be a battle wizard."

"Oh, he did?" She looked down lovingly at her son. "Ever since you arrived yesterday, he hasn't been able to keep his eyes off you. Pardon me for saying, but aren't you too young to be a battle wizard?"

Alli's face reddened slightly, but before she might say anything in anger, Gorn stepped in.

"She may still be an apprentice, ma'am, but she is one of the most powerful battle wizards in all of Alaris."

Alli raised her eyebrows at him.

"Sometimes we forget that pure wizard power doesn't have anything to do with age. She stopped this battle today and did it without losing any more innocent people."

It was a rare day when Gorn praised her so.

"That's what I want to do, Mama, help the in…the inno…the…" The young boy was having a hard time saying the word *innocent*. "Good people," he said, his ears turning red.

"Well, then start doing your chores and eating healthy," Alli said to the boy. His mother led him away with a smile.

Gorn turned to Alli. "I'm sorry about what I said before. There has never been anyone like you. Well, there are a few others like you also—a new generation of apprentices that seem to exhibit extreme talent. We, the wizards at the Citadel, are not sure how to handle you."

"Wow, quite an admission, coming from such a great wizard." Alli flashed a large smile at him. "Maybe there is hope for you yet."

"Now, despite the apology, what you did back there, with the white flame—"

"I know. I know. It's dangerous, and I shouldn't do things like that. But, Gorn, it was the only way to end this infantile conflict. Fewer died this way than fighting until the last man falls. You might think I reacted without thinking, but I didn't. I thought about it, and it made sense. I thought it was the right thing to do."

"The right thing to do is not always the best thing to do." Gorn pulled a pail from the well and lifted a waterskin from his side. His stomach rumbled, and he ran his hand over it.

"Hungry?"

"Don't try to change the subject. But, yes, I am. I don't see how you can do all that fighting and expend so much energy without getting hungry. You need to gain some weight. You are too thin to fight all day like this."

"You are the one tiring. I am doing fine." Alli stood with hands on her hips.

Gorn laughed and motioned for Alli to follow him. "Allison Stenos, you might very well be one of the most dangerous people I know. One minute, you are comfortably ordering a man's execution; the next, you are sitting with a young boy and giving him advice. You wield mercy as quickly as you dispense justice. You are going to be extremely difficult for a future husband to figure out."

Alli grew serious and stopped. She put her small hand on Gorn's arm and stopped him. "Gorn, don't ever think my swift justice is comfortable. Don't think I like killing or deciding to take the life of a war criminal. Don't make me into a monster for dispensing justice."

Gorn took a step back, and fear flashed in his eyes for a brief moment. "Alli, I didn't mean it that way. I just meant that you are complicated to understand. I'm sorry if I offended you."

Alli relaxed. "Two apologies in one day? I'm beginning to think you are getting soft in your old age."

"Ouch."

"Now, let's go find you a good meal." She pushed him forward and headed toward their camp on the edge of town.

"Now, *that's* something I can understand."

"You'd better hurry and take your fill. It's a long road back to Cassian. The Chief Judge will want a report as soon as possible."

CHAPTER TWO

In the middle of a small practice yard inside the Chief Judge's castle, in the capital city of Cassian, Roland Tyre danced around his opponent and flashed quick smiles to the sidelines—all to the delight of his many female onlookers. Their squeals and cheers motivated the sixteen-year-old more than did his instructors.

Brushing his blond hair out of his eyes, Roland parried the sword of his opponent, one of the more seasoned guards in the castle, and beat him back a few feet. He gazed up at the crowd with his dark blue, penetrating eyes and noticed one of the more lovely girls wiggling her fingers at him in a friendly wave. He pursed his lips at her in a mock kiss, sending ripples of giggles through that clique of teenage girls.

It was a warm summer day, and Roland was getting hot and thirsty. Sweat beaded on his forehead and dripped down the sides of his handsome face and square chin. Then his opponent swept toward him with a fierce blow. Roland jumped up into the air—higher than a normal man should be able to— and followed this with a quick wave of his hand. The guard opened his eyes wide in astonishment as his sword seemed to leave his hand of its own volition, flying upward, and then crashed to the dirt.

"That's not fair." The guard reached down to grab his

sword.

But Roland put his foot down on the blade. "War is not fair."

"What do you grasp of war or battles?" the seasoned guard sneered. "You are going to be a counselor wizard."

Roland's jaw clenched. The guard had hit a sore spot "I know that if I need to fight, I will use everything at my disposal to win."

"There is no honor in what you did, apprentice." Onius Neeland, a thin, older man with long, graying hair, approached the pair. "Yes, in a real battle, you may need to use all of your resources. But, in practice, with someone who is helping you learn, you should restrain yourself."

"I don't need lectures, Onius," Roland snapped as he removed his foot from the guard's sword. "And I don't need any more practice today. I was hot and wanted a drink, so I ended the fight."

"You should apologize."

Roland cringed inside. Onius Neeland could be so infuriating with his sense of honor and patience. Roland stared into the older man's blue eyes. Being a wizard slowed his aging so that, even though he was close to eighty, Onius looked like he was in his fifties. Onius, a third-level counselor wizard, had been guiding judges for a generation before Roland was even born.

Continuing to put on a show for his spectators, Roland bowed deeply to the guard and, in his most gracious voice, said, "My dear good man, I apologize for any slight I have given thee. My intentions were not to offend. I'm afraid that, with the hot weather and the looks of the beautiful damsels upon me, my thinking became irrational this day." He bent down with a flourish, picked up the dirtied sword, and handed it reverently to the guard.

"No offense taken, Sir," the guard said with a forced smile. He knew to tread lightly around the young wizard apprentice.

Roland turned and bowed again to the ladies, making sure he gave a special wink to the one who had waved at him so nicely earlier. Hopefully, he could meet her later that evening in a corner of the town square for a few kisses.

Then Onius pulled Roland off the field, moving toward the kitchen. "Well done," he said in a mocking voice.

"Oh, Onius, don't be so stiff. You're letting your age get the better of you. I was only having fun out there."

"Your magic is not something to have fun with, Roland. All wizards have a responsibility that needs to be taken seriously."

"Now you sound like our stuffy Chief Judge." Roland rolled his blue eyes upward, toward the castle. "All about *duty* and *responsibility*."

"Chief Judge Daymian Khouri is a good man—better than most of us." Onius stopped and glared down at Roland. His tall, thin frame still stood a few inches above the growing youth's, but Roland had grown tall in the last year.

"I know he is good and honorable and responsible, but maybe, if he tolerated more fun, the people would relate to him more and not be wanting a king instead."

Onius seemed to grow serious and surveyed the area before saying in a lowered voice, "You mustn't talk about that in the open, Roland. You should appreciate—as much as anyone—what a touchy subject that is right now. Things will work out for the best."

Roland considered Onius with suspicion. "You know how it's going to work out, do you, Onius? I haven't run across that power yet."

Onius opened his eyes wide at this implication, his gray eyebrows rising on his wrinkled forehead. "I don't know what you mean, Roland. Now, move it. You will need to learn to be more responsible in your training before you can figure out the doings of the government of Alaris."

Roland pouted. "I was only having fun out there," he said under his breath.

"Roland!" roared Onius.

Shaking his head to get the sweaty hair off his neck and out of his face, Roland felt a flash of anger. "I *would* take some responsibility if you gave me something interesting to do, Onius. Sitting around and reading about history, judges, and negotiations is tedious." He barely controlled the urge to stomp his foot. "You and the Council at the Citadel know I'm more powerful than any other apprentice. Besides skill I have learned as a counselor I also have strengths as a battle and scholar wizard. Raise me from an apprentice and treat me as a full wizard, and I might show some responsibility."

A servant came out of the kitchen then, saw the two wizards arguing, and with a small yelp, turned and ran back inside. The arguments of Roland and his mentor were notorious in the castle.

Roland toppled forward as a swat of air smacked his

backside. "Ouch. Why did you do that?"

"Because you are acting like a spoiled child, Roland." Onius shook his bony finger at him. "Do you know why the Wizard Council hasn't raised you to a full wizard yet? It is exactly because of what you just said. You think you possess all of this power, and you think you deserve those titles and responsibilities and that everyone loves you and swoons over you. When you can get your head on straight, use your powers responsibly, show some humility, and accomplish something of note, you might earn the right to move from apprentice to a level-one wizard. Great things could be in store for you, Roland; you do have potential. But you need to figure out what you want soon. Changes are coming."

"What do you mean *changes*?" Roland asked.

Onius closed his mouth tight, as if he feared saying too much. "Things are happening in the kingdom, Roland, if you haven't noticed, and you might not have much time to straighten yourself out."

Roland hung his head low for a moment, feeling actually surprised at this outburst from the usually even-tempered wizard. Something was bothering his mentor of late. He was more uptight than normal.

What Onius had said, about taking responsibility, made sense. But Roland couldn't change who he was. The power was so strong in himself he didn't know how to handle it sometimes. It was a part of him, like his arms or legs or ears. None of the other wizards understood. Maybe though—just maybe he did need to find something good to accomplish. He made a mental note to find something to work on that would show Onius he was ready to be a full wizard.

Onius stood, glaring down at him, clearly waiting for a response.

Roland lifted his head in a slow and deliberate motion, his eyes growing big. The corners of his mouth turned upward, and he began to laugh.

"And, what is so funny now, my spoiled apprentice?" Onius forced a smile.

"You used your magic to spank me. I've never seen you lose your temper so. It's actually quite funny."

Onius joined Roland in barking out a laugh at the situation..

After a moment, the young apprentice wizard glanced around and, much to his dismay, saw that his gaggle of girls was gone. He frowned for a second, until he thought of one of the cook's helpers, a finely shaped, dark-haired girl only slightly younger than himself. He smiled again.

Saying a farewell to Onius, Roland walked through one of the back doors of the castle and into the hot kitchen. Responsibility could wait until the next day.

He grabbed some freshly baked bread off of the large wooden counter in the middle of the warm kitchen. Fetching a tall cup of ale for himself to go with the bread, he was disappointed to learn that only the cook, a large woman older than his mother, tended the ovens that afternoon. So he headed off to his room to change and relax before heading out to the city to find the girl from the practice yard. She had such a nice smile!

Passing by the Chief Judge's chambers on his way to his

own made Roland rethink the conversation with Onius. So he decided that, before going to town, he would go to the library and ask Bak about the history of wizards and where he actually fit in.

* * *

Inside the Chief Judge's chambers sat Daymian Khouri himself. Always amazed at the amount of paperwork needing to be done to oversee the other judges and the people of Alaris, he shook his head to clear it for a few more minutes.

There were four other judges, spread throughout the land. The people democratically voted for all five judges, with the Chief Judge being voted on by the other judges. They kept the laws of Alaris along with support from the captains of the armies and the constables of the smaller cities. But there never seemed to be an end to the petty squabbling. Sometimes he wondered if he had made a difference. He had been in Cassian now for seven years, three of those as Chief Judge.

"Sir, do you need anything else tonight?" His head steward had stepped into the room, without Daymian noticing.

"No. I will be retiring soon. Please leave a message for my wife. I will be done within the hour."

The steward left, and Daymian rose from the padded chair. He stretched his tall, tired back and ran his hands down his long, thin sideburns, ending at his short, brown beard. The white speckles in his once black hair stood out in contrast with his light brown skin. His back hurt more now than when he was younger. Being a large man, he didn't like to be crouched down in the small office chairs for hours on end. But that seemed to be happening more in recent days.

He walked over to a window. It was still light outside, though the sun had just set behind the farms and fields to the west. A few lamps in nearby homes began to show as the summer twilight settled in. The pink sky reflected off the Corwan River to the east, forming a colorful ribbon, running from the Dunn River in the northeast, then back southwest to join it again near Corwan. The Corwan River supplied all the water for the city's needs.

The city of Cassian was as old as they had histories for, but it had only been the capital of Alaris for the past one hundred fifty years, ever since the barrier had gone up around Alaris and the new government system of judges had been enacted. When the old king and government had been replaced by the system of judges, the capital was moved from Whalen, near the wizards' Citadel, to Cassian, a beautiful and peaceful city in the middle of Alaris. Daymian had worked hard to minimize the poor and beggars. And, though crime would never be totally eradicated, he felt proud of all his accomplishments during his time as a lower judge in Orr and now as Chief Judge of the land.

He watched the people walking home in the warm summer air as vendors closed up their neatly organized shops for the day. Then Daymian felt a strange breeze blow by him and thought he heard a noise in the room. He turned and ran his eyes over the room. It all seemed in order. He took in the large tapestry on the wall next to the door, the stone fireplace he had not used since late spring, the shelves of books outlining the history of the law of Alaris, and then his desk. The feeling that something in the room had changed lingered in the back of his exhausted mind.

So Daymian closed the window and leaned back over his desk to straighten his papers. Then a letter caught his eye. He hadn't noticed it before. He opened it with a quick tear and cringed. Wizard Kanzar Centari had invited—no, that was too nice a word for it—*commanded* Daymian to the Citadel for a meeting.

Daymian threw down the letter in disgust. He needed to talk to Onius first thing in the morning. Onius understood Kanzar more than anyone. Daymian knew that others plotted behind his back because some of the people wanted a king, and he would bet Kanzar was involved. The man plainly loved power.

As Chief Judge, Daymian needed to visit one more place this evening before retiring to his living quarters. He needed to see Bakari in the library. There were rumors of the magical barrier weakening in places, especially along its eastern edge— the boundary they shared with Elvyn. The wizards, including Onius, had remained closed-lipped about it. If anyone knew the information, it would be Bakari. In the past year, Daymian had learned many times to rely on the young scholar wizard's memory and wealth of knowledge.

Daymian reached over to pick up the cup sitting on the edge of the table. As he brought it to his lips he paused for a moment and frowned. The cup, still chilled, dripped with condensation. He didn't remember having asked for anything to drink recently. He reasoned that it must be from the steward anticipating his needs and bringing it in before leaving for the evening.

He took a swallow from the silver cup and brought it with him as he headed down the darkening corridors of *his* castle. This thought startled him. He had never thought of it as his castle before. That was dangerous. He knew he served here for only a five-year term. And he was only a servant of the people, a judge. There was a big difference between that and a king. From what he understood of history, kings only brought problems. Kings brought wars. And the last king of Alaris, before the barrier went up, was a powerful wizard. The main purpose of creating the barrier was to protect Alaris from greedy kings in nearby kingdoms.

Two guards fell in behind him as he walked to the library. Their footsteps were quiet on the long run of blue woven carpet running down the middle of the halls in this part of the castle. As he rounded the last corner, Daymian bumped into someone, and a portion of his drink splashed out, dampening the carpet. The other man stumbled but put a hand to the wall to keep from falling down

"Watch where you're going," the other man said before looking up. The guards tensed and moved to intervene.

"Roland?" Daymian reached a helpful hand over to his apprentice counselor.

Roland's face turned red, and he apologized. The guards relaxed. They recognized Roland and nodded their heads to him.

"What are you doing in this wing?" Daymian asked.

"Oh, just hanging around, waiting to be knocked over,"

Roland said with a wink, trying to use laughter to diffuse the awkwardness of the situation.

Daymian didn't laugh. Roland needed to be more serious about his duties if he planned to be a counselor to one of the judges in the land. Taking a long drink from his cup, Daymian motioned for Roland to follow him to the library.

"That's where I was going," Roland mumbled.

As Daymian reached for the handle of the door, a wave of dizziness washed over him and he swooned to the side. One of the guards reached over and tried to steady him. He began to choke and felt his eyes starting to roll back in his head. Then his fingers relaxed around the cup, and it fell to the floor, bouncing twice, spilling its remaining cool liquid on the carpet in front of the library's door.

CHAPTER THREE

"Bak!" Roland yelled, pushing the door of the library open with a bang.

The young, dark-skinned youth with short, dark hair and homemade glasses came running to the door. He seemed out of breath and almost tripped on his long scholar's robes.

"Roland?"

"The Chief Judge has collapsed."

Bakari stood for a moment, staring at the fallen judge. Then he took off his glasses and pinched his nose.

"Bak, stop standing there and help us!" Roland shouted. "Pull your head out of your books. We need a place to lay him down."

"Of course. Of course. On the couch here." He motioned them to a well-built brown couch in the sitting area of the castle library. Books lined a multitude of shelves around them.

Since Bakari was already a level one wizard, protocol dictated he take the lead—even though Roland was more powerful. So Roland watched as Bakari ran his hand over the Chief Judge's body.

"He's been poisoned."

Brilliant deduction was what Roland wanted to say. He could tell that. Sometimes Bakari's head was so far into his books it took him a while to return to the real world.

"The cup was in his hand."

One of the guards started to fetch the cup from the doorway, but Roland flipped his hand out and brought the cup through the air to them. Bakari sniffed it and closed his eyes.

"Well?" Roland urged. "What is it?"

Bakari didn't acknowledge Roland except to hold up his finger to tell Roland to wait a moment.

Roland sat impatiently, looking across at the young scholar wizard. Bakari had grown up at the Citadel as an orphan and, during that time, had won the respect and favor of most of the other wizards for his ability to recall anything he had seen or read. And his being named a full wizard a year earlier, at fourteen years old, got on Roland's nerves. Roland ground his teeth together. While Roland did everything quickly and impetuously, Bak moved slowly, thought slowly, and took his time doing everything.

"Maloak," Bakari said.

Roland was once again amazed at what Bakari could remember from the many books he had read. Maybe there was still hope for the kid after all.

"Should we find the physician?" one of the burly guards asked. The man clearly didn't want to be held responsible for the Chief Judge dying on his watch. He would end up, at best, working along the magical barrier.

"The antidote can only be made through the use of a magic spell," Bakari said. "We must get Onius. The Chief Judge doesn't have much time."

Bakari stood up to go find the older wizard.

"Bak, no. Wait." Roland closed his eyes. "I will."

To the obvious surprise of everyone in the room, Roland remained there and kept his eyes closed. He pictured Onius in his mind, concentrated hard, and then spoke to his mentor's mind.

Onius, come to the library now. The Chief Judge has been poisoned.

He felt a response, as if Onius had actually jumped up in surprise. So he reiterated the point. *Hurry.* Then Roland opened his eyes and saw Bakari holding his head in his hands.

"What did you do? My head is killing me."

"I called Onius with my mind," Roland said matter-of-factly.

"Well, your power washed over me on its way there. You need to learn to focus better."

Roland grunted and furrowed his eyebrows at the young wizard standing opposite him.

Bakari smiled. "Sorry, Roland, I didn't mean it wasn't amazing. It's just that you killed my head. I don't know of anyone else with that ability... except for a few level four or five wizards. How did you do that?"

"Yes, how?" boomed a loud voice as Onius rushed into the room, his robes swirling around him. "A great scholarly question but one that can be answered later. Now, what happened?"

Bakari showed Onius the empty cup, in which the residue of the poison, mixed with a chilled juice, still lingered.

"Water. We need water," Onius informed them. "We need to dilute the poison before it gets farther in his system."

Roland glanced down and frowned. "I can't move water yet," he mumbled. *At least, not without making a mess*, he thought to himself. So he jumped up and ran down the hall to a small common room that was on the same floor. He returned in moments with a full mug.

Onius put his large, bony hands under the Chief Judge's head and brought it up a foot from the cushions of the couch. He lifted water to the Chief Judge's lips and watched as his reflexes swallowed automatically. Then the old wizard leaned down and listened to Daymian's heartbeat.

"Slow and fading," Onius said.

By this time, others had heard the commotion and begun to gather around. Daymian's wife, Mara, came in and collapsed on the ground in tears. Bakari tried to comfort her but didn't succeed much.

"Papa?" The sound of Daymian's ten-year-old son reached their ears from the hallway. "What happened to Papa?"

"I need quiet here to work," Onius grumbled. He motioned for the guards to take the child away. "Roland, get me an oak leaf."

"What?"

"This is no time for your questions." Onius's expression was grave. "Go. A few oak leaves and more water."

Roland motioned a guard to come with him. After telling the man to fetch the water, Roland ran down three flights of stairs to gather the oak leaves. A group of girls squealed and jumped out of his way, almost falling down the stairs.

"Sorry," he said, giving his attention to one in particular. Her soft blonde curls hung down in ringlets to her shoulders. He hadn't noticed her in the castle before.

He refocused himself as he took the last three stairs with

one jump. He needed to do what Onius had asked him and show his level of responsibility to his mentor. The leader of Alaris was on the brink of death, and it all rested on Roland getting the leaves for the antidote. The Chief Judge seemed like a boring man to Roland, but he would never have wished him to die.

Slamming the ornate castle doors open—to the chagrin of the two guards—Roland ran out to the lawn in front of the great, four-story castle. He raced past more guards at the bottom of some steps and ran to the big oak tree out front. He paused and caught his breath.

The castle grounds were filled with waves of colorful flowers. To Roland's left, dahlias larger than his hand bloomed in gardens surrounded by freshly cut grass. To his right, lavender asters stood over bright purple petunias. The leaves of the oak tree stood on enormous branches high above his reach. So, without thinking it through, Roland gathered his power and pushed out his hand to bring a few leaves down.

In his urgency, Roland caused the entire tree to lose all its leaves within a matter of seconds. He cringed inside at his lack of control. But he jumped to catch two large leaves, floating down through the air above him, and then ran back toward the castle. The guards' eyes were wide as Roland ran back inside.

He paused only a moment to glance back outside and then wished he hadn't. Oak leaves drifted to the ground, soon to cover the entire garden area around the central portion of the lawns. Roland groaned out loud and took the stairs up, two at a time.

He shoved the leaves into Onius's hand along with the

water the guard had already fetched for him.

"The Maloak is a rare oak, whose leaves, when mixed with healing magic, can slow down the heart rate until, eventually, the person will die." Onius crushed the oak leaves into the mug. "This oak, being a relative of the Maloak, along with a spell, should help to combat the poison."

"I hope he survives," Bakari said softly.

Daymian's wife moaned, and one of the guards picked her up off the floor and helped her to a nearby chair.

Roland watched Onius carefully. If he was to be a counselor to the judges, he would need to protect them as well. Onius settled his right hand over the top of the mug and chanted some words. Roland felt the effects of the words in the air, but the spell seemed incomplete to him. He didn't know why.

Onius began to lift the mug to the Chief Judge's lips.

"Wait," Roland said with so much authority that Onius stopped. His gray, bushy eyebrows rose in question to Roland's outburst.

Roland put his right hand over Onius's and pulled both hands back over the cup. "Say it again."

"Roland, we don't have time for you to learn this right now."

"Just do it," Roland said with such force that Onius complied, and Bakari took a step back at the command.

When both of their hands hovered over the cup, Onius chanted his spell once again, and then Roland added two words to the end: *Kaolam Novis.* He didn't know why, but he knew it was the right thing to do. The power flowed through him immediately and into the cup. This was one more reason to talk to Bakari about his magic.

Onius had jumped when Roland spoke those last words. "Kaolam Novis?" Onius asked. He frowned and then added softly, "*Maloak* backwards and the spell word for *reverse*." He brought the mug to Daymian's lips and forced a cupful into him. Everyone waited in silence.

"How did you know?" Onius gazed at Roland with wide eyes. "You haven't learned that yet."

Roland only shrugged.

"We'll talk about it later." Onius gave Roland a look that brooked no argument.

Moments later, color began to return to the leader of Alaris's face, and his heart rate strengthened. Onius told the guards to take the Chief Judge to his bed and informed his wife that, after a good night's sleep, the Chief Judge should be fine, although still a little weak for a few days. With that, the guards carried Daymian from the library with his wife and son in tow.

Onius, still sitting on the floor, leaned his head back against a chair and closed his eyes. Using magic always took a toll on the user. The more strength the spell held, the more weak the person's body was after using it.

Roland watched his mentor and wondered what he thought about Roland's ability. He liked Onius and learned a lot from him, but he knew he had done things today that couldn't be explained. Roland walked over to a sizeable window and put his hands on the sill, the residue of power still coursing through his veins. He was not tired, as he should have been after such a feat of magic. In fact, he felt invigorated.

Bakari rose and made himself busy cleaning things up, then bid farewell and left the room.

Roland continued to gaze out the window. In the dark but torch-lit evening, he could see the comings and goings of guards and of others around the castle grounds. They went about their routines as normal, not realizing their leader had almost died that evening. Then Roland felt a hand on his shoulder and turned around. Onius looked exhausted.

"Roland, we will talk tomorrow. I think we all need some rest now, and I need time to think."

"I..." Roland tried to speak.

"Don't say anything. Tonight, I saw and heard things I never thought I would see and hear from you, Roland. I need to think about this."

"But…" Roland tried again to speak. He thought his mentor must be angry with him. "I tried, Onius. I really did. I tried to be responsible and help out."

Onius softened his gaze and stroked his mustache and short beard. He sighed deeply and then spoke. "I'm proud of you, Roland. You acted tonight without thought for yourself, and you put yourself at risk to help another. You acted rationally in a potentially dangerous situation. I will rethink our conversation from this afternoon."

Roland bowed with a slight flourish. "Thank you, Counselor."

Onius glanced out the window for a moment before leaving the room. With a flourish of his silk robes swirling around him, he turned back to Roland and gave a questioning glare to his young apprentice, one eyebrow raised higher than the other.

"What?" Roland asked, wondering what he had done this time.

Roland followed his mentor's gaze out the window. The gigantic oak tree stood bare and leafless in the night air. His cheeks reddened, and he shrugged his shoulders.

Onius laughed out loud, turned, and walked out of the library. His booming laughter echoed back through the hall and down the stairs. Roland glanced outside once more and saw a few latecomers pointing to the enormous bare tree. He smiled and blew out the candles, closed the door, and then headed down the stairs himself.

Now, where did that lovely lass go that I passed earlier on the stairs?

CHAPTER FOUR

"So, what is it you wanted to learn about, Roland?" Bakari asked.

Roland sat opposite him in the library with his legs sprawled over the side of an overstuffed chair. The center of the large library was arranged like a sitting room, with colorful couches and chairs and a small table, for readers to relax in and discuss things they had studied and read.

It was the day after they had saved the Chief Judge's life. Bakari hung on the top rung of a ladder, putting a book away on the top shelf. This library, the second largest in Alaris, held more books than anywhere else, except for the wizards' Citadel. Books rose from floor to ceiling here, with study rooms off to each side. And scribes worked constantly to make sure the books were continually preserved and recopied.

"I want to understand more about the history of wizardry and if there is a difference between wizards now and wizards in the past."

"Quite a scholarly question, coming from you, Roland."

"Bak!"

"I was joking. I thought you liked jokes. You told me I needed to be more personable. I believe what you said was I need to *get my nose out of my books more often*."

Bakari, a year younger than Roland, was the closest thing

to a friend that Roland had in Alaris. There were plenty of girls who wanted to spend time with Roland, but he didn't get along with the other young men very well. Bakari thought it was probably because Roland thought himself better than everyone else and far more advanced of a wizard than he was being given credit for. But Bakari ignored his friend's attitude and tried to find the good in Roland. He had decided Roland wasn't such a bad person, deep down inside.

The two fellow wizards couldn't be more different from each other. While Bakari was dark-skinned with short black hair and a broad nose, gangly, and not interested much in anything that wasn't a book, Roland's chin-length blond hair framed his light face, blue eyes, square jaw, and thin mouth, one that usually held a smile for the girls his age. Roland didn't take much seriously, in contrast to his studious friend.

"I do like jokes. It's fine." Roland winked as if to reassure Bakari. "Look, you remember everything you've read, and I know you have spent the last ten years, since you were a small child, studying at the Citadel and now here. So I expect that, if anyone has the answers, you would." Roland leaned forward and rested his chin on his hands. "So, what do you know about wizards?"

Bakari sat down opposite Roland and crossed one leg over the other. He thought about what Roland had done the day before with the Chief Judge, and wondered who should be teaching whom. But Bakari did understand more about history than his friend. So he took a deep breath, removed his glasses, and spoke with authority from memory.

"From the few histories written prior to the barrier going

up one hundred fifty years ago, wizards were more plentiful in the past and more powerful. All the kingdoms had powerful wizards and were organized more by the type of powers they held. Some wizards worked off of the earth, some were stronger with their minds, and others worked magic from their hearts. Loosely, those now translate into our Battle, Scholar, and Counselor wizards. A few held special telepathic abilities."

"Don't get too technical on me now, Bak."

"All right. Special mind abilities. Like the kind you exerted when you called Onius."

"So I do have special abilities." Roland bounced up in his seat. "Go on."

Bakari rolled his eyes at Roland's continued insistence that he was *special*.

"There is not much said about these wizards in the time leading up to the Great War, only that a few became very powerful. But it is understood that a wizard of Alaris ruled as king for many years. During the Great War, most of our powerful wizards died, including the king at the time. The final act of a group of minor wizards was to put up the magical barrier that has kept us separated from other kingdoms. In that final act, most of the remaining level-four and level-five wizards died. It has only been recently that we have seen a higher level of powerful wizards emerge—and they are getting younger."

"Like me!" Roland said proudly.

"Like you," Bakari admitted.

"How did they create that much magic for the barrier?"

"Nothing is said about it, at least, not in any book I have found yet. I would like to take a trip to some of the smaller libraries along the barrier and see what I can find. There is quite a gap in our library's histories during the time the barrier went up." Bakari furrowed his dark eyebrows and quit talking for a minute.

"Bak?"

"Sorry, I was just trying to sort through my memories to make sure. It is strange. There are no history books here from that time. The next thing we read is about the organization of our new form of government—the judges."

"But you haven't told me anything I hadn't learned in the Citadel, except that they are not as candid about the missing histories. Do you think some of the early wizards possessed all of the powers: mind, heart, and earth?"

"I would expect that their leaders did, maybe even the head of the Citadel. But I haven't seen any evidence in our libraries. There are bits and pieces that suggest a fourth power also used to exist."

"Hmmm." Roland stood up and walked to a window, the same one from the day before. The stark, bare oak tree still brought a grin to his face. The leaves had now been raked up and disposed of somewhere. His light eyebrows furrowed as he thought of an idea.

Bakari joined him at the window. "You're not thinking about trying to re-bud the tree, are you?"

"Are you sure *you* can't read minds now, Bak?"

"No. I just know you and your way of thinking," Bakari snorted.

"Well, the thought did cross my mind," Roland said.

"You really shouldn't," Bak said. "You can't force things

like that. You would destroy the balance of nature."

"You can't tell me what to do, Bak," Roland said. "You know nothing about the world out there. You stay cozied up with your books all day long."

"Actually, Roland, I can tell you what to do," Bakari said. "You are still an apprentice, and I am a full wizard."

"Ouch, Bak. Now that hurt." Roland's face turned a slight shade of red. "You don't need to get so personal. You do realize that I am more powerful than you?"

Bakari nodded and took his glasses off. "But becoming a wizard is not merely about having strength in magic. It is about learning how to use it responsibly."

Roland slapped his hand on the windowsill. "But you saw the things I did with my power. Even Onius didn't know how. He's been avoiding me since then. I think he's afraid of what he doesn't understand."

"As we all should be. Magic is not a game. I've studied it for years and have still barely scratched its surface." Bakari loved studying and discovering past truths from their histories. He was born to learn and to help pass on the knowledge of Alaris to others. His recent obsession was to find out what had truly happened when the barrier went up. There were rumors that it was starting to weaken lately, and no one would admit to knowing how the barrier had received its power to surround Alaris and keep them safe all these years. But he wanted to find out. Needed to find out.

"I saved the Chief Judge with my abilities. What have you ever done with all your knowledge?"

Bakari ignored this jab, put his glasses back on, and headed across the room. "Sometimes, Roland, you are not a very nice person."

"Bak, I'm sorry. I got carried away. I just don't understand what is happening to me. The power flows through my veins, and I can hardly contain it. I don't think I fit into any of the disciplines anymore. I am not merely a Counselor or a Scholar or a Battle wizard. I am something more. I can't tell the difference between the magic and myself anymore." Roland went quiet and plopped himself down onto a chair. "It's one and the same. Me and magic. Bak, I *am* magic."

"What did you say?" Bakari almost tripped coming over to the front of Roland's chair. He steadied himself against an oak table in the center of the library's sitting area. "That phrase is in a book from a long time ago. I can touch its echoes in my mind. There might be something to what you are saying, Roland. I have to search my books. Somewhere, the leaders of the Citadel used to refer to themselves in such a way."

Bakari ran back across the room to a smaller study and began leafing through volumes of books. In the back of his mind, he heard Roland get up out of the chair. A tiny smile tugged at the corners of Bakari's mouth. Roland knew him too well. Soon Bakari found himself lost once again among the many books of the library, any frustrated thoughts toward Roland long gone.

CHAPTER FIVE

Roland realized it would be hours, or even days, before anyone saw Bak again. Maybe the scholar wizard would find something to help Roland describe clearly how he felt inside. It frustrated him, to say the least. He was tired of being an apprentice. He was more powerful than so many other wizards. This thought made him crave the power even more.

He decided to tell Onius that he was going to go to the Citadel and request to be named as a full wizard. This had been a thought in his mind for a while. And, now that he'd actually decided to do it, he felt better.

A loud noise outside the library window caught Roland's attention. A long column of soldiers marched up to the castle gates. Their uniform patterns of marching impressed Roland. Their flags were red, which meant they were from the Chief Judge's battalion.

In front, he saw two figures in wizard's robes. The first was an older man with receding gray hair and an impressive array of weapons hanging from the belt around his solid body. The sunlight forced Roland to put his hands up to block the early morning glare so he could see the second figure more clearly. She was stunningly beautiful. She looked younger than he and had short dark hair—not usually his type—but her lips were bright, her cheekbones high, and her skin pale.

He would have described her as exotic, compared to the girls who followed him around the capital city lately. He extended the touch of his mind out toward hers and felt the edge of her awareness – a new trick he had discovered lately. The raw power there amazed and surprised him. So he pulled back before she would notice him.

Then the young girl turned and gazed up at the castle, right at Roland. Her visage was stern but incredibly intelligent and stunning. She carried a sword and dagger on her hip in a way that said she knew how to use them. He doubted she could see him, but his heart leapt again. Now here stood a conquest he would enjoy! A few kisses from those pouty lips would make for an enjoyable distraction from his counselor studies.

Without bidding farewell to Bakari, Roland turned and ran out of the library and down the stairs, his red robes floating behind him. Skidding to a halt as Onius came around the corner from the Chief Judge's private rooms, Roland put his hand out to stop himself from falling.

"Good. I'm glad you found me. The Chief Judge will be meeting with the battalion leaders in the throne room, and we are to accompany him."

Roland fell in beside his lanky mentor. "Onius, did you know there are two wizards with the battalion? A man and a girl; a pretty one."

Onius rolled his eyes. "The wizard is Gorn Mahron, a battle wizard, and the young girl is Allison Stenos, his apprentice."

Roland had to almost run to keep step with Onius's long paces. "She is training to be a battle wizard? Are you kidding?

She's just a girl." Roland frowned. "I mean, a beautiful one at that, but still…"

"Just a girl?" Onius laughed. "Yes, she is still an apprentice like you. But, from what I hear, Roland, you may be soon meeting your match in terms of power and attitude."

"What's that supposed to mean?"

Onius paused right before entering the room. "Please behave, Roland. My head still hurts from your escapades yesterday, and I am not in the mood for any of your games today."

Roland's face reddened. He opened his mouth to voice his complaints, but Onius stepped into the ready room, and Roland followed him in dutifully.

The room was a considerable area, big enough for hundreds of people. Ten marble columns held up the large, white domed ceiling. Windows and tapestries alternated along two outside walls. The tapestries depicted scenes of battles intermixed with fantastic depictions of fairy tale creatures, like dragons. No such creatures actually existed in Alaris.

In the middle of the bright and regal room, the battle commander stood at attention, waiting to give his report to the Chief Judge. Flanking him on either side stood the two wizards Roland had seen through the windows of the castle.

"Captain," started Onius, "the Chief Judge will be with you shortly." Onius then turned his attention to the wizard. "Gorn, good to see you again." They clasped hands. "How is the training of your apprentice going?"

Gorn glanced at Alli, who stood still, taking inventory of everything in the room that might be of danger to them. He turned back to Onius and, with a wink, said, "She tries my patience and is unconventional in her fighting but is doing well enough."

Alli glanced at Gorn without breaking a smile. She looked even more striking up close. Roland couldn't take his eyes off her. Her full, pouty lips and small nose made her young face look vulnerable, but the power in her stance was unmistakable. He saw in her eyes an intriguing intelligence and an understanding of everything going on around them.

Onius pointed to Roland with a broad smile. "This is my apprentice, Roland Tyre. He, too, can be trying at times, and unconventional, but he has some remarkable powers."

"Tyre?" Gorn asked. "Are you from the Westridge area? I've heard of a Tyre family from there. Seems like a lot of wizard power is coming from the edge of the barrier lately."

Roland still looked at Alli.

"Roland!" barked Onius a little louder, taking him out of his daze.

"Yes, Onius?"

"I introduced you to my friend, Battle Wizard Gorn Mahron, and his apprentice, Allison. Gorn has asked a question of you."

"I know, and I was going to answer." Instead, he turned to Alli and, with a flourishing bow, said, "I could not help drinking in thy beauty. Ye make all the other ladies in the castle pale in comparison."

Before Roland could grasp what was happening, Alli had stepped forward, drawn her dagger, and pressed it to his throat. "I'm not your toy, Counselor Apprentice. I have heard that

Roland Tyre thinks he is God's gift to women."

"Alli," Gorn said sternly. "We are their guests. What has gotten into you?"

She turned to Onius, who was trying not to laugh. "I forgot my manners, Counselor. I'm tired and thirsty after the long march from Orr." Then she moved back to Gorn's side.

Onius gave Roland a stern glare, telling him to behave, but Roland was not going to take that kind of embarrassment. He moved his fingers lightly and sent a push of air toward Alli's feet as she walked away from him.

She tripped and fell, scanning the area to figure out what had happened. The sound of her knee hitting the hard marble floor had been unmistakable, but she didn't even wince. With fire almost blazing from her eyes, she glared at Roland.

Roland smiled in delight. "May I help you up, Battle Wizard Apprentice?" Roland reached his hand down to raise her up.

Alli brought forth a small spark of fire from her fingertips and shot it at Roland's hand. He yelped and jumped backward, shaking his hand, only to find her leg sweeping in an arc around his. He hit the ground with a thud and winced. With only a moment's hesitation, he rolled to the side and jumped back up. The two apprentices moved toward each other, determination on both of their faces.

"Enough!" bellowed Onius, his voice echoing off the solid stone walls. He picked both of them up with magic and brought them to stand in front of him in the air. "This is why you are both still apprentices. Now, put your pride and childish ways aside. The Chief Judge will soon be here."

Alli and Roland both looked at their feet, their faces the same shade of red.

Onius lowered them to the floor and released his power over them. "Now, go and get all of us something to drink from the kitchen."

"But—"

"But nothing, *Apprentice*," Onius said. "If you act like children, you will perform childish errands. Now go."

"Both of you," echoed Gorn, displeasure covering his face as well.

Roland stomped out of the room and down the hall toward the kitchen. What an infuriating girl. Maybe he should stick to the boring court ladies. Alli was going to be harder to win over than he had first thought.

"Did I hurt your ego, Roland Tyre?" Alli caught up to him and met him stride for stride, though she pushed her shorter legs to do so. "I'm not such an easy conquest, am I?"

Roland's eyes widened, and he slowed his pace. There was no way she had read his mind. Or was there? She was indeed a dangerous lass.

"No, I didn't read your mind."

Roland was surprised at her honesty and straightforward attitude. She was quite unlike the gaggle of girls hanging around the castle these days. "At least we have one thing in common," he mumbled.

"And that would be?" A sly smile lit her face. Roland didn't want to look, because he wanted to stay mad at her, but that feeling had already faded. Not one to hold a grudge long against a pretty young woman, he resumed the flirting.

"We are only apprentices but should be at least level-three wizards. Level four, in my case. I hold powers even Onius doesn't understand."

"Level four, huh? You do think highly of yourself."

Servants in the wide halls walked to either side of the apprentices on their ways to their daily duties, but Roland didn't give them any notice.

He reached out to Alli's mind as he had to Onius' when the Chief Judge had needed them the day before. It was easier this time because Alli stood right in front of him.

I do have some special abilities, he spoke to her mind.

Alli physically jumped in front of him, trying to shake his voice from her mind.

"See?" Roland smiled smugly.

"Get out of my head, Roland." She slapped his arm, more in amazement than in anger.

Roland complied. They were almost to the kitchen, made evident by the aroma of freshly baked bread wafting down the hallway toward them. It hung in the air, tickling Roland's senses and making him hungry.

"Why haven't they tested you yet?" Alli asked. "You are older than I. And you aren't a girl." Her own words brought a slight blush to Alli's cheeks.

For once, Roland decided to bite back a retort.

They soon entered the kitchens. The young blonde girl he usually flirted with was there this time, but she seemed less refined and beautiful than she had before. The two apprentices asked for her help in getting some refreshments for the captain and their mentors.

Roland peeked at Alli out of the corner of his eye and felt the need to be honest. "They think I am not mature enough to be tested."

Alli snickered behind her hand. "Ahh. I see." Her green eyes were captivating and full of a power that drew Roland in.

"Yeah, well, I'm trying," he grumbled, but he couldn't help broadening his smile. He pushed his long bangs out of his face and laughed. One thing everyone knew about Roland Tyre was that he couldn't stay in a bad mood long. Life was too short to stay angry.

They placed the refreshments on a tray and headed back to the ready room.

In the doorway, before entering the room, Roland turned to Alli. "Sorry about earlier. I don't know what got into me."

Alli looked surprised. "I shouldn't have been so jumpy. I'm sorry too." Her smile seemed genuine, but her eyes mocked him still.

Roland motioned for Alli to precede him into the room. Then he leaned in and whispered, "But I guess you couldn't help being drawn to my breathtaking looks and grand personality, could you?" Alli almost dropped the tray. Roland laughed from behind.

Roland noticed the Chief Judge standing in front of the group. Color had returned to his face. But he supported himself with the arm of the red stuffed chair next to him.

"You two seem to have made amends," the judge spoke to the two apprentices. "Roland, I wouldn't think I would need to remind my counselor apprentice of how to treat our guests."

Alli eyed Roland and then cocked her head to the side, a

grin slowly spreading across her face.

"The captain has been telling me how Alli helped tremendously in their battle against some of these King-men we have been hearing so much about. He was astonished, as was Gorn, at her strength and abilities. The captain mentioned her grace as she flowed over the battlefield."

Roland's blue eyes popped open wider. She wasn't just a pretty face after all. Alli nodded her head to the Chief Judge and offered him a cup from the tray. He, in turn, motioned for Roland to serve the captain, Gorn, and Onius.

Roland silently fumed. He hated being treated like a servant—and, to make matters worse, right in front of this young female wizard. He clenched his jaw and sought control. When done serving the others, he set the tray down roughly on a side table and returned to stand next to Onius, as was his place in these types of proceedings. Then he glared at Alli, though she didn't appear to notice.

Daymian continued, "Roland also has shown some amazing abilities these last few days. He saved my life yesterday, for which I'm of course grateful beyond measure."

Now it was Roland's turn to gloat. He thought he saw Alli looking at him in surprise, her face full of questions, but, when he turned his head, she had turned hers away just as fast. He smiled at her obvious interest in him.

"I have been invited by Wizard Kanzar Centari to visit with him in the Citadel," the Chief Judge informed the small group. "The captain and a few of his men will escort me, along with Onius, Gorn, and you two."

Both of the young apprentices' eyes widened. They stood

straighter, trying to make sure they had heard correctly. It would be a great honor to travel in the Chief Judge's entourage and to meet the High Wizard. They shared a look and instantly forgot their earlier skirmish. Neither held in their smiles.

"The High Wizard," Roland said under his breath. It must be a sign it was time for him to be tested.

"That is a name he uses for himself, Roland," the Chief Judge said. "There is not a *High Wizard* title that I am aware of." He looked to Gorn and Onius for confirmation.

Roland noticed Onius's mouth tighten, and then relax. He didn't think others had seen it, except for maybe Alli, who turned her head with a questioning gaze.

"It is a title he has earned through the years," Onius said. "He is one of the most powerful wizards since the barrier rose. There is no harm in showing him respect."

"He pulls too much power to himself, Onius. I will not be intimidated by him." The Chief Judge sat down in the chair and took a few deep breaths. "We will leave in a week's time. Prior to that, I want to gather as much information as we can on these so called king-men. Another judge has gone missing or has been murdered. That means two elections now that we must hold this autumn to keep peace among the people."

"Sir, you must be careful," Onius said. "We still do not know who tried to poison you."

"That is why I am taking all of you with me. Surely this group of wizards can protect me." Daymian looked at each one seriously.

Roland stood taller and nodded. He would protect the Chief Judge. This trip would be one more way to show Onius that he was ready to be tested.

The Chief Judge turned to his counselor. "Onius, please inform Bakari that he will be accompanying us also, and I want to know everything about the barrier before we leave. I need to be prepared to ask our esteemed *High Wizard* what he is doing about that danger, on top of everything else. You are all dismissed."

CHAPTER 6

Erryl Close strolled away from the wall that surrounded the city of Celestar. He knew he couldn't go out of sight of the sentries at the gate. Another wall kept him from going too far, anyway—a wall that none of the guardians were allowed to cross. He carried his medium-sized frame lightly, even though he'd just finished his noon meal. The breads and fruits had tasted delicious, as always. All of the guardians—of which he was one of — were well provided for.

He climbed the grassy hill, which stood between the city and the outer wall, and breathed in deeply. The scent of pine grasped at his senses.

He found an enormous, thousand-year-old mountain spruce, its circumference wider than four men holding hands, and sat down a few inches from where the trunk met perfectly manicured grass. Streams of sunlight filtered through the thick branches far above, warming his closely shaved head. He leaned his head back against the thick, brown bark and gazed straight up through the never-ending branches.

Erryl always did what others expected of him, but he was wrestling with thoughts of boredom again. He understood the importance of the job he performed as a guardian of the Orb, but, as he grew older, he wanted more. Others around him seemed content to live lives of peace and tranquility up in the forests of the North. So he kept his restlessness a secret, especially from his parents, likewise guardians, who viewed what they did as an honor.

From his vantage point on the top of the hill, he stood and overlooked Celestar, the city he had lived in his entire fifteen years. The breathtaking white spires and domed glass roof of the building where the Orb sat rose over the gleaming white walls of the city. The sun sparkled off the rooftops of the other buildings and homes, creating an aura of white and gold hovering above the city. It was beautiful. Who wouldn't want to stay here?

Pain and pride pierced his heart: pride, because he knew that, as guardians of the Orb, they performed a special duty for others throughout Alaris It was a secret and sacred duty that few outside of Celestar would ever know about, but a duty nonetheless. And pain, because, even though he realized it was wrong, he wanted more.

The power in the Orb had kept the magical barrier intact around the kingdom of Alaris for one hundred fifty years. The barrier was the final sacrifice of a small group of wizards before they died. The current guardians, although they had no magical powers of their own, were descendants of those wizards. Each new generation became guardians. The cycle had continued all of this time to feed the Orb's ability to protect all within the kingdom.

Erryl rocked back on his feet, turned, and then walked around the giant tree to face away from Celestar. He gazed down the other side of the gently sloping hill. Soft, green grass filled his gaze until it met the outer wall. On the far side of that man-made barrier stood a mixture of spruce, pine, and aspen trees, leading to the magical barrier.

He wondered for the hundredth time what transpired on the other side of the barrier. They lived so close to it, here in Celestar. It was only a short walk away, physically, but felt so much farther otherwise. Nothing went in, out, or through the barrier. That's just the way it was.

Erryl found himself clenching his hands and squeezing his eyes shut in shame. He felt embarrassed for wanting more. The guardians had everything they needed here. The city was bright and clean, and food was provided for them by the protectors, who took care of their every need. No crime or poverty existed, the weather was always perfect, and he had loving parents.

Physically fit and healthy, educated in reading, writing, and the arts, he shouldn't have much to complain about. However, he gazed intently toward the magical barrier and wondered what life might hold for someone normal, someone who didn't have the burden of such a great responsibility.

Erryl wanted to leave Celestar and find out what existed in the rest of the world or, at least, the rest of Alaris. He was curious, a trait he found harder and harder to deal with lately. Leaving Alaris was not an option, with the barrier in place, but guardians were not even allowed to leave the city of Celestar. Ever. That was the accepted rule for all guardians. Their lives were too sacred and the location of Celestar too secret to let someone leave. There was the source of his pain.

Just then, Erryl was torn from his thoughts by a shimmer appearing around the farthest trees. He walked a few steps down the hill, shielding his pale blue eyes with his hands. Then the magical barrier became thinner for a brief moment. He squinted and tried to peer closer. He swore he could see something. A figure. No, two. They were tall and thin but appeared strong. They held bows across their backs and had long, silky hair hanging past their shoulders.

He took another step forward. "What should I do?" Erryl said out loud to himself. He knew they were not from Celestar. Maybe they knew about the outside world. His heart pounded, and a thrill ran through him. He took a few more steps forward. But, as fast as they had silently emerged, they disappeared, fading back again across the barrier. Then the barrier returned to its normal, opaque look.

A voice called to him from behind, back down the other side of the hill toward the city. He turned, walked back to the top of the hill, and saw Geran Armada, one of the protectors of Celestar.

A nice-enough man, Geran seemed content to live here in Celestar with his books. Geran was not a fat man but largely built nonetheless. He sported a speckled, thinning beard and round glasses and looked to be toward the end of his middle years.

But it was always so hard to tell with older people.

From what Erryl knew, Geran was a rather weak scholar wizard, a descendant of those wizards who first created the barrier.

Only one reason would send Geran out to the city walls to fetch Erryl. It must be time, time to fulfill his daily duty as a guardian. Erryl covered up a long sigh, forced a smile, waved, and then shuffled back toward his duty.

"Daydreaming again, young man?" Geran asked when he got close enough to be heard.

"What do you mean, Geran?"

"Come now, Erryl, I am not as naive or unobservant as you must think I am. I can see your restlessness and your desire to know more."

"It shows, huh?" Erryl smiled more warmly at the protector this time.

Geran patted him on the back as they turned to walk back through the city's northern archway. They walked silently for a moment. Gardens of bright colors lined either side of the paved streets. Everything was built in white. Erryl spotted a few gardeners working and waved to them.

"Erryl," Geran said, "you understand the importance of being a guardian, right?"

"I have been taught about the Orb my entire life, Protector," he replied.

"Then you know that what we do here is beneficial to all of Alaris, that the Orb gives life to the magic that keeps the peace of this land."

"But, how do you know?" Erryl took an apple from a cart outside of the white building they were about to enter.

"How do I know what?" Geran stopped with his hand on the door.

"How do you know it's so important? How do you know it keeps the peace? We never get to leave. How do you know we aren't prisoners here? How do you know we wouldn't be better off without it?"

Geran's face darkened with alarm. He pulled on Erryl's

arm and took him around to the side of the building instead of entering. No windows appeared on this side, and the afternoon sun kept them in the shadows.

"Erryl, you ask too many questions. You must not say these things. This is blasphemy concerning what we do here. You are taken care of and live a good life, and you think you are a prisoner? These thoughts could get you into trouble, young man. I warn you because I care for you, but watch your wayward tongue."

Erryl felt afraid of Geran, for the first time in his life, and afraid of what they did in Celestar. The protectors here also descended from minor wizards one hundred fifty years ago. Some possessed magical powers; others didn't. They took care of Celestar and the Orb and, as far as he knew, did not ever leave either. They were as much prisoners as he was.

He now wondered about those who disappeared from time to time. Did they doubt also? Geran's soft demeanor had lulled Erryl into confessing his innermost secrets. Now he would be watched more closely by the council of protectors.

"I'm sorry, Protector, for my foolish thoughts; I am still young and learning," Erryl said humbly, hoping the incident would soon be forgotten.

Geran smiled again. "Yes, you are. My outburst was uncalled for, but I do ask you to heed my advice."

"I will, Geran."

They walked together, back to the double doors, and entered the building housing the Orb of Life. Even though Erryl held no magical abilities, he still recognized the pulsing of the Orb's power as soon as he had entered the foyer of the building. He turned his face upward, still amazed at the sight. The ceiling grew taller as it worked its way to the building's center. And the walls held grand murals, depicting various landscapes of the world. Erryl was always drawn to one mural of what he had been told was the Blue Sea. The picture of the water seemed so peaceful and so powerful at the same time. He doubted he would ever see it in person.

Other protectors, ones older than he, led them both into the inner sanctum. The ceiling, even higher here, was domed and made of glass, held up by far-reaching columns. Rather than repeating the murals of the foyer, here the walls bore no decoration other than that of the architecture itself.

The other guardians in his sector already stood gathered. He glanced around the room and noticed those he had grown up with. He remembered again that, over the years, some of the guardians had disappeared. His mother and father were also there, along with other older guardians.

As he had been instructed since he was ten years old, Erryl took his place among the others, holding hands with those to either side of himself in the circle. Until last year, he had always been with only the younger guardians and a smaller orb. A *training orb* they called it. Now he noticed that a few of those newest ones with him here in the circle today. Both guardians to either side were a year younger than he and gazed up at him with rapture and pride in their faces. He smiled back, trying to show an enthusiasm he didn't feel.

They held hands and walked toward the Orb, bringing their arms down, close to their sides, as they moved closer together. He noted that the Orb had grown larger over time. It used to be the size of a large pumpkin, but now it was the size of a tall bush. It was round and smooth and sat on a golden pedestal, which, in turn, sat on a small red carpet that covered a portion of the white marble floor. It glowed with a soft, iridescent blue light. He wondered if its growth was normal or even expected.

Erryl closed his eyes, and the raw, pulsating power of the Orb reached deep into his breast. This instantly washed away his doubts, and he wondered how he could have been so foolish. Its power was mighty, and what they did was an honor among all men. He felt infused with love and compassion as they stopped walking.

Now, one by one, each of them took a turn, reaching their right hands to the Orb. To not break the chain, each guardian held hands with the person to the left, while one guardian fed the Orb his or her life source.

His turn came, and he reached his hand out steadily, settling it on the cold, smooth, almost glass-like surface. He still bore the feeling of peace, but he also felt his own energy leave his body and enter the Orb. Then he perceived gratitude from the Orb.

Erryl was young and strong, but each day the Orb took that energy into itself, leaving him feeling tired and weak for hours. He had noticed that it took longer and longer each time now to become fully drained and also longer to recover than when he had first started. What used to take an hour or two to recover now sometimes took several hours or even the rest of the day. And some guardians only came every other day as they got older.

He sensed something he'd never felt before: a presence inside the Orb. Not a person but something bigger and more powerful. He scanned the group to see if anyone else had noticed. They looked content, with no apparent traces of alarm.

It was time for Erryl to pull his hand away, for the next guardian to continue the routine, but he found that he couldn't remove it.

Erryl, a deep voice said to his mind, and he almost jumped away. Only Erryl's sheer determination kept his shaking hand in place.

"Erryl," one of the protectors called out. "Let go. It is time."

But he couldn't. Not yet. Something had called to him.

Find him. Find the one. It is almost time, the voice whispered to his mind.

Who? he tried to ask back, wondering if whatever it was would hear him.

"Erryl," said one of the protectors. "You must let go, or you will drain yourself."

He opened his eyes and saw a protector walking toward the circle. Energy continued to drain from his body. His legs weakened, and his heart raced.

Who am I supposed to find? he asked the voice again, his mind barely able to focus now.

I will show you. The quiet, yet deep voice echoed deep inside Erryl's mind.

A vision began to open up to him, but before he could see anything, his legs buckled and he slid down next to the orb. Guardians scrambled forward to stay with him and not break the link. Light from the Orb flared, and Erryl felt himself blacking out. He closed his eyes tighter, trying to see what he was supposed to have seen.

The vision had gone. But his pain did not leave. His head hurt, and his heart raced. He heard someone begin screaming. He slumped farther to the ground and then realized it was he who screamed.

"Erryl!" his father yelled. It was the last thing Erryl heard.

CHAPTER SEVEN

"Where is Roland?" Onius asked Bakari as they stood together outside the castle stables in Cassian.

Bakari glanced up from the small book he was studying with a blank look on his face.

Onius flung his hands into the hair. "Put away the book, and pay attention, Bak. We're almost ready to leave, but Roland is nowhere to be found."

Blushing, Bakari put the book in a side pocket of his pack. "I'll go find him, Counselor. Probably down in town."

"No doubt saying good-bye to the girls." Onius shook his head and barked a laugh. "Take my advice, Bak, and please don't follow in Roland's ways."

Bakari's cheeks turned an even darker shade, and he gave Onius a nervous smile. "I've got my books to keep me company."

Onius patted him on the back. "Good man. Though it would do you good to get out a little more. You don't want to be a hermit for all your life."

"Yes, Sir," Bakari said. He couldn't tell if the counselor was serious or not.

Bakari ran through the south gate of the castle compound and scampered to the shipping district. This was not a place he frequented, as he didn't enjoy the pastime of visiting much, but this was where Roland usually found the girls.

The late-summer day was hot, and Bakari slowed down and wiped the sweat from his forehead. Shops lined the cobblestone street, their colorful awnings and flags hanging out in front to advertise their wares.

The district consisted primarily of two-story brick and cement buildings, with a few older wooden clapboards down at the end. Each building housed a shop on the lower level and living quarters on the top. Dirt-packed side streets led off to smaller shops and more homes.

Bakari wandered around the streets for a few minutes, until he saw a group of girls standing next to a bakery. The laugh of one girl floated through the air, followed by a deeper voice. Roland! It had to be.

Coming closer, Bakari saw that it was indeed his friend, telling an entertaining story to four girls. The girls laughed and screamed in delight. Their frilly, colorful dresses, with lace detailing, marked them as highborn.

Bakari caught Roland's attention, so Roland called his friend over to meet the girls. Bakari felt awkward in his riding attire.

"Um…nice to meet you," Bakari said to the group, stumbling through his words.

They were polite but seemed unimpressed and soon turned their attention back to Roland.

"I'm sorry, girls, but I must go off with the Chief Judge to meet the High Wizard."

"Oh, Roland," said a tall, brown-haired beauty while touching Roland's arm with her gloved fingers. "What a great honor that must be for you."

Roland smiled and clasped her hand in his. "Not as much of an honor as spending some time with you ladies."

Bakari rolled his eyes. "Roland," he called to his friend sarcastically. "The esteemed company is waiting for you to return to the castle so they can leave."

"Right you are, Bak, my friend." Roland turned back to the girls one last time. "Wizard Bakari, here, reminds me I am needed back at the castle. Farewell, ladies! I will see you in a few weeks, when I return."

Roland gave a flourishing bow, and then the two young men hurried back toward the castle grounds.

As they walked up the road that led to the castle, Roland turned to Bak and slapped him on the back. "Have you seen that fetching young wizard yet, Bak?"

"Roland!" Bak sighed and pushed his friend's hand away. "Is there nothing else you think about these days?" Roland fell silent while the two of them entered the castle gates and headed toward Onius and the rest of the group.

"Well, I do think about how powerful of a wizard I am going to be."

"And a humble one at that," Bakari said. "At least being with you should make this trip more exciting."

"You got that right," Roland said, winking at Bakari.

The two found their horses, mounted, and, with a stern eye from Onius, headed out with the group.

Hours later, Bakari sat on his gray quarter horse with his head once again in a book, oblivious to the scenery around them. He reviewed his own compilation of facts about the barrier and the magic that sustained it. It seemed to be showing signs of weakness recently.

Something didn't seem right to him, so he poured back over his notes. Where did the barrier get its power? Why was it weakening? Those two questions kept him up late each night, reading by the side of the fire.

Three days into their journey north to the Citadel, Bakari's horse stepped into a small dip in the dirt road and the book in his hand went flying through the air, landing on some tufts of grass along the side of the road.

The farmlands and grasslands were primarily open in this part of Alaris. But, up ahead, the road curved around a large copse of trees. As Bakari watched, the rest of the group disappeared in front of him. He hadn't realized he had fallen so far behind.

He stopped the horse and hopped off. Then he picked up the book and wiped the dust from the cover. Sighing to himself, he pushed his fists into the small of his back to try and rid it of the tightness riding had caused. He did need to get out of the library more…and exercise. He was weak and out of shape.

His horse stood patiently, with its head down, chewing a few mouthfuls of grass growing next to the hard-packed road, which would lead to River Bend and then northwest to the Citadel.

"Adi," Bakari said, then called the horse over to him with a cluck of his tongue. He liked the temperaments of the female horses better than those of the males. Before he could climb back onto his horse, he heard a sound up ahead, between himself and the rest of the group.

A dozen men on horses emerged from the trees a few hundred feet in front of him, riding cross-country. They turned away from his direction and charged in a fast gallop up the road, toward the rest of the Chief Judge's party. If they had noticed Bakari standing there behind them, they didn't seem to show any interest in a lone traveler standing next to his horse on the side of the road.

Bakari felt his chest tighten. He didn't possess the magical ability to communicate with other wizards through his mind as Roland had done. Bakari thought about yelling a warning, but his voice wouldn't travel that far, and this would only call undue attention to himself. So, instead, he decided to travel at a slower pace behind the men and keep his eyes open.

Putting away his book, he traveled behind the men and noticed that their horses were thoroughbreds, the types found mostly up in the northern regions of Alaris. They were popular in the Citadel, and Bakari remembered riding one once, only to discover that they were too big for his comfort. His rump didn't have enough padding.

He proceeded now to push his smaller horse faster so as to keep them in his sight.

Before the riders caught up to the Chief Judge and his traveling group, they turned around another bend in the road. Soon both groups ahead of Bakari were out of sight, hidden behind a small forested area. The Dunn River roared not too far away behind the trees. Bakari rode harder so he wouldn't miss anything.

Loud voices and the sound of clashing swords filled the air before Bakari grew too close. He slowed down and inched up behind a group of great oaks. The riders had indeed surprised the Chief Judge's group and were now fighting them. Other riders from the north also joined in, boxing in the group from Cassian.

A loud swooshing sound filled the air, and bodies went flying. Bolts of light flew through the air at the attackers. Bakari smiled. Two powerful wizards, in Onius and Gorn, along with the apprentices, Alli and Roland, would be more than a match for these apparent rebels.

Bakari stayed hidden, knowing his skills were not in the area of fighting. Men ran and screamed, trying to push into the center of the group. Adi snorted and stomped her feet, so Bakari leaned over and quieted her down with a small pat to the top of her head.

The battle seemed to be going well for his friends, when, over the din, Daymian Khouri's voice cut through the air.

"Stop the fighting!" the Chief Judge repeated twice.

The fighting slowed, and Bakari watched as two burly men walked out of the circle of fighters with the Chief Judge held between them.

Roland marched toward the two men, but Onius put his arm out and held him back with a shake of his head. Instead, the counselor wizard himself strode forward.

"What is the meaning of this?" Onius's face was still red from the recent fighting. "This is treason."

One of the men holding onto the Chief Judge stepped forward. "We have no fight with you, Wizard. In fact, we hope you will one day join our cause."

"And what cause is that?"

"To be like other kingdoms, with a powerful king. The judges are too soft. There is no pride in Alaris. We must break through the magical barrier and become more than we are. We must once again show the world that Alaris is in charge."

It was the same old argument that had been used for a dozen years now

Onius brought his hand up toward the rebels, but one of the men holding the Chief Judge brought out a small bottle of liquid and forced its contents down the Chief Judge's throat. The Chief Judge coughed and spit, but soon his body fell limp, and his head lolled to the side.

Bakari took a step forward, then changed his mind and moved back behind a tree. These must be the same people that had tried to kill the Chief Judge ten days earlier, in the castle. At least, they must be working for the same people. He couldn't imagine this rebel group being the brains behind both attacks.

"Your leader has been given a poison," the captain of the mercenaries began again. He held his sword outside its scabbard next to his leather-clad body. "We have the antidote hidden nearby. If you attack us, he will die."

The Chief Judge's eyes were still open and appeared to understand what was happening. But, without the use of his body, he could do nothing about it.

The mercenary leader gave a toothy grin. Black hair and beard covered most of his face and head, and muscles bulged around his black leather armor.

"Good, I see we have an understanding. In the morning,

we will all take a little trip together. Be mindful that your Chief Judge's life is in your hands. We will administer the antidote in small doses, and he will renounce his position and step down as Chief Judge."

Bakari heard a gasp from Roland and saw the Chief Judge's eyes grow darker and his face muscles twitch. Bakari knew then that the Chief Judge would not obey their terms but would protect the system of government over his own life.

Shouts from angry voices spread throughout the Chief Judge's party. Then Onius stepped up.

"What assurance do we have that the Chief Judge will actually live?"

"You personally will stay by his side and observe him. You can monitor his health. But, I assure you, if you try anything, he will die!" the mercenary spat. "The antidote only works within the first forty-eight hours."

Bakari's shoulders slumped. An extreme burden had just settled upon his young frame. He was the only one free, the only one with a chance to save the Chief Judge. He knew the rebels were not to be trusted to keep their promises. Bakari also knew Roland well enough to know that he would try something. Roland wouldn't be able to sit still through this ordeal. He possessed too much power and pride.

As the rebels took the prisoners farther back into the forest, the setting sun sparkled on something on the ground where the men had been. Bakari dismounted the horse, and with quiet steps and slow movements, crept forward to find out what it was. After being sure he had not been seen, he moved closer to the object.

Lifting it up and turning it around in his fingers, he recognized it as the small bottle for the poison that had been administered to the Chief Judge. He brought it to his nose and took a small whiff. His head snapped back with the pungent smell and his nose wrinkled up.

Bakari moved back into the trees and started to cipher through his mind for the type of poison the bottle had contained. His mind worked methodically, analyzing the smell and breaking down the ingredients, then comparing this information to the notes and books he had read over his short fifteen years.

After a few minutes, a broad smile spread across his face. He removed his glasses and rubbed his tired eyes, trying to think of the best way to save the Chief Judge. Luckily for them, the rebels were bluffing to some degree. The poison was debilitating for sure, and the Chief Judge wouldn't be able to move his body much for about forty-eight hours, but it was not as deadly as they had let on.

This fact meant that wherever they were going to take the group wasn't too far away. However, even after the effects of the poison wore off, the Chief Judge would still be weak and sickly if he didn't get some type of antidote and herbs to help strengthen him.

Bakari needed to figure out something he could do. They all depended on him to find help.

CHAPTER 8

Thinking about Roland's experience of healing the Chief Judge a few weeks before, Bakari took his horse and headed back toward a small nearby village, an hour off the main road. He hoped to find the village healer or a medicine woman so he could buy some herbs to speed up the Chief Judge's healing. He left his horse tethered by a patch of grass and a small spring, out of sight of the village gate. He took off his wizard's cloak, folded it up, and placed it inside his pack.

Walking into the village alone was unnerving. Bakari was rarely by himself, unless it was with his books in the library, so he glanced around in quick motions. The town was small, with one wide dirt road heading through the middle of it. A few shops and houses lined this street. Smaller paths, only wide enough for a person or a horse, led off to the sides, presumably to other homes. Normally, in the evening, he would have expected more movement around the town as people finished their shopping or headed to the ale houses or inns for an evening of entertainment and conversation.

"Good Sir, could you tell me the way to a medicine man or woman's home?" he asked the first adult he saw.

The man glared at Bakari with a look of nervous suspicion and said nothing. Maybe they weren't used to seeing someone of his dark heritage. There were not a lot of his people south of

Whalen.

"The city seems quiet for this time of day," Bakari observed out loud.

The man turned his head, as if looking for someone. "What is your business here in our town?"

"I need some herbs for a friend of mine who is sick," Bakari offered. "We were traveling and an insect bite has given him a fever." He hoped this small lie would suffice. He wasn't good at making things up like this.

"You're from the city?" the man asked, referring to Cassian, the only city of size in the area.

Something felt wrong. So Bakari took in his surroundings again and noticed a band of men walking down the road from the other side of town. They wore the same black leather armor as the rebel mercenaries had. He then realized they had left backup in this little town.

Lowering his voice, he took a chance by stating, "I serve the Chief Judge in Cassian. I need to get to the medicine woman."

"Strangers are not much appreciated here, son." The man sighed and lowered his voice even lower. "Down the main road, two houses past the inn. But hurry, then leave town when your business is done." The man glanced back at the men walking up behind him, still about a block away. "We don't want any more trouble here."

Bakari understood: the rebels had taken over the village. Giving his thanks, he turned and headed off in the indicated direction. He sensed the eyes of the rebels on his back. But, when he glanced behind him, he noticed them entering a shop.

He knocked on the door of the medicine woman's house. A moment later, the door swung open, and he was greeted by a young, dark-skinned girl a year or so younger than himself. Bakari felt self-conscious seeing the girl all by himself. He reached up and patted down his hair. For some reason, he wanted to appear presentable.

"I am here to see the medicine woman," he said, surprised to see someone else with dark skin south of Whalen. History said their ancestors came from a mountain region north of Alaris—in Mahli. Since the barrier had closed off any new travels for such a long time, much of that history was now lost.

Peering back and forth down the street, the young woman nodded and moved aside for him to enter. She motioned him to a small sitting room. The sky had darkened on his way there, and the room was lit by a few candles and one oil lamp. Two worn but sturdy stuffed chairs sat in the center of the room with a small, low table between them.

A few books and decorations lined a wall of shelves, with another wall devoted to bottles and canisters of herbs and medicines. The aroma of peppermint and lavender, mixed with dried herbs like catnip and echinacea, among others, tickled his nose. He shook his head to ignore his natural impulse to catalog each scent in his mind.

The young woman sat down opposite him. She wore plain clothes, her straight black hair falling in a gentle cascade to the top of her shoulders. Her nose was thinner than his, and, though she was not a great beauty, her face held a kindness and a serenity that Bakari admired immediately.

"I am Kharlia Attah, the village medicine woman." Her

brown eyes were intelligent and sparkled as if holding back a secret.

Bakari's body twitched with a sudden movement, which gave away his surprise at her being so young. He adjusted his glasses and said simply, "I am Bakari. Some call me Bak for short."

"Well, Bakari, what can I help you with today?"

"I didn't expect you to be so young," he blurted out, then blushed. Kharlia laughed, and Bakari felt himself relax.

"My mother died a few years ago, and I took over for her. I assure you, I do know my trade."

"Oh!" He smiled back in silence for a few moments, admiring her soft brown eyes and smooth skin.

The young woman couldn't have been more than fourteen, but Bakari was drawn to her. Remembering Onius's warning from three days earlier, about not getting distracted like Roland did, he shook his head to clear his thoughts. He did hope she knew her trade. Kharlia cleared her throat, and Bakari was brought back to the task at hand.

"I have a friend who accidentally took a mixture of tags weed, yellow bark, and grants root, and I need an antidote."

"Accidentally took?" Kharlia looked skeptical and frowned. "I don't think anyone *accidentally* takes that concoction. You know what it does, don't you?"

Bakari nodded. Before he could say anything else, they heard a loud commotion down the street. The two stood up and peered through the lace-covered window. Down the road, Bakari saw the leather-clad group pushing their way into the homes along the street, apparently searching the houses.

Kharlia turned to Bakari with a fierce gaze in her eyes. She stood only two inches shorter than him. "What have you brought to our village? Who are you?"

Bakari fell back a step at this fiery response. "I am a friend of the Chief Judge. Are you?"

Kharlia opened her mouth, closed it, and then opened it again. "I don't support these rebels, if that's what you're asking." She peeked out the window again, then moved swiftly to her shelves. In a matter of moments, she had gathered up a few packets and jars of herbs and had put them into a satchel.

"Thank you," Bakari said, reaching toward the bag of herbs. "How much do I owe you?"

Kharlia snatched it back from him with a frown. "You don't think you're going to give this to someone by yourself, do you? I'm coming with you."

Bakari frowned. "I'm thankful for your help, Kharlia, but I need to do this myself. This is too dangerous to take you along. I assure you, I can access the knowledge I need to administer them correctly."

Before Kharlia could respond, the two of them heard loud voices and banging at the door of the next cottage over. So Bakari took a step toward the bag that Kharlia held.

Kharlia grabbed Bakari's hand and pulled him toward the back of her cottage. A strange thrill ran through his body at her touch. She picked up another bag in the small hallway and directed him out the back door.

It was dark now, and a breeze blew, but the air was still warm. Within a few dozen steps, they had cleared a small vegetable garden and had entered a narrow dirt trail leading into the nearby trees.

Bakari's head swirled with activity. The black-clad men began banging on Kharlia's door and ordering her to open it. Bakari hoped that, once they found her not at home, they would assume she was out helping someone in need. After they jogged down the trail for a bit, the dim lamplight from the village receded, and only a patch of partial moonlight showed through the full trees.

They moved silently around the village toward his horse. Yells from the mercenaries faded into the wind behind them.

"Adi," Bakari called to his horse a short time later. Adi lifted her head from a tuft of grass with a look of contentment.

Kharlia let Bakari's hand drop, and he felt disappointment at the loss of her touch. He untied his horse's rope and returned it to the pack he was carrying. At the same time, he pulled back out his cloak and draped it across his shoulders.

"You are a wizard," Kharlia said. Her chest still heaved from the exertion of the quick sprint there.

"I am."

She pointed to the cloak. "Are you an apprentice?"

Bakari shook his head. "Full wizard. Only a level two, though." Bakari stayed busy with the horse, for he didn't want to meet her eyes. Then he motioned for Kharlia to tie her two packs to the side of the horse.

"What's in the other pack?" he asked.

"Personal things. You never know when you will need to leave in a hurry." Kharlia smiled. And, once again, Bakari was calmed yet intrigued by her demeanor.

Kharlia didn't seem to want to say anything more about

her bag, so Bakari let the subject drop. He jumped up on his horse and looked back down at Kharlia. "I appreciate the help, Kharlia, but you must understand…this is dangerous."

"You are such a gentleman to worry about me so, Bakari. But those men back there, in the village, looked like the more dangerous option to me."

Kharlia put her left foot in the stirrup and grabbed Bakari's offered hand. As she swung her leg over the animal, her full-length cotton dress became tangled for a moment. After getting situated behind Bakari, she hugged his waist with her arms. Bakari proceeded to direct Adi back toward the main road out of town, taking off at a quick gallop. There were only a few hours left to figure out exactly how he would rescue the Chief Judge and administer the antidote.

CHAPTER NINE

Bakari found Kharlia to be a nice traveling companion. Despite the distractions of feeling her sweet breath on the back of his neck and having her arms wrapped around him, he liked that she was talkative, affable, and knowledgeable about many things. Most of all, Bakari was delighted at her love of learning. In this, they quickly shared a deep bond.

"Bak, how did you become a part of the Chief Judge's party?" Kharlia asked.

"Well, I am a scholar wizard serving in Cassian," Bakari told her.

"But, aren't you a little young—no offense—to ride with him?"

Bakari didn't know how to explain, without sounding like he was boasting, but he trusted Kharlia. "I enjoy a unique ability to remember everything I see or read."

"Ooh." Kharlia's breath came out onto the back of Bakari's neck. "That is amazing, Bak. I will need to remember not to say anything wrong, or you might bring it back up later."

Bakari stayed silent. He wasn't used to talking to girls and didn't know how to react. Then he felt a light tap on the back of his head.

"Bak, I was kidding." Kharlia laughed.

"Oh," Bak said in return. "Sorry, just thinking about the Chief Judge."

Kharlia breathed in a quick breath. "Oh, I'm sorry. Of course you would be worried about him."

As Bakari spoke of his dilemma to her, she was quite astonished and disturbed by his report of mercenaries kidnapping and poisoning the Chief Judge.

"So what will you do?" she asked.

"I need to free Roland." He decided to talk through his plan with her. "He is the most powerful wizard in the group. His raw talent exceeds that of many of the other full wizards. Just don't tell him I said that, or it will go to his head."

Kharlia laughed, and once again Bakari found himself pleased at the glee in her voice.

"But, how will that free the Chief Judge? They must have guards on him."

"If I can sneak up behind where Roland is and untie his hands, he will be free to pick up the Chief Judge and move him. I will need some type of distraction to lead them away from him for a few moments. Once Roland has the Chief Judge, the other wizards will act against the rebel group."

Kharlia road in silence for a few minutes. Bakari wondered if she had fallen asleep. But then, in a small voice, she said, "I will cause the distraction. Drop me off on the other side of their camp. I will walk in, pretending to be lost and hurt. I should be able to grant you enough time."

Bakari almost stopped the horse. He turned his head sideways to see her face. "Kharlia, I can't ask you to do that. These are dangerous men. If they have no compunctions regarding killing the Chief Judge, what would they do to you? I can't allow it."

"You can't allow it?" Kharlia said in a brisk voice. "I will make my own decision of whether I can help the Chief Judge or not, Bakari. I believe in his cause."

Bakari let out a long breath. He had seen Roland get into many a squabble with a young woman, and he wasn't wanting to find himself in one now. "I'm sorry if I spoke poorly," he conceded. "I only meant for you to understand the potential harm that could come. This is not your fight."

"This is anyone's fight who wants peace and freedom," Kharlia said.

Bakari nodded. "You are right, my lady, of course. We only have a few more hours until daylight, and it must be done before then."

"Why do these men want a king so badly?"

"They think a king will give them prestige. Many of them want to wield power under a king. They also think it will make this more like other kingdoms, once the barrier fails." Bak winced over his last remark. He hadn't meant to let that slip.

"The barrier is failing?"

Bakari breathed in deeply. "Let's simply say it is weakening. I need to find out more information before I can make a full assessment."

"So what is so wrong with being like other kingdoms?" Kharlia asked.

"Nothing, I guess." Bakari thought a moment. "We've had good kings and bad kings in the past: kings who brought prosperity and glory to the land and those who brought death and destruction. The judge system keeps that from happening. It balances power."

Their conversation trailed off after that.

Soon they arrived at the place where Bakari would have to let Kharlia dismount. She hopped off the horse first. Then, when Bakari dismounted and opened his mouth, she pointed a finger at him.

"Bak," Kharlia interrupted, intruding on his thoughts with a shake of her head, "I know what I'm doing."

Bakari tightened his jaw. "I know." He paused. "Just be careful."

"Of course." Kharlia smiled, and Bakari noticed for the first time a dimple in her right cheek.

"I only need a few minutes," Bakari added.

They stood in front of each other for a moment that seemed to stretch into longer. With a sudden step, Kharlia grabbed Bakari in a brief hug, then turned and walked off through the trees.

With one last look in Kharlia's direction, Bakari jumped back onto his horse and rode it around the edge of the camp to the south side. Sliding off his horse, he tethered her there and motioned for her to stay quiet.

Invoking a simple spell of silence, he walked with careful steps up to the sleeping camp. Through the outline of the dying fire, he saw two guards standing watch; neither seemed to be overly alert as they stood in boredom over the sleeping group.

Moving from tree to tree, he worked his way closer to the sleeping men. He recognized Roland's form and was happy to see him sitting in the back of the group, leaning against the trunk of a birch tree. His hands were tied behind him. Bakari couldn't see the Chief Judge and hoped they hadn't moved him far away.

Bakari snuck up behind Roland and whispered in his friend's ear. Only Roland's strict wizard training kept him from crying out in surprise. A small twitch in his neck was the only sign of his surprise.

"Bakari, what are you doing? Where did you go?" Roland whispered, his voice barely audible to Bakari.

"I went for some herbs to help the Chief Judge. He wasn't given a deadly potion, only a temporary debilitating one. I'm going to untie your hands. Soon there will be a distraction. When that happens, you will have only a few moments to get to the Chief Judge and run with him out of the camp."

"What distraction?" Roland asked very softly.

"Don't worry." Bakari had kept his voice low. A rustle of leaves in a slight breeze helped to hide their conversation.

Roland gave a small laugh. "You say *don't worry*? You've never been a covert operative type of wizard before, Bak. What do you know about plans?"

Bakari grunted at Roland's usual pomp. "Just because I haven't done it doesn't mean I don't know how to do it."

As soon as Bakari had finished untying Roland's hands, voices came from the other side of camp.

"Help!" came Kharlia's small voice.

Bakari felt his heart beat faster with apprehension for his new friend.

Roland began to move, and Bakari pushed him back down with a touch of his hand on Roland's head.

"Not yet," Bakari directed. "And, Roland, you are to save the Chief Judge. That is all. Don't worry about the fighting or anything else. The others can handle that well enough. Your job is to carry the Chief Judge to safety. Then we will heal him."

Bakari felt rather than heard Roland's grunt of frustration. He knew his friend would instead want to jump up and blast every one with an immense show of power.

In mere moments, the two guards moved to intercept Kharlia as she wandered aimlessly into their camp. Their backs were to Bakari and Roland. Bakari held Roland back once more, waiting for more commotion to ensue.

With a few loud words from Kharlia, other mercenaries gathered around her, with their leader coming out in front. He did not look happy at being woken up in the middle of the night.

"What is the meaning of this?" he asked his men.

The rest of the Chief Judge's party woke up now and watched the exchange with interest.

Kharlia suddenly slumped to the ground with a groan and began to cry. The mercenaries were now fully distracted.

"Go," commanded Bakari to Roland.

Roland rose from the ground and slid sideways behind a copse of birch trees. Then Bakari watched him run around behind a small grove of firs. A strangled sound met Bakari's ears, then a yell, followed by the uproar of running and shouting.

Roland came around a tree with the Chief Judge hanging over his shoulder, a guard chasing after him.

"This way," Bakari motioned.

Roland yelled loudly to his fellow wizards, "Onius! Gorn!"

The two wizards turned their heads toward him, as did the rest of the mercenaries. The wizards immediately understood what was happening. They broke their bands, stood up, and faced the mercenaries, their power already gathering. They had only remained where they were for the safety of the Chief Judge. Now that Roland had their leader, they fought back.

More men began chasing after Roland, who now followed Bakari away from the mercenaries. Their pursuit was quicker than Roland could run while carrying the Chief Judge.

Behind them all raced Alli, who had loosed her own bonds. She threw a dagger, catching one man in the side of the neck, then grabbed a branch and swung herself forward, her power accelerating her leap. Her legs grabbed another man by the waist and pulled him down. Twirling around him, she hit him with the hilt of a sword she'd managed to grab.

Another man approached Roland's back. He lunged for Roland's legs and took him to the ground, knocking the Chief Judge hard against a tree. Roland stood and brought his hands out in front of him, fire forming in them. But, before it could be released, Alli jumped up onto a nearby tree stump, somersaulted into the air, and came down hard on the mercenary, shoving his face into the dirt. After a quick hit to the head, he fell motionless.

The three young wizards rushed to the Chief Judge's side. His eyes were open, looking at them, but his body still failed to respond. Hearing noises from the direction of the camp, Bakari jumped up and saw a trail of fire, weaving its way through the trees.

A sudden cry pierced the air over the loud sounds of the battle.

Kharlia! Without thinking, Bakari raced back toward the fighting. One of the mercenaries held the girl with a knife at her throat. Bakari stopped in his tracks. He couldn't live with himself if something happened to her.

"Onius!" Bakari yelled.

Onius turned to the man holding Kharlia, and the man pushed the knife closer to the girl's skin, drawing a thin line of blood.

"Don't come any closer, or she dies," the man said.

"I don't even know who she is," Onius said back.

Bakari's face went pale as he realized that Onius would indeed allow Kharlia to die to save the rest of them.

"She is my friend!" Bakari shouted. "Help her!"

Onius turned to him. "Bakari, the Chief Judge is more important than her. We must get him away and get help. If this buys us time..."

Bakari felt astonished at the counselor's lack of empathy and tried to explain, "She *is* the help!" His face now turned red as he became angry, angrier than he could remember ever being. He felt protective of Kharlia. He wasn't a particularly strong wizard, but hadn't he told Roland just minutes before that he knew how to do it all? His mind filled with information, and he sifted through it for a solution, all in the blink of an eye.

Kharlia squeaked, and her dark brown eyes bulged with a pleading look. It was his fault she was here. If anything happened to her, Bakari couldn't bear it. He closed his eyes to think more clearly.

Bakari heard every sound independently. His mind followed the footfalls of the mercenaries retreating through the forest. He could hear Roland and Alli with the Chief Judge, moving him farther away. Then he heard a bird, a large vulture, that had previously been resting peacefully up in a tree, and a thought came to him.

Bakari reached back inside his mind to a book he'd read once; it was almost a fairy tale. He reached with his mind toward the bird as the character in the book had done and commanded the creature. A loud squawking ensued, but the bird obeyed him. Bakari led it through the air in swift silence toward the mercenary.

The rush of wings and the air blowing against his face consumed him as he became one with the bird. Then, into his mind, the mercenary appeared in front of him. He was a small man from this new point of view. Swooping down, still one with the creature's mind, Bakari plunged toward the man's face.

Only moments before being struck, the man glanced up and screamed. The bird, with its large beak and talons, ripped into the man's face, clawing at him and poking him with its beak. The mercenary dropped his knife, and Kharlia fell away from him. Gorn gathered the girl away, and Onius moved in front of Bakari.

"Bakari!" Onius yelled. "Stop this now!"

Bakari remained with his eyes still closed, pecking the man's face through his connection with the bird, barely registering Onius's voice. Bakari was so angry and frustrated that Kharlia had almost been killed that he now lost control of himself within the vulture. The bird's head turned and stared at Onius.

"Bakari!" Onius raised his voice. "This must stop."

Bakari could hear Onius's yell. What right did Onius have to tell him to stop? He lifted the bird's wings and started to move toward Onius.

"No, Bak. I'm all right now," Kharlia said.

Bakari stopped the bird mid-flight. The voice of Kharlia penetrated his mind. His eyelids fluttered open, and the bird dropped to the ground as their minds' contact severed. After a dazed moment, the poor vulture flew back up into the trees, its own simple mind back in control once again.

Kharlia grabbed Bakari into a big hug. "Oh, Bakari. What did you do?"

"I saved you," he said. His anger had abated, and he wiped sweat from his forehead. It felt good to hold her in his arms. He felt something new and exciting around her.

Onius took a huge step up in front of him and, with little compassion, pushed Kharlia out of his arms. "That is forbidden, Bakari. You know it's against our laws to bond with a creature. It's unnatural." Onius stood fuming a moment. "My boy," he said, taking his voice down a notch, "you could have become lost in that creature. Where did you learn to do that?"

Bakari was exhausted, but he stood his ground. "Counselor, I remember everything I read. I just know things."

Onius took a step back, and Gorn joined him.

"I did what needed to be done. The outcome was what matters. I saved Kharlia and the Chief Judge."

At the mention of the Chief Judge, everyone turned in the

direction that Roland and Ali had run off.

"This conversation is not over." Onius looked troubled. "We will discuss this later, when the Chief Judge has been healed. I forbid you any use of magic until that time."

Bakari only nodded his head. He understood Onius's concerns. But saving Kharlia was worth the price. With a sudden flash of thought, he realized that he could indeed do so much more with his magic. What good was studying if you couldn't use the knowledge to help someone? He reached for Kharlia's hand and walked toward where the horse and bags were tied up.

Within fifteen minutes, Gorn, Onius, Bakari, Kharlia, and a few other guards stood gathered around Roland, Alli, and the Chief Judge. Bakari brought Kharlia's medicine bag over and motioned for the others to back away. He soon found himself standing next to Roland as Kharlia prepared the healing herbs.

"Why does Onius keep watching you like you are the plague?" Roland asked.

Bakari recounted what he had done to save Kharlia.

"A rule breaker now? Bakari, I wouldn't have thought possible of our quiet scholar." Roland smiled.

Bakari blushed, his dark cheeks growing darker.

"Ahhh. It was the girl, wasn't it?" Roland tried unsuccessfully to hold back a laugh. "It's always a girl that gets us in trouble, Bakari. Remember that."

The others turned toward Roland with a frown. Then Alli stepped up to him.

"Seems like a girl *helped you* quite a bit back there, Apprentice. Without me, those mercenaries would have killed you and the Chief Judge."

"I had the situation in hand, Apprentice," Roland retorted. "I was about to blast them all away."

Onius stepped forward. "Children," he chided the two apprentices. "This is why you are still apprentices. Roland, you should know better. Apologize to the young lady."

"Me, apologize?"

Onius glared at his young student.

With a deep breath, Roland turned to Alli and, in a sweet voice, said, "Alli, my lady, I apologize for my lack of appreciation for your efforts to help me. Your help was timely and appreciated." He then winked at her before turning back to Onius, as if to say, *Was that good enough?*

Onius huffed, but the rest of the group smiled.

Then Kharlia stood and turned toward Roland. "Bakari has told me you may have abilities to heal."

Roland regarded the rest of the group smugly. "Yes, I think I might. Last time I helped Onius, I felt that I could have given more." He walked toward Kharlia and knelt down by the Chief Judge. As before, he placed his hands on him, and everyone watched. "I can feel the poison inside him."

Onius turned to Gorn and raised his brows. All watched Roland in silence. After fifteen minutes, the poison began to spill out of the Chief Judge's pores and onto the ground.

The gathered crowd gasped.

Onius and Gorn stood off to one side, alone, but their words were loud enough for others to hear.

"We have three powerful young people here," Gorn stated.

"Powerful and very dangerous," Onius said back, his stern eyes looking over at Roland, Alli, and, last of all, Bakari.

Bakari heard Onius's words and looked down at his shoes. It was true: the three of them *were* powerful, beyond what the older wizards had expected. But he didn't think he was very dangerous. He was just a scholar of little consequence to the land.

CHAPTER TEN

Two weeks later Alli rode in the back of the Chief Judge's party alongside Roland, Bakari, and Kharlia. She looked ahead at the Chief Judge. He was doing better, though he tired more easily now. A week of rest for him and delays due to rain meant the party from Cassian was now entering the city of River Bend much later than expected.

Two nights previous, a summer storm had severely dampened their evening and had put everyone into a sour mood. However, this day dawned bright, and the temperatures rose quickly throughout the day. Being closer to the Elvyn Forest and the Dunn River kept the heat from becoming too unbearable, though, it did increase the humidity.

After a brief stop here in River Bend, they would take the road in a northwesterly direction another four or five days to reach the Citadel.

"Things are too quiet." Alli turned to Roland from her horse, which was next to his. "I don't like it."

"Paranoid," Roland said with a smirk.

"It's not right. It's still early enough in the evening that there should be children running around and people carrying their food home to prepare for the evening meal."

"Maybe they are tired and resting," Roland said, not paying much attention. "Same things I want to do: find a nice inn, eat some food, maybe watch a nice lass do some singing, then go to bed."

Alli glared at him.

"So, Bak, what do you think?" Roland turned to his other side, where the young scholar wizard rode next to his new friend, Kharlia. Bakari and Kharlia both had their faces stuck in books and didn't pay Roland any attention.

"Bakari?" Roland said, raising his voice. When no acknowledgment from him was forthcoming, Roland held his hand up and pushed a spark of power into Bakari's shoulder. The scholar wizard jerked his head up in surprise and fumbled his book, which fell to the ground.

"What did you do that for?" He rubbed his shoulder with a frown as he stopped his horse to retrieve the book.

Kharlia glanced up at that point and smiled. She apparently hadn't heard Roland either.

"Never mind," Roland said. "I would be surprised if either of you even knew where we actually are."

"Don't pay attention to him, Bakari." Alli came to his aid.

Bakari grunted in agreement. "Where are we?"

Roland laughed. "Oh, Bak, you are priceless." He looked toward Kharlia and smiled. "And it appears you have found a match. Her nose is farther in her book than yours."

Both Kharlia and Bakari blushed.

"Roland, don't tease her," Bakari said.

Roland seemed to want to say something, but the guarded visage on Bakari's face stopped him.

Alli moved her horse closer to Bakari. "We are in River Bend, Bak. But I was telling Roland that it feels wrong: too quiet."

"Didn't you grow up not too far east of here?"

"Yes I did, just northeast of here." Alli smirked over toward Roland. "At least someone pays attention to things I say."

Roland rolled his eyes. "That's not fair; he remembers *everything*. It's his greatest power as a scholar." He lightly kicked his heels into his horse, spurring it forward toward Onius.

Alli turned her attention back to Bakari. "I don't like the feel of this place."

"You are a battle wizard, Alli. You should say something."

"Gorn?" Alli called up ahead. But before Gorn could respond, a group of men clad in chain mail came around a building and stopped in the middle of the road.

The captain of the Chief Judge's guard moved out in front and ordered some of his men to keep the Chief Judge and the other riders safe. Onius moved up next to the captain.

"What is this?" the captain barked at the leader of the new party.

"Order of the judge," said the apparent leader of the opposing group. "All parties must be inspected."

"This is the Chief Judge's party. We are traveling to the Citadel to meet with Wizard Kanzar Centari, at his invitation."

"This is not the Chief Judge's jurisdiction," the man said.

The sounds of swords being drawn rang down the road as the Chief Judge's guard drew their weapons. Alli felt nervous and moved up next to Gorn.

Onius nudged his horse forward. "The Chief Judge's jurisdiction is all of Alaris. You have no right to stop, search, or hinder this party."

Three other men rode out from behind the group of soldiers. These were not dressed in chain mail, ready for battle, but instead in robes of silk. They were of differing ages, but the youngest one held the airs of being in charge and rode out in front.

"Please excuse my general here; he gets rather protective of me."

A warning sounded then in Alli's head, with the mention of a *general*. She remembered that only the Chief Judge commanded generals in the armed forces of Alaris. In fact, there were only two generals: one stationed in Cassian and the other in the training camp at Lake Corwan. As far as she knew, this man was not one of them.

"I am Mericus, the western judge."

At this declaration, the Chief Judge rode forward and sternly said, "Mericus, I have not met you yet. I was not informed an election had occurred."

Mericus bowed with a slight nod to Daymian. "Chief Judge, these are difficult times, as you realize. I have been recently appointed to fill the vacancy left by the untimely death of our last judge."

"That is not in accordance with the laws of Alaris. An election by the people determines the judges." The Chief Judge frowned.

"In normal times, yes. However, with the barrier failing and battles and unrest breaking out all over Alaris, it seemed better to fill the position as soon as possible."

Alli turned and glanced at Roland with a worried look in

her eye.

Roland took the hint and stepped his horse forward. "Who appointed you to amend the law?"

Onius glared at Roland.

Mericus brought his horse another step closer. Both sides tensed.

"Roland, isn't it?"

Roland, taken aback by the knowledge of this stranger, shifted in his saddle and nodded.

"Well, Roland, I am appointed by High Wizard Kanzar Centari. You do acknowledge his authority, don't you?"

The Chief Judge's party gasped. Onius tried to restrain Roland but he rode closer to Mericus. "I do acknowledge his authority over dealings with wizards and magic; however, he has no authority over the Chief Judge and the laws of the land."

Mericus snorted loudly and regarded his two fellow companions. "This young wizard seems to be educated in the fine art of diplomacy." After a brief chuckle, he turned back to the Chief Judge. "The people in the North, East, and West acknowledged his wisdom and his desire for the good of the people. Through local meetings and city councils, they have given him the authority to choose new judges that will be able to protect the people during these difficult times. It is all perfectly legal, I assure you."

Roland's face turned red. Alli noticed him watching Onius carefully. The counselor wizard should be stepping forward and helping his apprentice. Bakari took that moment to break through the crowd and lean in next to Roland. Alli also moved closer to hear what he would say.

"Roland," he whispered. "It is legal. The people's councils can vote for someone to act as a proxy for them to appoint at least a temporary judge until elections can be held. It was a provision inserted into the law to be used during times of war or other maladies in which it was deemed *unsafe* or *impractical* to hold elections."

Roland looked up at Onius, who had listened to Bakari's information. Onius motioned the young wizards back a dozen steps to confer with the Chief Judge.

"Chief Judge," Onius said to Daymian, "these are dangerous times. I counsel you not to start a fight here. All three of those judges are wizards also. Mericus is a powerful wizard. The other two I do not know. I've not been to the Citadel lately, but Kanzar appears to be pushing events forward on his own."

Overhearing the conversation, Alli pulled a sword off her back. "We have me, Gorn, Onius, Roland, and Bakari plus the best of the Chief Judge's guards here. I would call it a fair fight." The air crackled with her power, which was trying to come forth. "I could level their general and his men with one word."

"Alli," Gorn said. "This is not your decision."

"Chief Judge, let me go up and talk to them privately," Onius offered graciously. "I hold no small reputation among the wizards. I would like to see this end peacefully."

All eyes turned to the Chief Judge. In the end, it was his call. After a moment of silence, he gave an almost imperceptible nod toward his counselor wizard.

Roland clicked to his horse, but Onius grabbed the reins.

"I will do this alone," Onius said.

They stood quietly as Onius approached the three opposing wizards. They talked in hushed tones so neither side could hear what was being said.

Bakari motioned the Chief Judge over to where he and Alli stood. "Sir, you *are* still the Chief Judge even though, technically, they were appointed lawfully. You still have authority to override them in certain things. One of those things is being in command of the armed forces. They are breaking the law by naming a general without your permission."

"I know, Bak. I know. But I need to be careful. I underestimated the hunger for power that has been stirring. I do not want to start a civil war, especially against wizards. I have sworn to uphold this land, not destroy it. I will not break that peace easily."

Bakari stood up taller and took off his glasses. Then he glanced over at Alli, who nodded her assent.

"Chief Judge, I would not fight against you," Bakari began, "and I think many other wizards would be on your side. Please do not presume that all wizards vie for power against you."

Daymian put his hand on Bakari's shoulder while watching Alli. "Thank you for reminding me, my young scholar. You have been a good friend for a number of years. And, Alli, I see you agree with Bakari here. I do not think, however, that all of your kind thinks the same way as you two."

"I'm afraid you're right." Bakari moved his eyes to Onius and the three wizards who had usurped the judgeships. "But know there are many on your side, Sir."

Onius turned around and headed back toward the group.

Before he arrived, Daymian pulled Bakari aside and whispered something into his ear that Alli couldn't hear.

"I negotiated a settlement," Onius said to the group around the Chief Judge.

Daymian motioned for Onius to continue as Alli, Roland, and Bakari moved closer to hear.

"As it is late in the day, we will stay here this evening: all of us in one inn."

"So they can guard us?" broke in Alli.

"Let me finish, Apprentice," chastised Onius.

Alli's cheeks reddened. Ooh, how it grated her when Onius said that. Gorn had, at moments, put her in her place, but *he* was her mentor. She had tolerated that. But Onius Neeland, wizard though he was, was arrogant and belittling to her. It was not something she would take for very long. She would play it down as being from a stressful situation for now, but she wouldn't take much more.

"As I said, we will stay here this evening." Onius motioned toward the city. "In the morning, one of the judges and the general and his men will escort us to the Citadel. If we all ride hard and the weather holds, we can be there in four days' time. At that point, the Chief Judge can meet with the High Wizard and sort things out for himself."

Alli noticed Onius's use of *High Wizard*, Kanzar's self-proclaimed title, and alarms went off in her head for the second time. Was Onius on the side of this *High Wizard*? The two men had known each other for a long, long time. It wouldn't be hard to grasp. She looked around. No one else seemed to have noticed his reference to Kanzar as *High Wizard*.

"And, what do we get in return out of this settlement?" Roland asked. "It seems fairly one-sided."

"We get to keep our heads on our shoulders and to be escorted in safety, Apprentice!" Onius' voice boomed. "And, Chief Judge, I would submit that both of our apprentice wizards here should not be included in these privy councils if they cannot control their wagging tongues."

Alli watched Roland take a step back on his horse. He, too, she knew, was tired of being called an apprentice. Bakari shrugged his shoulders and spread his hands out to his sides when Roland looked toward him.

"Onius," the Chief Judge growled. "Though young he is, your *apprentice*, as you refer to him, has spoken correctly. What kind of negotiation did you procure for us? I will not submit to an escort that is virtually holding us prisoner. I am still the Chief Judge of this land."

Alli smiled over at Roland. It was nice to see the Chief Judge censure the great counselor wizard for once.

"As Chief Judge, these are my demands: One," Daymian said, counting it off on his fingers, "I am the only person authorized to promote a man to general. This so-called general of theirs will either step down himself or be named as a captain by me. Two, I will have my guards stationed outside of the inn along with their guards. I expect no trouble. And, three, I want to know where the other two judges are going to be and will send an armed escort with them, to ensure their safety, of course." Daymian smiled meaningfully.

Onius's face reddened. He bowed his head slightly and returned on his horse to speak with the trio of wizards. Voices were raised, and arms waved around in the air.

Onius rode back to the group. "Chief Judge, this is their final resolution, based on your demands: Their general will be demoted and will leave at first light. As you pointed out, their two judges will need an escort. So, this newly demoted captain and a few of his best, handpicked soldiers will follow Mericus and another judge to Cassian to maintain the laws and peace there while you are away. Your guards can stand outside the inn tonight, if you think they need to, but River Bend is a safe place. That should cover enough of your demands, Sir."

With all of his demands apparently swept aside, the Chief Judge's cheeks grew red above his short beard. "Onius, counsel me. What do you think we should do?"

"Sir, I have served you and those before you for years. I have always guided the Chief Judge to keep the peace and the law. Things are moving forward more quickly than we thought, and I would advise caution at this time. Keep a level head, and get to the Citadel. I assure you, I will have words with Kanzar immediately upon our arrival."

Daymian raised his voice to his people. "We will stay here tonight and leave early in the morning, resuming our trip to the Citadel. You will treat the people in this town with respect and pay for any services used. Captain, have your men secure the horses and find someone to feed and brush them, and then report back to me. All of you others may leave for the inn."

Alli walked with Roland, Bakari, and Kharlia toward the inn.

"I still think we should fight," Alli said.

Roland grinned. "Me, too. I'm itching to use some power."

"You fight too?" Alli asked. "I thought you were a counselor."

"Alli, dear, I assure you I am much more than a counselor. Maybe we could spar sometime."

Alli took a step closer to Roland, spinning a knife in her left hand. "That would be my pleasure." She would like nothing more than to put this arrogant boy in his place.

"Don't do anything stupid, you two." Bakari moved between them. "You are still apprentices."

Alli and Roland both scowled at Bakari.

He laughed. "I was kidding."

Roland then spread his hands wide to the side. "First, you find yourself a girl and take over the power of a vulture; and now, you're making jokes. Bak, you might just turn out all right after all."

CHAPTER ELEVEN

Bakari couldn't sit still at the inn when he knew there was an old library in River Bend that he had never visited before. And it didn't take much convincing for Kharlia to agree to come along with him.

It wasn't hard for the wizard to escape the guards around the inn. The night was clear, with stars shining down that lit their way to the library. Bakari basked in the warmth radiating from Kharlia as he walked by her side. It was a strange feeling he had for her, strange only in the sense that it was new. He admired her and felt protective of her well-being.

She glanced his way and smiled, and he felt his face redden in the starlight. He thought back to the night when he had saved her from the mercenaries by merging his mind with the vulture's mind. He had known it was forbidden, but in the moment of his need, it had come to him. It had been the only solution he could think of.

Thinking back now, he realized that the hardest part had been separating his mind from the animal's after he was finished. But there was still no evil taint in him or foul sensation. In fact, the ability continued to intrigue him.

He pushed aside his thoughts on that subject for now. What he needed to find out was how the barrier had been created, what kept it powered, and why it was now failing. In his methodical mind, he knew there must be a connection between the rise of the King-men, the move by Kanzar and his judges to assert more control, and the failing of the barrier. Too many coincidences didn't sit well with him.

He and Kharlia soon came upon the small stone library and walked around its dark exterior. Their dark skin and clothes would help them to blend into the shadows of the night if anyone looked in their direction.

"How do we get in?" Kharlia asked. Finding that the doors were all locked, she kept glancing around, worry on her face.

Bakari wondered how she was holding up in this situation, so far from her home. He smiled and walked up to a back door again. He only felt mildly bad as he pressed his hand to the door's lock and used his power to unlock the mechanism. They weren't there to do any harm, only to find out some information.

Bakari look around once more and then pushed the door open, motioning for Kharlia to follow him inside.

"That's cheating," she whispered with a twinkle in her eye.

Bakari raised his shoulders. He had never thought of it as *cheating*. It was an inherent power he held, a power he undertook to use for good.

Closing the door behind them, he gazed around the dark room. Starlight gleamed through the windows, highlighting bookshelves and tables. He took a moment to breathe in the aroma of the books and scrolls, and his heart leapt inside him. This is where he felt most at home: surrounded by knowledge. He stepped toward a nearby bookshelf and ran his hands lovingly over the spines of the books.

"Isn't it wonderful?" Kharlia said, her voice floating across the dark room.

Bakari smiled. "Yes, it is. It's larger than I would have thought for a small town. Many of the libraries in border towns close to the Elvyn Forest hold more books about pre-barrier life. This might be the result of Elvyn influence and desire for learning."

They both took separate directions as they walked around the room for a few minutes to get their bearings. They came back together on the room's far side and found two other smaller rooms, windowless and dark.

"I will light a candle in one of those rooms. We can study in there without being noticed," Bakari said. "The Chief Judge wants to know more about the barrier."

Kharlia nodded, but she was only half listening as she moved around the room, probably hunting for books on healing or herbs. Bakari watched her walk, her dark cloak swirling softly around her homespun dress, and marveled again at her poise. He had to turn away to remember why he was there.

Fortunately, hundreds of years ago, a few scholar wizards had designed a system for cataloging scrolls and books. This system was implemented throughout most of the land, and, indeed, this library used the system he was used to. That would make searching for the right books easier.

Focusing his attention on the history section, he noticed several books he had not read before, a few going back prior to the barrier. He picked up a sampling of them and settled into a chair in the reading room. Kharlia soon joined him, and the two sat in comfortable silence, each immersed in their own worlds.

Eventually, Bakari took off his glasses and leaned his head back in his chair. "Very interesting, but nothing about the barrier," he said out loud, mostly to himself.

"Have you tried the scrolls?" Kharlia asked.

"No, but I will. We need to head back soon. I was hoping to find something useful."

Bakari headed over to the cabinet that held the scrolls. Dragging his hand down the cabinet, he read the catalog numbers. There were some scrolls here about herbs, so he pulled them out for Kharlia. When he came to the historical section, he found three other scrolls. He took all of them back to the smaller room, handing Kharlia the ones on herbs. Her cheeks colored in excitement, and the corners of her small mouth turned upwards in a large smile.

He took the three historical scrolls to his side of the table and opened the first one. On it, he found a map already known to him. The second held a treatise on different forms of government and their advantages. And the third was a historical and factual account of the weather.

"Nothing again!" Bakari furrowed his brows. "I'm taking these back, and then we should be going. Did you find anything?"

"Oh yes!" Kharlia smiled up at him. "Wonderful things." She had brought along a small bag with parchment, ink, and a quill and was frantically taking notes. "Quite a few herbs that I hadn't thought to mix together."

Bakari walked back to the cabinet with his shoulders

slumped. He had hoped so much for some additional insight. He was afraid of what might happen to them when they reached the Citadel. He slid the scrolls back into their place, but the third one didn't fit anymore and poked out farther than the others.

"Hmmm," Bakari murmured. "They fit before."

He slid it in again, but still the scroll wouldn't go in any farther. Pulling back out the other two, he crouched down and peered into the cabinet. Then he reached inside the dark cube and felt around. He was surprised to find something in the back, so he pulled it out. He held it in his hands: a small scroll, edges frayed, tied with a tiny strap of leather. It must have fallen down earlier, when he had removed the three larger scrolls.

Taking the newfound scroll back to the lit room, he sat down and rolled the leather tie off of the scroll. Then he opened it up flat on the table. It was a map, drawn with thick, unskilled strokes. The entire scroll was only about twelve inches tall and six inches wide.

Kharlia moved around the table and walked up behind Bakari. He tried not to be distracted by her presence, even though she was hanging over him, her body slightly touching his shoulder. He smoothed out the scroll again.

"What is it?" Kharlia asked.

"I'm not sure," Bakari admitted. "It is not a map I recognize." He ran his fingers over portions of it, trying to get his bearings. "Wait, I think this is where we are right now—River Bend—and this is the Dunn River." He pointed down the length of the map.

"And this is Cassian." Kharlia pointed to a large circle on the map closer toward the center and farther down the scroll than River Bend.

Now that Bakari had found his bearings on the map, he picked out many landmarks he knew. He worked his way up and down the scroll. The Citadel, marked in red, had lines from the top right of the scroll pointing down to it. Following these lines up, Bakari gasped.

"I've never heard about a city here." Bakari pointed to a spot that would now be the most northeastern portion of Alaris, a portion on the other side of the Dunn River. It was marked with a blue circle and a symbol next to it. Light lines extended from it in the form of a sunburst, then broadened out and circled all around Alaris in its entirety.

"What does it mean?" Kharlia asked.

"The writing is in an abbreviated language form called *symbolus*, in which symbols refer to a string of words. It's a more compact form of taking notes. This one means *Celestial Star* or *Celestar*."

Kharlia looked at Bakari with questioning eyes.

"And then, these lines here, around the symbol, are drawn around the map to represent what seems to be the barrier." Bakari's voice rose in excitement. "This is the first thing I have seen linking the Citadel to the barrier, and it seems to go through this spot, called Celestar."

Hunching closer, Kharlia pointed to the blue spot on the map. "Something was drawn underneath the blue mark."

Bakari inspected it closer and agreed. He held up the scroll and moved it in front of the candlelight, being careful not to get it too close. His mouth hung open as a shape began to appear under the blue circle. Unmistakable in its form, it appeared to have been drawn in far greater detail than the rest of the map.

"A dragon!" Bakari let out a gasp of joy. "A dragon, Kharlia. Do you realize what this means?"

Kharlia sat down next to Bakari at the table and shook her head.

"Numerous books at the Citadel mentioned dragon-like creatures, but many dismiss these references as exaggerations. The few tidbits we do have never tell us about where they came from or where they went to or if they actually existed at all. They do mention these creatures' tremendous power and might: enough power to overcome dozens of wizards."

Kharlia ran her finger over the spot. "Do you think they were real?"

Bakari took a long moment before answering as his mind ran through the numerous books he had read since he was five and had been dropped off at the Citadel door. He tried to piece together the images on the map in front of him and what it all meant. The conclusion or answer eluded him at the moment, but this information was more, far more than he had hoped for. Celestar was the first place he had ever seen marked on a map that might hold the key to the barrier.

"Bak?" Kharlia prodded him again for an answer.

"Sorry, Kharlia, just trying to put it all together. It's so exciting. The only other sure reference I have read about dragons comes from Mahli, where our people are from. It was a story about people who rode on dragons and about how the greatest rider became a king, the king of the whole land."

"When I was little, my mother used to tell me stories of dragons and magic, passed down to her from her parents." Kharlia's eyes glistened in the candlelight, and she paused before speaking again. "I sure do miss her sometimes."

Bakari didn't quite know what to say. He rubbed his hand across the top of hers. "I hardly knew my parents." He spoke softly in the quiet room. "They, or someone, dropped me off at the Citadel when I was only five years old. I remember my mother's soft voice, singing to me, and my father's long, braided hair. The wizards say I was left by the front gate with a note that said to call me Bakari."

"I'm sorry," Kharlia said. She sat quiet for a moment, then looked back at Bakari. "So, the dragons? Do you think they are real…and not just children's stories?"

"Maybe, but maybe not. I don't understand it all, but I need to tell the Chief Judge. He could send some wizards from the Citadel to this place, Celestar." He turned his head back to the map again, memorizing every detail. It wouldn't be right for him to take the scroll away from its rightful place.

Then they snuffed out the candle, returned the scrolls and books to their shelves, and headed through the dark room toward the back door. As Bakari reached for the doorknob, he heard voices outside. He turned back to Kharlia with his finger to his lips, and they both crouched down to not be seen through any of the small windows. Then they listened to the voices talking.

"Mericus, what are you doing here as a judge?" Bakari recognized Onius's voice.

"Onius, good to see you again," Mericus said, his tone arrogant. "You have not been around the Citadel in a while."

"And, what does that mean?"

"Onius, don't get so upset," Mericus said as if trying to calm him down. "I am sure Kanzar has plans for you too."

"Plans?" Onius asked.

"You know Kanzar…he always has plans. I'm not always privy to them, but I don't mind being a recipient of his generosity: first, as a judge," the voice of Mericus dropped lower, almost to a whisper, "then, who knows?"

Before Onius could say anything more, another voice spoke.

"Wizard, you owe me some money," the gruff voice said.

"I owe you nothing," Mericus said. "Your job was to take the Chief Judge, and you botched it."

"Mericus, what have you done?" Onius said, raising his voice.

"We kidnapped him as agreed and administered the poison," the third man said. "It was your wizards who interfered. Pay up as you agreed or else there might be new problems that you can't control."

Bakari turned to Kharlia and mouthed the word *mercenary* to her. She clearly understood: Onius and Mericus were talking to the captain of the mercenaries who had kidnapped the Chief Judge. They turned their attention back to the conversation.

"Don't threaten us," Mericus said.

The mercenary captain laughed. "You wizards need me. You are too high and mighty to get your own hands dirty."

"That is where you are wrong, Captain," Mericus said.

A bright light flashed through the outlines of the door, and the night fell silent for a moment.

"Mericus," Onius growled. "You didn't need to kill him."

"I didn't like his attitude, and, anyways, he isn't dead, merely stunned," Mericus said. "People need to learn their place. Their attitude toward wizards has grown complacent during the reign of judges."

"Be careful, Mericus." Onius spoke with barely concealed contempt. "Don't climb too high, or you might fall."

"Oh, I see," Mericus said. "You want the power for yourself."

"I have been serving judges for more years than you have been alive, Mericus. Don't be greedy. These are dangerous times. I obviously need to talk to Kanzar. Things have moved far ahead of me while I have been away from the Citadel."

"The plan is still the same, Onius. We must have a king. And that king will be a wizard. Are you getting a conscience now?" Mericus said.

"The Chief Judge is a good man. I don't want to see him hurt by greedy wizards," Onius said.

"You have been away from the Citadel for too long, Onius." Mericus's voice faded as the two walked farther behind the building. "You have grown soft in Cassian. You care for the Chief Judge too much. And, from the look of things, you are losing control of your little apprentices."

"I have not lost control of anything, Mericus." Onius's voice also got softer, and Bakari tried to follow the voices by moving around the room to another window.

"So you do have them under control. I hear brilliant things

about those three from Cassian. News has reached us in the Citadel. They'd better not get in our way."

"Their powers are considerable," Onius agreed. "All three are moving ahead faster than normal. I admit, they do need to learn better their roles as wizards, especially Roland. Their powers could upset the balance of the Citadel."

"You need to discuss their abilities with Kanzar and the Council, Onius," Mericus directed.

"Don't worry about them, Mericus. I've got it covered. We just continue to appeal to Roland's vanity. And Gorn has Alli under control. She is powerful, but still young. She can't do anything on her own. Then Bakari..."

Bakari perked up at the mention of his name, his head already reeling from the traitorous talk of the two wizards. Kharlia looked at him more intently, and he realized that he was breathing hard and clenching his fists.

Onius continued, "Bakari, I might have underestimated. The merging of his mind with a creature could be dangerous for us. I hadn't realized that all his knowledge was so accessible for him."

Bakari couldn't believe his ears. Him, dangerous? Onius was much more powerful than he was. Bakari didn't understand what Onius was afraid of. It didn't make any sense. This was the second time the Counselor wizard referred to him as being dangerous.

The two wizards then moved too far away for Bakari to hear anything more. He slumped down onto the floor, his back to a wall. Kharlia slid over next to him and took his hand in hers. Bakari didn't know what to say. She would be in danger now because of him. He needed some time to think this through. And, he needed to leave before Onius found out that they had listened to this conversation between the two wizards.

"Celestar," Kharlia said softly.

Bakari turned his head. "What?"

"We need to go to Celestar," Kharlia repeated. "You were wondering what you should do. The best way to help the Chief Judge now is to go to Celestar and find out what is happening to the barrier."

Bakari was amazed. "How did you know what I was thinking?"

Kharlia smiled back at him. "Bak, you are not a hard person to read. You carry your emotions on your face. And, I also heard the conversation. It's too dangerous for you to stay here. I don't know Onius well, but Mericus seems dangerous enough. You can't go to the Citadel right now, and you can't go back to Cassian. That's where Mericus is going."

"But I don't even know where Celestar is, Kharlia. I'm a scholar, not a battle wizard or an adventurer. I've hardly even been outside the palace for the past two years. This trip is making me wish I had never left Cassian."

Kharlia frowned at that, and Bakari realized what he had said. "I mean..." he stumbled over his words. "I am glad I met you, Kharlia. I really am. But I'm not cut out for these types of adventures."

"But you *are* a wizard, Bakari, and the smartest person I know," Kharlia said, holding his hand in hers as she praised him. "Together, we will find a way to get there."

"We?" Bakari caught on to her line of thinking. "No,

Kharlia. I can't drag you into this. You could be in danger."

Kharlia dropped Bakari's hand. "There you go again, thinking you can make my choices for me." She smiled to soften the words. "Like I told you before, this is a fight we must all be a part of. I want to help you."

Bakari didn't know what to say. He did enjoy being around Kharlia. Her presence made him stronger. But this task could be dangerous. He opened his mouth to argue with her.

But Kharlia spoke first. "And I want to be with you," Kharlia said in a timid voice. "I like you, Bakari."

Bakari hoped Kharlia didn't notice his burning face. He had never had a girl tell him that before. Why would someone want to be with him, a boring scholar? He opened his mouth to speak, but Kharlia had a different idea and moved in closer. She kissed him hastily on the lips. Her lips, soft and warm, made Bakari forget what he was going to say.

"We need to find some provisions and then get out of town tonight," Kharlia said. "I'm glad I brought my pack with me." She motioned to the pack on the floor next to her. "But we need to find you a few things."

"What about the Chief Judge and my friends?" Bakari asked. "I need to warn them. They need to know. We need to think this through more. I need more time."

"I don't think we have time to think this through more, Bak. We need to act now."

Bakari slowly released a big breath. Then he adjusted his glasses, stood up, and walked back toward the back door. Putting his hand on the door knob, he turned it quietly.

"Let's go, then."

CHAPTER TWELVE

L eaving River Bend was easier for Bakari and Kharlia than they thought it would be. Most of the guards had been assigned to watch the inn where the Chief Judge's party was staying. And they'd all relaxed as soon as they had realized the Chief Judge did not mean to cause any problems.

Bakari snuck around the back side of the stables. Peering into the stalls, he found Adi. The stable hands had finished their work for the night and now sat outside in the warm evening air, playing a game with dice.

With Kharlia on the lookout, Bakari bridled and saddled his horse in silence. Then, grabbing a sack of oats and a brush he had found in the stall, Bakari motioned for Kharlia to mount the horse. He led them in a slow walk out the back door of the stable and into the dark summer night.

Following a loose trail, he kept a steady pace through a nearby pasture. A gate on its far side let them out into the Dunn Forest and closer to the banks of the river. Once they were clear of the town, he mounted the horse as well, and they began a slow trot, keeping the sounds of the Dunn River on their right-hand side.

Bakari didn't like riding at night. There were too many things unseen and a much better chance for the horse to stumble on unsure footing. But he knew they needed to get as far away as possible. They rode on in a slight strip of tall grass next to a small trail, trying to hide their passing as much as possible. Kharlia wrapped her arms around him from behind, and he recognized the scent of lilac — *How did she manage that?*

For the next two days, they rode as far as they could each day, resting at night under the trees along the bank of the river. Bakari suspected that they were far enough from River Bend now that they wouldn't be found.

On the evening of the third day, Kharlia led Bakari to a small copse of trees next to the river bank, where Adi could drink and they could get some much needed rest. Giving the horse a few handfuls of oats to replenish her energy, Bakari sat down and laid his head back against a tree. Then Kharlia walked back from getting a drink in the river.

Bakari watched her approach. She was slender and shorter than he, but not by much. Her face still held a hint of youth, but her walk held a confidence that was not usual in a fourteen-year-old. Before they had left River Rend, she'd changed into leather pants, which were more suitable for riding. He began to wonder about everything she kept in her pack.

"Kharlia, what happened to your family? Won't someone miss you if you are gone too long?"

Kharlia came over to Bakari and sat down next to him, the side of her leg touching his. "My mother and I left our town up north five years ago and settled outside of Cassian in Forest Way—the town you found me in. She was smart and had a way with medicines and herbs, but last year, she came down with something we couldn't cure." She stopped for a moment to compose herself.

Bakari felt rather than saw her eyes fill with tears. "I'm sorry," he said.

"I tried everything I knew. And, although we prolonged her life as much as possible, she never got well again. Eventually, she passed on."

"That must have been hard," Bakari said.

"The townspeople accepted us well enough, but I was the only dark-skinned person in the town, once my mother had passed. They still came to me for remedies and help, and I tried to do my best, but things began to get uncomfortable, being there all by myself. So I traveled around the countryside more and more, finding and helping those in need who weren't able to travel to town."

Bakari marveled at her resilience after her mother had died. "Kharlia, that is one of the nicest things I have ever heard. You must really care about people." Bakari turned his head to look at her.

Kharlia smiled back softly. "I just want to help others. I feel a drive, a need to heal and to comfort."

"You're a rare person indeed, Kharlia."

She blushed at this compliment and lowered her head.

"What about your father?" Bakari asked, venturing further into Kharlia's life. He wanted to know all about her.

Kharlia shook her head. "I don't know much about him. My mother never spoke about him, except to tell me he had died in an accident up closer to the barrier. I never pushed her on this subject. Her pain was too deep. I think he might not have been of our same heritage, but I don't know for sure."

Bakari felt bad for dredging up something painful from her

past.

"What about your family, Bak?" Kharlia said after a moment of silence.

"I was raised by wizards."

"Sounds exciting!" Kharlia's eyes grew bigger. "What stories you must have."

Bakari laughed. "I was kind of a loner. I didn't stay around people much. Books are what drew my attention—and learning. I'm not so much for adventure."

"I understand that. I love books." She closed her eyes for a moment, as if remembering things. "I love their feel and the scent of the paper." Her brown eyes opened back up and held a deep sparkle. "My mother taught me to read early on, and I used that skill to try and learn more things about herbs and healing."

Adi wandered back over to them and hung her head down low. The night air was cooler by the river and made for a comfortable evening. Bakari listened to the peaceful chirpings of frogs, crickets, and other nocturnal creatures and rubbed his eyes. "I don't know how good of a traveling companion I will be." Bakari stretched out his arms and yawned. "I'm not one for the out of doors, but I'm glad you are here with me."

"I will teach you all I know, Bakari. I've gotten used to traveling and living off the land."

"Can you teach me more in the morning?" Bakari's eyes started to close.

The two young teens both closed their eyes and used the tree to keep themselves sitting up. Kharlia's right hand and Bakari's left filled the space between them. Resting against each other, they each took comfort in the small touch. Bakari fell into a deep sleep for the next few hours, dreaming of little and letting his body rest.

All of a sudden, Adi neighed loudly. Bakari opened his eyes abruptly and tried to make sense of what he saw: two men trying to lead Adi away.

Leaping into action, Bakari began to yell and chase after the two men. One continued leading the horse away at a fast pace, while the other turned and brought out a dagger in front of him.

Bakari slowed as the man approached. He was in his mid-thirties, Bakari could see in the moonlight, with dirty, long hair and missing a few teeth. "Don't be stupid, boy."

Bakari tried to stay brave. He wasn't used to this type of activity. Alli would be more at home in this situation. She probably would have already taken the man down. "That's my horse."

"Not anymore," the man said. "Stay where you are, and no one gets hurt."

Bakari was a scholar wizard, but a wizard nonetheless, and had been trained in all the disciplines of magic to some degree. Bringing his hand up in front of him, he tried to push out against the dagger the man held, but nothing happened. He shook off the remaining sluggishness in his brain and used his mind to think of what to do. Then, with renewed strength, he pushed again, and the blade flew out of the bandit's hand.

The man's eyes widened, and a look of fear crossed his face momentarily. Without warning, he rushed Bakari. Not prepared for the sudden action, Bakari was thrown to the ground. As the man brought up his fist to hit him in the face, Kharlia appeared behind him. She swung her bag in front of herself and knocked the man off of Bakari.

Rolling on the ground and coming up in a crouch, the man pulled another dagger from his boot and lunged toward Kharlia. She backed away but tripped on a tree root and fell down, tangled up in her bag. The man jumped toward her and grabbed her leg.

Bakari didn't know what to do; he was plain scared and wanted nothing more than to be back in the city, sitting in the library. A sound to his side alerted Bakari that the other man had now circled back around to help his fellow bandit. He came through the trees at a run and jumped toward Bakari. But Bakari stepped aside at the last minute, and the man missed.

Kharlia was still struggling with the other man on the hard ground.

"Bak!" she screamed and pointed toward the abandoned dagger on the ground.

Bakari leapt toward the dagger, bringing it up in his hands. The second man regained his feet and pulled his own knife out.

Bakari was tiring physically, which always affected his powers. Then he saw Adi through the trees, took a deep breath, and reached out to the mind of his horse. The connection came easier this time. He didn't take firm control, only made his gentle thoughts known to his horse.

Time slowed as he reached into his horse's mind. He felt a source of comfort there, a mind he had known for the last few years, and her will came easier to him than the vulture's had. The bandits seemed to stop moving, and Kharlia still lay on the ground next to the first bandit. Bakari sensed everything his horse could: the smell of the earth, the panic of being taken by the men, and adoration for Bakari himself.

The horse was much stronger than the men, so Bakari directed his thoughts to her. The horse jumped into action and sprinted with her powerful legs, running into the man standing in front of Bakari, knocking him down.

Kharlia continued fighting with the other man, rolling across the ground. Bakari directed Adi there next. The horse kicked the man with her hind legs, splitting open the side of his head and knocking him away from Kharlia.

Time resumed its normal pace once again, and Bakari felt light-headed and sick to his stomach. He pulled his mind back out from his horse's mind and leaned over, with his hands on his knees. A blackness crept over his vision, making everything blurry. He tried to breathe deeply, but it was too much. He glanced up briefly to see that Kharlia was all right, but then he began to faint.

He looked back up and made eye contact with Kharlia but couldn't bring himself to say anything. Blackness continued to engulf him until he fell into a crumpled heap on the ground.

CHAPTER THIRTEEN

Chief Judge Daymian Khouri rode next to Roland. The boy's mentor, Onius, was farther in front, holding a conversation with Mericus and Gorn. After riding for three days, they were now only a day out from reaching the Citadel.

Daymian turned to Roland and quietly said, "Roland, you are Bakari's closest friend. Are you sure you don't know where he ran off to?"

Roland took a deep breath. "Chief Judge Khouri, as I told you numerous times these last three days, the last time I saw Bakari, he was sitting in the corner of the inn with that new girl of his. Maybe she talked him into sneaking off."

"Roland!" Daymian reprimanded. "This is a serious matter. He's a scholar wizard with great knowledge. He was researching something for me. If he fell into the wrong hands, it could be dangerous for us all."

"You mean *dangerous for you,* as Chief Judge?" Roland questioned. "Is that what this is all about?" He waved his hands around the group. "Our being taken to the Citadel like prisoners. Is it the fight between you and the King-men you are worried about?"

"It's not just my fight, young man; and have some respect for the law."

Roland sat silently for a moment, then spoke with a serious

demeanor. "I have served you well as an apprentice, haven't I?"

"There have been no problems," the Chief Judge agreed. "Onius has been a good mentor for you; though, I hear some trepidation in your voice."

"I try to do my best, and I am sorry if I sounded angry a moment ago, but this is all so frustrating to me. Things are changing rapidly around here. I am as powerful as many wizards, yet they still treat me as an apprentice. I healed you twice." Roland gave a quick glance around himself to see if anyone else listened. "Even Onius cannot do that. Why am I not a full wizard?"

"Hmmm." Daymian took a few minutes to think. "Roland, have you noticed anything different with Onius lately, since we left Cassian?" He purposely did not answer Roland's question. He had left it for the Citadel to deal with, and he didn't want to get in the middle of that.

Roland looked as if he was hiding something. "What do you mean?" he answered Daymian with his own question.

The Chief Judge gave Roland a stern look. "Roland, you are my counselor apprentice. It is your duty to me to tell me anything you know that could affect the peace of this kingdom—even if it has to do with counselor, Onius."

Roland glanced around again. The party was riding spaced out on the road, and no one was around to overhear them. "When I healed you in the forest, Sir, Onius and Gorn were talking. They said something about all of us—Alli, Bak, and myself—being *dangerous*. I think they are afraid of the power we have."

"Or afraid of what it will do to their standing. This stinks of Citadel politics."

"Sir?"

The Chief Judge sighed. "I'm sure you will learn someday, Roland, that the Citadel is as much involved in the politics of this land as are its rightful leaders—maybe even more so. Their hands are in everything."

Onius still traveled between Gorn and Mericus, their heads bent together, conversing. The Chief Judge hoped Onius didn't have anything to do with Bakari's disappearance and that his aloof attitude was only from the stress of the situation.

"Roland, thank you," the Chief Judge said to calm the young wizard's fears. "I am sure Bakari is all right. He must have Kharlia with him also, as we haven't seen her either."

"The sly dog." Roland smiled. "Who would have thought it would be Bakari who ran away with a girl?"

"Indeed," the Chief Judge said. "I would have thought it would be you."

Roland's eyes twinkled as he seemed to regain his normal mood. "Me? It would be hard for me to decide which girl to run away with. They are all so beautiful."

Daymian laughed. "Watch out at the Citadel; the girls there aren't as timid as those in Cassian."

Roland rubbed his hands together as if in anticipation.

The Chief Judge then turned serious once more. "And, Roland, watch out for yourself also. Things might not be what they appear to be right now."

With that, Daymian kicked the flanks of his horse to move up in the line toward his counselor. He needed to see what was being planned in his absence.

Riding up behind the three wizards, the Chief Judge watched as their backs stiffened. Onius was the only one to turn around.

"Welcome, Daymian. We were discussing how things will be at the Citadel. We will be arriving before the evening meal. What were you and young Roland speaking about?"

"He *is* my counselor also, Onius," the Chief Judge said.

"And, did he counsel you?"

"He gave me a few insights."

"Ah, good," Onius said, but he acted as if he was nervous. "That's good for him."

The Chief Judge knew from this that something was going on that he wasn't privy to himself, but he understood politics and subterfuge. He could play the game as well as the rest of them.

"Have you found anything out about young Bakari yet?" he asked Onius to gauge his reaction.

"No. Quite strange. The boy never wanders off without a specific reason." Onius flicked a quick glance at Mericus.

Seeing this, Daymian hoped Onius was still trustworthy. "Roland thinks it was the girl," he said.

"The girl?" Onius asked. "So that is what you were talking to him about."

"Yes. He thinks Bakari might have run off with Kharlia." Daymian pushed out a laugh. "Maybe there's nothing to worry about. Boys have done worse things for a girl than to run off with them. They did seem fond of each other, and Bakari was never one to get much attention from the girls."

Onius visibly relaxed. "Yes, Chief Judge, that must be it. I wouldn't think it of Bakari, but you never know. We won't worry anymore. I am sure he will find his way back to the Citadel at some point. A shame, though, to lose such a good mind. He could remember anything."

* * *

Later in the evening, the large party rode into the Citadel. It sat as a separate complex of buildings north of Whalen, the closest city. The Citadel used to be the capital of Alaris, before the barrier went up and the system of judges came to be. An imposing structure, the Citadel stood with a fifty-foot-high wall, thirty feet thick in places. Its gleaming spires extending from the wall's corners, could be seen for miles.

Now they passed under the city walls, through a short tunnel, and into the greeting courtyard of the main complex. The buildings stood tall, clean, and architecturally unique, compared to the rest of Alaris. The Citadel was rumored to be the oldest city in the southern kingdoms, outside of Lor'l in Elvyn. Parapets, gargoyles, and oversized stone carvings covered the main building of the Citadel itself.

The Citadel had been the headquarters of wizards and kings for thousands of years. And, since the war, it had been the training grounds for the wizards of Alaris. It was indeed an ancient and imposing group of buildings.

After the war and the formation of the barrier, the ranks of wizards had been decimated. Wizards usually lived long but did not procreate in abundance. There were few wizards still alive from that fateful time, and they seemed to keep to themselves— whether by preference or by decree from the Wizard Council, the Chief Judge wasn't sure which. The wizards, in part, divided themselves between the young apprentice wizards and the older, fully trained level-two-through-five wizards. Within the wizard ranks, scholar, battle, and counselor wizards also trained in their own groups.

Once inside, the citadel guards and men-at-arms left the Chief Judge and the wizards to brush down their horses and find some food for themselves.

Daymian ascended the steps first, as was the Chief Judge's right by law, to present himself to the Council of Wizards. But, upon reaching the top step, Mericus stepped in front of Daymian and assumed control.

"Here to see High Wizard Kanzar Centari," Mericus said, using the self-proclaimed title of that powerful wizard. "Chief Judge Daymian Khouri has arrived."

The Chief Judge would not allow himself to be intimidated by Mericus, so he moved to step around him. The doors opened to him.

Being led down a wide marble hallway, Daymian noticed the gold and crystal lamps lining the room, placed every few feet. At the end of the long hallway, they were admitted to a sizeable room. As soon as Daymian stepped inside, he saw Kanzar, seated on what could only be described as a throne. Kanzar was a broad-shouldered man with a large, shaved head. His dark eyes and his goatee gave him an intimidating look.

"Ah. Daymian Khouri. Good of you to join us." Kanzar stood and put on a smile that did not fool the Chief Judge or cover up the wizard's omission of Daymian's full title. "I hope your travels were pleasant enough."

Daymian was not in the mood for social niceties. "Kanzar, what is the meaning of your naming judges of your own choosing? That is not Citadel business."

"Right to the point, I see. Get it out in the open, and get it done." Kanzar nodded to Daymian. "Very well, then, may we at least retire to my rooms to discuss this…away from prying ears?"

The Chief Judge followed Kanzar across the hall to a set of doors on the opposite side. A servant standing nearby opened them for Kanzar after a short bow. The Chief Judge received no acknowledgment.

These rooms were more ornate than the throne. Crystal lamps and goblets, artwork, and marble statues surrounded the seating area, which held a grouping of red velvet chairs, trimmed in gold. An enormous stone fireplace sat to one side.

Kanzar offered Daymian one of the chairs to sit in.

"You seem to be doing well for yourself, Wizard Centari," noted the Chief Judge on his way to sit down. "You have accumulated more wealth since the last time we met."

"Ah. I do like the finer things in life, Daymian," the wizard said, talking down to the Chief Judge. "When you live as long as we do, you realize comfort and wealth are important."

"Is that why you are stirring up trouble in the land? To accumulate more wealth?" Chief Judge

The two leaders sat and a servant hurried over to pour drinks.

After a long gulp of wine, Kanzar put his head on the back

of the stuffed chair and sighed, deep and long.

"Kanzar," Daymian prompted.

"Please call me High Wizard. That is my title, and this is to be a formal affair, right?"

Daymian couldn't believe the arrogance of this man. "Excuse me. I have not heard of a new title being approved among the wizards."

"Ah, Judge Khouri," Kanzar began.

"That's *Chief Judge*, if this is to be a formal affair.

Kanzar barked out a loud, booming laugh. "Well played, Chief Judge, well played."

Daymian pushed through. "Now, *High Wizard*," he said with emphasis, stroking the wizard's ego. "Why the invitation?"

Kanzar smiled, and his narrow eyes almost disappeared into his fleshy face. "We share a problem, Chief Judge. The kingdom wants a king, and you are the Chief Judge. That puts you in a rather precarious situation, don't you think?"

Daymian had not expected such directness from the wizard. He firmly believed in the judge system. Fair to all, it spread out the power, and it had worked for one hundred and fifty years. Why change it now? He had an inkling of why, and it was staring right at him.

"Personally," Daymian began, "I think it puts those who are opposing the legal form of government in a precarious situation, like the King-men. Stirring up trouble and organizing two attacks on my life in the last few weeks could be considered *treason*. Do you speak for all wizards or only for yourself in this matter?"

Kanzar seemed legitimately surprised at this response from

the Chief Judge. "I speak for all those concerned in the kingdom of Alaris, Daymian," Kanzar said as he stood up in anger, his voice booming across the walls in the open room. "The time has come for a change—an evolution of sorts—a strong king who can lead us back out into the world."

"What about the barrier?" The Chief Judge wished he had spoken more to Bakari earlier. He knew the young scholar had a head full of information. And he wondered for the hundredth time where Bakari was but hoped he was gathering information about the barrier.

"The barrier is failing, as I am sure you have heard. Though, that is not your matter, as it is a thing of magic, which does not come under your jurisdiction." Kanzar spat in anger. "I am tired of these games you play."

Daymian rose to his feet. "If the barrier—which guards all of Alaris—is not my concern, as the chief political leader, then who governs this kingdom is not your concern, as the self-proclaimed leader of the wizard's Citadel."

Both leaders stared daggers at each other. The Chief Judge knew his own expression was dark and livid. He also knew Kanzar's powers could kill him anytime the wizard desired. The balance in the kingdom had come from the lack of sufficient numbers among the wizards' ranks. But he wondered if Kanzar's desire for power knew bounds.

Kanzar's entire frame quaked. "When the barrier falls, Alaris will resume its leadership among the other nations, and you don't have the ability to be that leader, Daymian. It is that simple." The great wizard took one step closer to the Chief Judge. Before any more words could be spoken, the door of the room burst open, and in walked Onius.

"I was not informed of a formal meeting between you two."

"I have the consent of the Council and the other judges to speak to the Chief Judge on political matters." Kanzar shot dark looks at Onius.

"We gave you authority to be the spokesman, not to speak on your own, in secret," Onius retorted.

The Chief Judge saw a power play enacted in front of him. Due to recent events, he didn't completely trust Onius, but at least Onius seemed to hold as much disdain for Kanzar as Daymian himself did. The Chief Judge decided that now was a good time to leave.

"I can see you two have some things to work out in the Citadel. I will excuse myself to clean up from my journey. You may inform the Wizard Council that I will address them after the morning meal tomorrow."

Both wizards turned to the Chief Judge in obvious surprise.

"Address us?" Kanzar asked. "About what?"

"About the state of affairs in our country," the Chief Judge answered back.

"I will go with you," Onius offered. "To help you prepare."

"There is no need for that." The Chief Judge waved a hand in dismissal. "I will not need your services tonight, Onius. If I need something, I will ask Roland. You trained him up properly, didn't you?"

Onius took a step back and then opened and closed his

mouth twice. Apparently, the wizard didn't know what to say to this abrupt dismissal, but, by the color of his face, he was none too happy about the situation.

The Chief Judge opened the door and walked out into the hallway. Two of his personal guards had stayed there for him, and they now accompanied him to his quarters, along with two Citadel servants.

Daymian took a deep breath and let it out slowly. He had no idea what he would say to the Wizard Council the next day. His announcement had been a ploy to grab the two powerful wizards' attention. And it had worked. But now he needed to figure out what he could say to diffuse the precarious standoff between the King-men and the government of judges.

CHAPTER FOURTEEN

R oland stood on one of the large balconies on the north side of the Citadel. As evening fell, the fields and forest around the wizards' city took on multiple hues of shadows. Far to the north, he could make out the faint silhouette of the Barrier Mountains, so named for the magical barrier that cut across their length, leaving the people of Alaris no access to the lands on their other side. Deep within the mountains was the kingdom of Mahli, along a few loosely held and little populated territories—at least, they used to be there. No one in Alaris had heard of or seen them since the barrier's creation.

Footsteps sounded behind Roland, making loud clicks on the granite tile floor. It was Onius, his teacher and mentor for the past year, a man who carried his age well and his power even better. The man must be over eighty years old, yet he still held youthful features on his barely wrinkled face. Roland wondered if this was what he had to look forward to: a long and healthy life. The problem was he found being a counselor quite boring. Of course a strong counselor could control a weak leader and be the puppet master behind the king's head. But he didn't want to be behind anyone; he wanted to be in front.

"Quite a view." Onius stood next to him. "The land looks so peaceful from here. You would think there are no problems."

"But there are," Roland said, feeling unusually somber.

"Yes, there are, Roland. And, in the days to come, I would like to know I have your support."

"My support for what?" Roland perked up and turned to gaze at his mentor.

"For whatever it is that I need your support for," Onius answered cryptically. "The Chief Judge will speak tomorrow morning to the Wizard Council. I fear his words will stir up division among the people."

"Can't you counsel him otherwise?" Roland asked.

Onius tightened his lips, and his eyes hardened. He took a moment, as if trying to compose his thoughts into words. The sun dropped below the few trees to the west, and dark shadows fell deeper across the land and, in turn, across the counselor's face.

"He dismissed me for the evening," Onius said, obviously not pleased, "and maybe for longer. I cannot tell."

"Dismissed you for what?" Roland knew, from his conversation with the Chief Judge earlier, that there was now some mistrust of Onius, but the old wizard had served faithfully for decades. A dismissal was serious business.

Instead of answering the question, Onius asked again, "Do I have your support?"

Roland sensed the tides of power beginning to shift. He breathed in deeply and knew this was a pivotal moment in his life, one that would define his future. If the Chief Judge and his counselor were having a falling out, then Alaris stood on the brink of something disastrous. Roland also knew that disasters sometimes brought opportunities. It was time to see how much Onius Neeland really wanted Roland Tyre on his side.

"I want to be tested," Roland said.

Onius's eyes opened wide. He surely had not expected him to push that at this time.

"I want to officially be a full wizard." *Then I might support you in whatever it is you need support in,* he thought to himself. He didn't need to say this condition out loud; Onius understood his meaning.

Onius nodded his head slightly. "It will be done tomorrow, after the Chief Judge's speech. But you will not be given any special treatment because I am on the selection committee, Roland."

"I would not expect that, Onius. But I would also not expect you to award me anything less than I will deserve. The test is based on power and knowledge, not age."

"Don't push things, boy. You are not all that special."

"Am I not?" Roland's eyes twinkled in amusement. "You know I have done things these past few weeks that surprised even you; and, as you are so quick to point out, I am still young. What might my powers become as I grow?"

Roland knew inside that he held more than the knowledge of a counselor. He didn't have the recall and memory of Bakari, but he did have a natural instinct for what to do. The potential of what he could someday do with his own magic amazed him. If Onius moved in for a place of power, Roland would be one step ahead of him.

Onius gave a loud humph and turned to leave. "You'd better study up tonight. It will be a big day tomorrow." With that, his mentor walked back across the balcony and disappeared through the ornate double doors leading into the Citadel.

Roland smiled and experienced a level of excitement he hadn't felt in a long time. He would get what he deserved: recognition for the power he held. He was sure to surprise them with his power. He would move past level two and three and go directly to level four or five. A soft laugh escaped his upturned lips, and he spun around with joyful delight.

"What's so funny, Roland?"

Without a sound, Alli had come up behind him, surprising him. He berated himself for not noticing her approach. He should have known this by her sweet, magical scent.

"Looks like I caught you daydreaming about something." She pushed a lock of dark hair out of her beautiful green eyes.

Roland peered down at her. She stood almost a foot shorter than his six feet, but he knew not to judge her by her size. He had seen her fight when the Chief Judge had been captured, a marvelous and magical thing to behold. She had flowed in motion with her weapons and power as one. Definitely a small ball of fire. One that made his heart race.

"I will be tested tomorrow." Roland saw no harm in sharing the information with a fellow apprentice, one who soon would not be his equal anymore.

Alli's eyebrows shot up in surprise, and then her eyes squinted with obvious consternation. "Why wasn't I invited?"

"Onius was just here. And I told him I wanted to be tested."

"You told him, just like that." Alli's hands sat on her hips, just above her belt of weapons so common for a battle wizard.

"Well, he wanted my support, and I told him I wanted to be tested. I think that's fair, don't you?"

A loud banging sound distracted them for a moment. They walked across the wraparound balcony and peered southward, toward the city gate. The thick wooden doors to the city had closed for the evening, with guards stationed out in front. Roland didn't remember them being closed before, when he used to live at the Citadel.

"How long did you stay here?" Roland asked Alli.

"My parents brought me here when I turned nine. I stayed here five years and left a little over a year ago. It feels strange to be back. The Citadel is like a second home to me." Alli ran her hands over the smooth railing in front of them.

"Wizards came to my town only three years ago to test everyone," Roland said. "Up until that time, I never knew I possessed the powers to be a wizard. Well, looking back, I did have a special knack for certain things," Roland reminisced. "But, once I began my training, it was like a block lifted from my senses. Then I could sense power flowing through my veins."

Alli eyed him with some obvious astonishment. "You only attended here two years before you were apprenticed out? And now they are going to test you for a full wizard?"

Roland smiled.

"Roland?" Alli frowned at him.

"I know you think I am full of myself and overconfident." Roland spread his arms out from his sides. "That's what everyone thinks. But none of you understands. None of you."

He felt his face redden as he brought his clenched fists to his sides.

"Understand what, Roland?" Alli asked, raising her voice. "You think you are the only apprentice who is powerful and feels ready to be a wizard? I may be only fifteen, but I feel that power every day, especially when I am in a battle. It flows around me and through me. It heightens my senses and gives me clarity of thought. I even feel that I am *at one* with the power at times."

This time, Roland was astonished. He wasn't quite sure what to say. "Quiet your voice down, Alli." He glanced back into a nearby window, where a few servants brought food now to some of the Citadel wizards. "Do you think they are afraid of us? Could it be possible that the older wizards are not as powerful as we and are afraid of what we are?"

Alli shrugged, and her black hair bobbed up and down over her shoulder. "I heard what Bakari did with the vulture and what you did to heal the Chief Judge. These are not powers the older wizards are comfortable with. I don't think they like that we can do more than they. Gorn is always trying to slow me down and telling me to *pace myself*. But I don't need to pace myself. I do not get tired when I am in battle."

Roland had frowned when she mentioned Bakari. He was a quirky, quiet fellow, but a good friend nevertheless. "Do you know where Bak went?"

Alli walked along the rail for a moment, glancing down at the bustling city below getting ready to settle down for the night. "I don't know Bak well. Even though I am stationed in Cassian, I am usually out with Gorn, fighting King-men or bandits. You know him better than I. Do you think he's in trouble?"

"Trouble?" Roland thought for a moment. Bakari was the only person he knew who was never in trouble. He stayed away from people and places that would cause him trouble. "I don't know. Not normally, but things are changing, Alli. He was fiercely protective of that girl."

"Maybe it was because he doesn't see many of his own kind around Cassian."

Roland chuckled. "I hadn't thought about that. You are right. Bak is one of only a few darker-skinned people in Cassian. He must have been surprised to find someone like him. Maybe that's it. Good for him!"

"How did he get to the Citadel?" Alli asked.

"He was dropped off at the doorstep here when he was only five years old—it is said—with a note saying his name was Bakari. He doesn't remember much from before then. Someone from up north brought him. North of Whalen, there are a lot of his people, being closer to the Barrier Mountains of Mahli. He lived here for a long time and moved to Cassian before I did. Then, last year, they raised him to a level-two wizard."

"Do you think they will test me?" Alli asked, bringing the conversation full circle.

Roland shook his head. "I don't know. You are even younger than I."

"But age does not mean strength!" Alli's eyes flashed.

Roland laughed. "That is what I told Onius. Tomorrow, I will show them. Then I will be promoted to a full wizard—level three or four!"

Alli shrugged her shoulder. "Don't be too cocky, Roland. You might be powerful, but to jump multiple levels is unheard of. It isn't done often, particularly at our age."

"It will be for me. You wait and see." Roland ran his hand through his hair, pushing it off his forehead. "I will run this place someday."

Alli seemed about to retort, then closed her mouth when the Chief Judge came out onto the landing. His light brown skin, common down south, near Orr, almost glowed in the torchlight. He stroked his graying goatee with his fingers and smiled at seeing the two apprentices.

"Ah, Roland, I have been searching for you," the Chief Judge said as he nodded a greeting toward Alli. "I see you two are enjoying the Citadel."

Alli blushed, and Roland found himself caught off guard. "Discussing our powers, Sir."

"Hmmm." The Chief Judge looked from one to another. "I hope you two keep good heads on your shoulders in regards to that. There is too much power being used to manipulate others as it is. In fact, on that note, Roland, I would like to speak with you."

With those words, Alli was dismissed, and Roland turned toward the Chief Judge.

The Chief Judge motioned Roland over to a set of wooden chairs next to a table, out on the corner of the balcony.

"Counselor, what do you know about the King-men?"

Roland sat in silence for a brief moment, surprised at this greeting. First, Onius; then, Alli; and now, the Chief Judge. Was his entire evening going to be taken up by surprise conversations? He glanced out over the city that had been built up around the Citadel. Farms and small homes now dotted the land outside the walls. "Sir?"

"Are you not a counselor, Roland? Are you not trained to counsel?"

Roland remembered from his conversation with Onius how the Chief Judge had dismissed him earlier. "I am trained to be a counselor. But, as you can appreciate, I am not a full wizard yet."

"But you have mentioned several times how powerful you are and how you should be recognized as a full wizard, correct?" The Chief Judge motioned for a servant in the building to bring out some refreshments for them. "You shouldn't worry about receiving a title if you know what you are and what you stand for."

Roland, however, did want the recognition.

The Chief Judge seemed to notice his hesitation and then continued talking. "I remember being young, Roland. You want the praise, the glory, and to be noticed, right?"

"Is that so wrong?" asked Roland, surprised that the Chief Judge was actually taking time to discuss these things with him.

"No, not so wrong; but, in time, you learn it doesn't matter what others think of you if you are acting in accordance with what you think is best. You are who you are, Roland Tyre—a wizard with growing powers. A designation doesn't change that. You will see this as you get older. But, for now, try to remember it is more important to have a conviction and live by that conviction and know that you are true to yourself, more important than to be someone you are not, just to receive the notoriety of a title."

"I understand what you are saying, Sir." Roland leaned forward in his chair. "I really do. You are saying that I shouldn't be a different person whether I am an apprentice or a wizard, that my principles and what guides me should be the same either way, and that I should take what is dealt to me and make a difference in whatever station I am in."

The Chief Judge nodded and smiled. "My, my, Roland, you do pay attention sometimes. That is nice to know."

He knew what the Chief Judge wanted him to understand, but Roland didn't know if he agreed with him. With higher titles came greater opportunities. One thing would always stay the same, though. It was what drove him. And the Chief Judge was correct in encouraging that him to remain dedicated to something—no matter what station he was in, Roland would continually strive for his goal of becoming the most powerful wizard in Alaris.

A simple goal. And the next day would afford him a large step on that path. The wizard test!

The Chief Judge then got down to the point of his visit. "Let's discuss the King-men: what they want, where their power comes from, and how we can survive the revolt and keep Alaris intact whichever way things go."

Roland's eyes widened. These were the subjects the leader of Alaris usually discussed with Onius. Then he smiled and realized that, once again, he was showing up his mentor. By tomorrow, he could be calling Onius his *former mentor.*

CHAPTER FIFTEEN

The next morning, everyone gathered in the great hall of the Citadel to hear the Chief Judge speak. Bright sunlight filtered through the high windows, and food and drinks were set around the hall's perimeter for the taking. The room was filled to capacity.

From up in the front of the room, Onius watched the Chief Judge walk through the austere group. Inwardly, he felt proud of Daymian. Walking through that many men and women of power was intimidating for even the highest-ranked wizard, let alone for someone who had no powers of his own.

The Chief Judge took the podium and began his speech. He was a master orator and captured the attention of all assembled with a brief history of the system of Chief Judges in Alaris.

"This system of fair government has been part of the heart and soul of Alaris for one hundred fifty years," the Chief Judge continued. "The barrier has kept other nations from troubling us, the wizards have supported the judges as their scholars, counselors, and battle generals, and together we have built a strong kingdom, a kingdom that is not dependent on any one person, but a government whose rule and law is upheld, shared, and run by the people."

Out of the corner of his eye, Onius watched Kanzar scowling at the Chief Judge. The High Wizard's jaw was set firm, and his eyes glared at his *current* rival for power in Alaris.

The Chief Judge paused and looked out over the crowd, almost as if looking at each person present individually. "This system has existed because of the trust between the wizards and the judges. And the people trust us to keep them safe and provided for. The recent rebels, referring to themselves as *King-men*, have set aside the law. In the name of wanting a king, they have killed peaceful followers of the law, spread anarchy, and endangered our nation's peace and prosperity."

Onius thought the Chief Judge was being a little dramatic about this threat to the land, but his words kept the attention of the wizards and apprentices in attendance. Onius hoped to stave off war, but he knew Kanzar's greed for power knew no bounds.

His mind wandered back to when he and Kanzar had first met, decades ago. Through the years, they'd had periodic conversations, the last time being many years ago, about the need for Alaris to have a king again someday, a king that must—by right of their power—be a wizard. But that didn't mean Onius agreed with the way Kanzar was going about it.

It had taken one hundred fifty years for the Citadel to find and train enough wizards to replenish what had been lost during the war when the barrier was raised. Kanzar, without consulting Onius, must have determined that it was now time to make their move; hence the King-men came into being. These were primarily groups of mercenaries and unscrupulous parties whom Kanzar had hired out to cause trouble in the land.

Besides the timing, Onius felt consternation over the fact

that he actually liked this Chief Judge, the third he had served. Daymian Khouri was a good man, a fair judge, and a highly competent leader.

A growing rumble in the crowd drew Onius's attention back to the Chief Judge's speech.

"I repeat," he said, his voice booming over the crowd, "the King-men are traitors to our land, and anyone found conducting business with them, supporting them, and colluding with them to take over the government will also be seen as traitors and will be tried as such."

Kanzar held his seat, seeming barely able to control himself. Most of the Council knew of Kanzar's plans, and they looked to him for direction.

"The very fabric of Alaris is built on law." The Chief Judge's voice rose louder. "The means for continued peace is the following of that law. And those who want to change those laws must work inside that system; to do otherwise will bring anarchy and disaster to this land I am sure we all love. May the bounties of Alaris and the peace we have enjoyed continue to be enjoyed by all."

Daymian slowly walked from the pedestal and down the aisle of wizards and exited through the gold-bordered double doors, with two guards holding them open for him.

Then Kanzar stood and, without any words, turned sharply, his robes flying out around his large body. He walked through a back door, and Onius followed. Then, throwing open the door to his own office and slamming it closed again after Onius, Kanzar went to a counter and poured himself a drink.

Kanzar excused the servant and turned to Onius. "The Chief Judge goes too far."

Onius knew he had to tread carefully now. "Kanzar, he is the rightful ruler of Alaris."

Kanzar threw his glass to the floor, and it shattered. Servants would be called in later to clean it up. "He has no right to call us traitors in our own house."

Onius frowned. "Kanzar, you seem to be moving on your own here. Why wasn't I consulted? I could have told you the timing was not right. The Chief Judge is a good man."

"The time will never be right with you, Onius," Kanzar bellowed. "You've become too soft in Cassian, serving with the judges. Don't you remember our discussions on the need for a king—a wizard king?"

Onius sighed. "I remember talking about it happening someday, when events had led to it naturally. Not like this, Kanzar." Onius rubbed his temples with his fingers. This was not going well. He needed to toe the line with Kanzar about the Chief Judge. Onius needed to appear to be enough in Kanzar's camp to stay in his confidence. But that could lead to alienating himself from the Chief Judge.

"Let me talk to Daymian privately this evening."

"After that rousing speech, of protecting Alaris and her stable government, I don't think the man will budge." Kanzar stood up to emphasize his point. "He even had the gall to say that anyone associated with the King-men would be considered traitors and treated accordingly."

"I heard the speech, Kanzar," Onius said, his voice clipped. "I have counseled him for years. I will point out to him the obvious: W*e are wizards, and he is not*." Onius would hate to throw that in the Chief Judge's face, but he needed to appear strong in front of Kanzar. He would placate Kanzar until the opportunity came to take him down.

"That we are, Counselor, and powerful ones at that," Kanzar boomed. "We will crush the government and place a king on the throne of Alaris once again. When the barrier fails, then let the other nations fear us as before."

Onius cringed inside but outwardly remained calm. "And, who would you propose for that king, Kanzar?" Onius knew full well the answer.

"Why, me, of course. Is there anyone more suited than the High Wizard of the Citadel?"

Onius had no problem thinking of plenty of others, even himself, who would be better. But he said nothing on that point.

A knock on the door interrupted Onius before he could say more.

Kanzar brought his great frame back out of his chair, with a glare that told Onius they were not finished yet. When Kanzar opened the door, Roland took a step forward into the room.

"Ahh, Wizards Kanzar and Onius," Roland said, forgoing their usual honorific titles.

Onius saw a flash of annoyance cross Kanzar's face, and he suppressed a smile. He had used Kanzar's *High Wizard* title in public, but, personally, it had grated on his nerves that the man had set his title all on his own.

"What brings you here today, apprentice?" Kanzar asked.

"Onius said that, after the Chief Judge's speech, I would have the opportunity to be tested as a full wizard," Roland said.

Kanzar turned to Onius with a surprised glance.

Onius stood, his robes flowing around his body as he took a brisk step toward the two. "That was the item I wanted to discuss with you, Kanzar. I agreed we would test Roland today, in exchange for his support."

Kanzar opened his mouth, but Roland jumped in. "The title of *wizard* was in exchange for me to *consider* giving you my support, Counselor Onius."

"You did not run this by me or the Council, Onius." Kanzar's face darkened with anger. "There are other items needing our attention more than testing this young apprentice."

Roland's face turned red, and he opened his mouth to respond, but Onius shook his head at him and jumped in instead.

"Kanzar, I am a member of the Council and do not need your permission to invite an apprentice to be tested. That is the rule of the Council, unless you have changed *that* recently also."

Onius realized that his time in Cassian, away from the Citadel for years, had allowed Kanzar to gather too much authority to himself.

"Apprentice Tyre is more than ready to be considered," Onius continued. "Given the uncertain times ahead, I think we cannot afford to wait any longer. Roland could be a powerful ally."

Kanzar snarled but nodded his head in acceptance. "Allies are good, if they can be taught their place."

Roland reddened and clenched his fists but kept his mouth

closed for once.

"So be it." Kanzar flipped his hand out with a dismissal. "Roland Tyre, report to the testing room in one hour. I will be interested to see if you have the makings of a level-one wizard or not."

Roland again opened his mouth, but, once more, Onius shook his head and, with a tight squeeze on his apprentice's shoulder, led him out of the room.

When Kanzar had closed the door behind them, Onius turned to Roland. "I am glad to see you were able to hold your tongue in there, Roland."

Roland scowled and pushed the hair out of his eyes. "It wasn't easy. That man is too arrogant with too much power behind him."

Onius nodded his head. "That I agree with. Though, you must learn to tread lightly around him and not let your own arrogance get in the way. He has powerful friends around here."

Roland hung his head.

They walked outside and through a garden patio. The dahlias were in full bloom, many of them larger than a man's hand. A small stream trickled by and wound its way through the gardens. Color and fragrance filled the air as the two walked to a secluded corner.

Onius motioned for Roland to sit down on a stone bench there. Limbs of a large apple tree hung behind them, with small apples beginning to grow. The Citadel sat in front of them, looming up into multiple stories, surrounded by parapets and balconies. The early afternoon air was warm and pleasant in the shade.

"Roland, during the test, you must control yourself. You must show discipline and, above all, a regard for the Citadel and its wizards."

"But I know so much, Onius, and hold so much power inside; they'll have to name me a wizard when they see what I can do alone."

Onius took a deep breath and let it out in a quick rush. "Being a wizard is not only about power, Roland, it is about thinking with a clear head, having discipline, and showing loyalty. We have been given a great gift and must be careful not to misuse it."

Roland shook his head, and his voice grew serious. "Onius, you speak of loyalty, but what you are doing now?" He searched for the right words. "It seems you are becoming closer to the High Wizard than to the Chief Judge of the land. How is that being loyal?"

Onius's face grew red. "Look, boy. What do you understand of the things of the world? I am loyal to the Citadel and all it stands for. There is loyalty among the wizards that you will learn in your test. I am loyal to the ideal that what we possess is a gift to be used to help others. I am loyal to preserving this kingdom with as little chaos as possible."

"Sounds cryptic to me, Onius." Roland stood face to face with the counselor.

"There is a hierarchy in loyalty, Roland," Onius said, lowering his voice to a whisper. "That is what the test is all about. I do not want to hurt the Chief Judge. He is a good man, and I will ask him to step down peacefully, if it comes to that.

But I truly believe that as the barrier fails and we are opened up to other lands once again, we will need a strong king. The timing may not be the best, but the situation may warrant it."

Roland waved a hand in the air. "And I am guessing that this king should be Kanzar?"

"That is none of your business, young man. If you pass the test—and I mean *if*—you will pledge your loyalty to the Citadel and its wizards *above all else*. You will serve whom you are expected to serve and none else. If that means serving a king, then that is what it will mean."

"I have no problem with a king, Onius. I do have a problem with people pretending to be something they are not or using their positions to intimidate others. You call me arrogant and spoiled. You have said I don't take things seriously, but this is a serious matter if you are talking treason."

Onius furrowed his brows at his young apprentice. What did this youngster really think? He was only sixteen years of age. Onius barely remembered back that far. Had he been as bad as Roland? He didn't think so; at least, he hoped not. Onius felt a momentary sympathy for his own past mentors and instructors.

Roland continued, "Well, Onius, I am arrogant because of the power I hold. I am not pretending to be something I am not or hiding my loyalty behind my rank or playing both sides of a conflict, hoping to come out on top. I am who I am. And I am simply one of the most powerful wizards you will ever know."

Onius couldn't control himself. He burst out laughing at Roland's dramatics. "My, my, my. I think you may be in for a rude awakening during the testing, Roland. Wizards from the fourth and fifth levels will be on the Council. They have been practicing this craft for decades upon decades. Your power will be nothing to theirs."

Roland opened his mouth, but Onius stopped him from speaking with a wave of his hand.

"Control your ego for an hour, Roland—during the test. Show your loyalty to them, and you may come out a full wizard. But don't reach for the stars, or you may get burned."

"And, what is that supposed to mean, Counselor?"

"That means don't be a brat and alienate the Council. They hold all the power over you right now. Don't blow this chance. Now, go prepare yourself. You would do well to try to meditate and calm down."

Roland stepped away but then turned back around. "Onius," he said softly, "I don't think Alaris would survive with Kanzar as its king."

Onius took a few steps closer to Roland. He examined the gardens. The colors and scents were so peaceful that it almost seemed incongruous with his internal struggles with chaos.

"Roland, these are stressful times for all," Onius said in a soft voice. After all this time together, Roland could infuriate him without a moment's notice, but he was still fond of the boy. "I agree with you, and I will do everything in my power to make sure it doesn't happen."

Roland looked surprised at this admission.

Onius put his hand on Roland's shoulder. "But, I do need to be careful," Onius continued. "You've seen Kanzar. Right now, he trusts me, and with that trust, I can be privy to information others can't access. There are plans that have been in play for decades which you know nothing about. Trust me, and don't think too ill of me in the coming days."

Onius didn't leave Roland room to say or ask anything else. Now was neither the time nor the place. He left Roland standing in the garden.

CHAPTER SIXTEEN

Roland walked into the testing room. One chair stood in the middle, and eight wizards sat in high-backed stuffed chairs on raised platforms, half on either side of the room. Onius, one of the eight, sat next to Kanzar. Both hardly sent a glance in Roland's direction.

Roland sat down in the chair and waited for instructions. He took a deep breath and forced his mind to relax, trying to take Onius's counsel to heart. There was no way he would fail this test.

One of the wizards rose from his sizeable chair. "State your name, your apprentice training, and the purpose for being here today," he said.

The man must have been over a hundred years old, his face full of wrinkles and his voice raspy. Roland wondered if the man had been around before the barrier went up. There were rumors of a few wizards surviving that long.

Roland stood, not knowing for sure what the protocol was, and pushed his blond locks out of his eyes. He smiled at both sides. "My name is Roland Tyre, from Westridge. I have been trained by Onius Neeland, as a counselor, but carry powers contributing to all disciplines…"

"This is not a time to tout yourself, young man, just answer the questions," interrupted the old wizard.

Roland ground his teeth but continued. "I am here to be tested to be a full wizard."

The old wizard turned to his colleagues and announced, "Be it known that Roland Tyre of Westridge, Counselor Apprentice, desires to be tested for wizard level one."

Roland shifted his feet. He knew he shouldn't say anything, but he felt that he had better speak up now, before it was too late. Level one was not his goal. Onius shook his head ever so slightly. Apparently, his mentor knew what Roland was thinking.

Needing clarification before he began, Roland raised his voice and said, "Speaker, excuse me."

The Council did not look pleased.

Then the old wizard spoke. "Apprentice Tyre, this is not a time for conversation. These proceedings have an order to them."

Roland was not deterred. He winked at the speaker, to the astonishment of the group. "My good wizard, I only wanted some clarification about the test. Sir, is this test merely for level one? Or, if I exceed that, will it suffice also for the other levels?"

The speaker's eyes almost popped out of his head. "Young man, as I said, there is an order to things. Wizard level one would be your first designation. Wizards can rise to new levels through experience and training, and only by the Council's words."

"But, what if I am stronger?" Roland blurted out.

"Enough!" blared Kanzar. He glared down at Roland. "You waste our time here, Apprentice. I warned Onius about overstepping his bounds and inviting you to test without our Council's consideration. Do we need to disband this meeting?"

Roland couldn't think of enough bad words for Kanzar Centari. The man was a bully and was trying to humiliate him as well as Onius. Roland glanced at Onius and noticed brief, but controlled hostility as Roland's mentor glanced at Kanzar. There was bad blood brewing there, Roland guessed. He vowed right then that Kanzar would rue the day Roland became a full wizard.

Gritting his teeth, Roland stated, "I will take the test now, if the Council will allow it." Then he added, "The test will show who I am."

Eyebrows arched around the room, and the Council looked at Kanzar for direction. Their High Wizard sat down and nodded toward the speaker to proceed.

The old wizard who had first addressed Roland continued. "You will be given a drink. This drink will take you into the test. You will be presented with two sessions as parts of the test. Each session will test your ability to become a wizard and your loyalty to the Citadel. Each experience will seem real to you, and you won't realize you are in a test, so your reactions will be genuine. We will be monitoring your responses, but you will not be able to communicate with us until the test is over."

Roland nodded his head.

A man came out from a door with a glass of light blue liquid. He motioned for Roland to sit back in the chair. So Roland relaxed and took the drink in his hand. With a slight wink at Onius, he drank down all the liquid. It felt cool and sweet going down his throat, but with a bitter aftertaste. He closed his eyes, wondering how long it would take to affect him.

Roland was still aware of the room around him, the touch of the chair underneath him, and the breathing of the Council, when all of a sudden, he found himself standing inside the home where he had been raised.

In Roland's mind he was thirteen years old again and, like most boys his age, didn't like to work but had to do as his father told him. His father, the town carpenter, had made all the furniture in the Tyre family home, with the help of his three sons. Roland was the youngest. As such, he was teased by his older brothers, Thomas and Cade, that he was spoiled and always got what he wanted. Well, why shouldn't he? He knew he was smarter, quicker, and more able than they. Things came easily to him.

Currently, he stood in the small living room of their home. He ran his hands over the smooth wooden walls as if remembering something. He couldn't shake the feeling that something was different—something was wrong.

He heard his father and his two older brothers coming across the front field. Soon they entered, wiping their muddy shoes on the mat before coming farther into the small house.

"Quite a storm brewing out there. I've never seen its like before. Wind's pickin' up something terrible," Roland's father, Jarryd, said.

"Roland, what are you doing?" shouted his oldest brother, Thomas. "You're standing there like you don't know what to do."

"Yes, Son, what are you doing? I asked you to make sure

all the windows were covered," his father said.

Roland thought a moment about what he was doing. He shook his head but still didn't remember. He opened his mouth and closed it again.

"Well, get to it." His father swatted him on the behind, and Roland went scampering to the windows. He heard the snickering of his brothers behind him.

Soon his mother came into the room. "Hurry and eat," she told them, "so we can get the dishes all packed away before the storm hits."

Roland sat down in between his two brothers, who were trying to keep the food from him. Instinctively, he reached out his hand and summoned the plate of pork toward himself, and it came. His brothers gasped, and his mother almost fainted.

Roland didn't understand what had made him reach out with his mind like that. But, once he had done this, he found it reassuring and gave a smug look to his brothers. His father stayed silent, and the rest of the meal went on without much conversation.

Wind rattled against the outside of the house, and the family could hear trees creaking out in the small yard. Lightning flashed through the sides of the small windows, and the sound of thunder soon followed—too soon. A bright flare lit up the sky around their barn. It had been hit.

"The barn's on fire!" yelled Cade.

Roland's father stood up and headed toward the door. "I will go and check on it. Cade and Thomas, you come with me. Roland, stay and take care of your mother."

Roland groaned. He was always the one told to stay and

take care of his mother. He was thirteen now, almost a man. He should be able to help.

When his father opened the door, Roland ran out ahead of them. As he ran, he thought about how he had summoned the plate of food to himself. It had come so easily once he had thought about it. He smiled.

As he ran toward the burning barn, he laughed and thought to himself, *Now I will show my brothers who is more important.*

Upon reaching the barn, he sent his mind out toward the flames. Just as he had summoned the food to himself, he now directed the flames to move away from the barn. Holding his arms in the air, he concentrated hard and moved his arms to the side.

As he did so, he heard voices in the air, voices expressing surprise at "the power of one so young." Then, off in the distance, he saw three riders approaching through the storm. They wore wizard robes and rode large black geldings. "Come with us, young wizard," they beckoned him.

But the barn still burned. He turned back to it and forced his mind to concentrate again. If their barn burned, his family would lose so much; his father's tools and wood were in the barn.

"You are one of us now, Roland. You must come with us," the riders called again.

Back at the house, Roland's mother screamed. Turning his head to the house, he saw a section of the roof fly off in the growing wind. It crashed into a nearby tree and broke into splinters. The roar of the wind grew louder, and Roland held on to a fence post for support. His body was now drenched, and his strength started to wane.

The three riders once again came closer. The storm did not seem to bother them. Their cloaks hung still on their stiff bodies. Roland blinked, trying to reason it out.

Using all the power he could, Roland finally persuaded the flames away from the barn. The back side was partially burned, but he could save the rest. His mother screamed again as another piece of roof caved in, smashing portions of their living room furniture.

Roland reached into the far recesses of his young mind to figure out what to do. Then he remembered where he really was, and jumbled thoughts raced through his mind: *The test. The three wizards calling to him. The voices were the Council.*

"He should not know about us," the council members whispers reached his mind.

But he could hear them.

"It's impossible, what he is doing," another voice said. "Come to us. We are your family now. We can train you to be so much more," the three riders said through the storm.

"Noooooooo," Roland wailed out loud. "This is not real. A wizard should help others with his power. A wizard should not leave his family like this."

"We are your family now, Roland. You must accept the Citadel as your family now, your brothers and sisters."

With a push of his mind, he pushed the riders away. He extinguished the fire and then ran back to the house to help his mother. She lay trapped under a piece of the roof. His father and brothers helped him to lift it off of her, and Roland stayed there to make sure she was safe.

He then ran back outside and stretched his arms to the heavens. He spoke to the Council through his mind. *What kind of test is this—to leave my family when they are in danger?*

"Roland, you shouldn't be doing this," Onius's voice cut through the loud wind. "This will break your mind. You can't be in two places at one time."

"My mind is stronger than you think, Onius! Power not only flows through my body. My body *is* power!" With one last effort, he pushed the storm away in his mind until only the sounds of dripping water from the trees up above could be heard. Then he turned to find his family, standing in astonishment in front of their front door.

"I love you," he said to them. "But I need to go and be more than a carpenter or a younger brother. I am going to be one of the most powerful wizards in the world."

With that, Roland summoned the three riders back toward him. The wizards squawked in surprise when Roland jumped out in front of them. He knew this was a test of his mind, so he was able to do things here that he couldn't yet do in real life. He ran in front of the three wizards, leading them east, to the Citadel.

"Now you will follow me," Roland commanded.

Suddenly, he found himself back in the chair in the testing room, and the noise was deafening. Every wizard spoke at once, most of them out of their seats. The three wizards still in their chairs slumped down, looking exhausted and worn out. They must have represented the three riders.

"Never before has this happened," Roland heard someone

say through the cacophony.

"It's impossible. He cannot control enough power to push that storm away," another said. "He led us here, instead of us leading him. That can't be. He is just a boy."

Roland stayed sitting, trying not to smile. He had shown them who was more powerful. He had accomplished their task to come with them, leaving his old life behind, but only after saving his family and ensuring their survival.

He heard footsteps through the noise, and a man brought him another glass of liquid. He took it and drank it in one quick gulp.

CHAPTER SEVENTEEN

Roland now stood at the edge of the Elvyn Forest. River Bend sat a hundred feet away, through the trees. Glancing to his left and then his right, he noticed that he stood within a company of wizards.

"Roland, the rebels are here," one said to him. The wizard that had spoken to him was older than Roland but was obviously a battle wizard. "We seek your counsel on the matter."

Roland was having a hard time remembering how he had gotten there but felt joy at the confidence they put in him. "How many?" he asked.

"About two dozen, including the Chief Judge and a young scholar wizard," came back the report.

The Chief Judge? Roland thought. That didn't seem right. Daymian Khouri wasn't a rebel. Roland surveyed the group of wizards again and realized they were all Kanzar's men. Then it dawned on him—*he* was one of Kanzar's men!

The jolt from this fact almost meant something to him, but he lost that thought while the other men clearly awaited an answer. Roland also had a good idea of who the young scholar wizard would be, and he had no intention of killing his friend.

"I will go by myself and scout out the buildings," he said to buy himself some time. "The rest of you will circle around the town, making sure there are no other reinforcements."

The other wizards nodded their heads in agreement to his plan. That felt good. Someone finally appreciated him for who he was: a great wizard leader.

The men took off, and Roland walked into town. Masking the sound of his feet and staying close to the trees, he had no problem getting close to the main building. It was an inn that he recognized, one they had stayed at on the way to the Citadel. This was a strange thought, and he couldn't place how long ago that was.

Roland peered through a side window and saw Bakari sitting next to Kharlia, the young girl he had grown attached to. Roland felt slightly envious of the young man. His own escapades with women always ended badly. Maybe it was only the conquest that held the allure for him, because boredom always followed.

Focusing back on the situation, Roland noticed the Chief Judge, his personal guard, and some other nobles, business owners, and political leaders gathered around a large table. The discussion seemed to heat up as one man stood up with his arms flapping in the air. Moving around to a window with a small crack in it, Roland tried to hear what they were saying.

"We cannot attack the Citadel," the Chief Judge said. "That would be suicide."

"Well, we shouldn't sit here and do nothing either," the man who had been so animated moments before continued. "Kanzar's men grow more powerful every day. They already control Whalen and Cassian."

"We will keep recruiting. We must go from town to town

and let the people choose whom they will follow."

"But Kanzar has set himself up as king. The people are flocking to a king," another man said. "The people want a king, Sir."

Roland blinked, surprised to hear that Kanzar was king. He shook his head to clear his mind. It was something he seemed to have forgotten. But it sounded wrong. He didn't trust Kanzar. But, remembering the wizards that were with him earlier, he surmised that he, himself, was one Kanzar's men. This didn't make sense to him. He wouldn't have chosen that.

"Maybe you should step down, Daymian." Bakari spoke for the first time.

Roland turned his head to where Bakari sat, away from the table. He smiled at how close Bakari was sitting to Kharlia. They both held books in their hands. They made a good pair, and Bakari did raise a good point.

A thought flashed through Roland's mind: *Wait—Bakari had left with Kharlia before the group left River Bend. No one knew where they went. How could they be back here again?* With that thought, Roland heard voices around him. Whipping around, he scanned the trees. *Nothing there.* Yet, he was sure he had heard something.

A large, meaty hand fell on his shoulder. Roland jumped and turned around to find Kanzar Centari himself, looming over him. The self-proclaimed king motioned Roland back into the trees.

"Congratulations, you found the rebels." Kanzar considered Roland with only a hint of a smile. "This will be easy. Once and for all, we will rid ourselves of the Chief Judge and his troublemakers."

Troublemakers? thought Roland. *That group? They were trying to find peace.*

"Are you ready to attack? Are the men in place?" Kanzar interrupted his thoughts.

Roland thought hard about the Chief Judge and the last time they had spoken in the Citadel. Wasn't it only yesterday? Wait, it couldn't have been yesterday if he was here in River Bend now. No. He had watched the Chief Judge's speech that morning, right before…his wizard test.

The test! That was where he was now, and this was, once again, only an imaginary scenario playing out in his mind.

"Kanzar, I am surprised that you came into my test yourself," Roland said. "Are you taking a personal interest in me?"

Kanzar's eyes opened wide in surprise. "You cannot be aware of the test. That cannot be."

"Surprised you again, didn't I?" Roland said, and he opened his mouth to say more.

But, at that moment, Kanzar bellowed, "Attack!" Kanzar yelled the command to his other men.

The other wizards came running in from the woods, surrounding the small inn. Two of them busted down the front door and, with ease, killed two surprised guards. The rest of the Chief Judge's men drew their swords.

Roland turned to Kanzar, but the man had disappeared. "Bakari," Roland yelled through the window in warning. He knew his friend didn't exhibit much in the way of fighting skills and would sorely lose in a battle against these men of Kanzar's.

Leaping into action, Roland busted through a window. The Chief Judge studied him with questioning eyes.

"This is wrong," Roland yelled. "Protect yourselves." In his mind, Roland screamed back to the wizards in the room, *This is not a test! This is a slaughter. I will not be part of this.*

"What kinds of powers does this apprentice possess?" they asked among themselves.

Roland didn't want to kill anyone, but he now knew this wasn't real, so he plowed into Kanzar's men with a vengeance. And, once again, realizing that he was only limited by his mind during the test, he performed tricks he normally couldn't have done.

Running up the side of a wall, he ran across it sideways and knocked out two of Kanzar's wizards with a strike of his hand. Two more ran toward Bakari, and Roland stopped them with a push of air, sending them head first through the wall. Was this how Alli felt when she fought? It was euphoric. Nothing could stop him.

"Kanzar!" he yelled. "Why did you run away before the fighting started?" Roland goaded the High Wizard.

Then, without warning, more men rushed into the building, with Kanzar in the lead. Roland jumped through the air, sending fire toward two of them, taking them down instantly. Then he threw a knife and hit another one.

The Chief Judge came up beside Roland, and, with Kanzar's attention elsewhere, the Chief Judge somehow managed to stab the High Wizard with a small hidden knife. Kanzar bellowed and tried to throw a stream of fire at the Chief Judge, but his pain seemed to have limited the use of his magic.

Two wizards picked up Kanzar and began moving him out of the building, protecting their master. Another one battled Bakari. Roland rushed to the aid of his friends, only to slip on something and miss the man by inches. The man then turned and sliced Kharlia down her thigh.

A scream pierced the building. Then two screams: Kharlia's pain and Bakari's anger. Bakari closed his eyes briefly, and a dozen birds came flying through the broken window. These pecked at the man that had stabbed Kharlia until he lay on the floor dead.

Roland turned around, ready to take on another attacker, to see that the only ones left were the two wizards with Kanzar.

"Come with us, wizard." They reached their hands out toward him. "We must get King Kanzar back to the Citadel in time to be healed."

"He is no king of mine," Roland spat and roared these same words at them through his mind. He knew the Wizard Council was now in upheaval. Many scrambled across the floor, Kanzar being one of them. The High Wizard had come into Roland's test too strongly.

Roland realized now that, although this test occurred in his mind, the wizards could be hurt still, not physically but mentally, magically, and emotionally. The strain he had put on them, with his knowledge of what was happening and with the ensuing fight, had exhausted them. This knowledge he kept in a part of his mind that they couldn't see. It was something he had over them—all of them—even Kanzar.

"Roland!" shouted Bakari.

Roland turned toward his friend. Bakari was kneeling down next to Kharlia, tears trailing down his cheeks.

"Heal her, please!" Bakari asked with such raw emotion that Roland himself could hardly hold back tears. Bakari was the closest thing he had to a friend. Roland had teased him a lot and knew Bakari would never be as great of a wizard as he, but Roland would help him, even if this was only in his mind—because this was the right thing to do, to help his friend.

"You need to come back with us, Roland," the other wizards said. "Kanzar is suffering and needs help. If you don't come with us, you won't pass the test."

Roland stopped dead in his tracks. What did they mean, he wouldn't pass the test? How could they not let him pass, after all the power and abilities he had shown them? He reached inward once again and saw the testing room. He still sat in the testing chair.

Looking up in the testing room, he saw Kanzar, writhing with pain. Onius sat nearby with barely disguised anger.

"Roland, she is losing too much blood," Bakari said, bringing Roland's attention back to Kharlia again, if only in his mind.

"Ahhhhhhhh," Roland roared with frustration. Why must everyone want him? It wasn't a fair test: to choose between becoming a wizard or helping his friend. He looked back and forth between the two groups and then fully realized what he needed to do.

He would heal. He had done it twice before; he would do it twice again. Running to Kharlia, he knelt down beside her. Her breathing was labored, her leg slick with blood. He placed one hand over her leg, sank his mind deep into her wound and chanted a spell. He felt the veins healing, and blood stopped leaking out. The tissue gathered together once again, and her flesh mended itself.

Opening his eyes, he saw a hint of color return to her face. Bakari reached his hand over to Roland's shoulder and thanked him, then turned his attention back to Kharlia.

Roland then stood, letting a small wave of dizziness end before he walked over to Kanzar and the other two wizards. In his mind, back in the Wizard Council, he could hear them marveling at his healing of Kharlia, especially after he had expelled so much energy in the fight.

"I will heal you, Kanzar, but only if you will name me a wizard, as is warranted by the power I have shown in these tests." Roland spoke these words out loud and in his mind.

"Boy, you have the gall to threaten me?" came the reply. "You have broken so many rules—"

"Rules? Rules you did not tell me. I've not broken any rules. I have only shown you things you never thought possible. You should be happy and excited to have my abilities as a wizard. I broke through the mind barrier, communicated with you, controlled a tempest, led the wizards back to the Citadel, and now healed someone. How am I not a full-fledged wizard?"

The wizards conferred among themselves. Some agreed with his argument; others not. He placed his hand on Kanzar's gut and felt the sword wound inside. Instead of healing it, Roland first prodded deeper, bringing more pain to this man who would stop him from becoming a wizard.

Kanzar roared deeply and reached his mind out to stop Roland, but he was too weak.

"I could take your life now, Kanzar," Roland said in anger and exhaustion.

"No, Roland. This is not what you want," Onius said, speaking up for the first time. "We all acknowledge your power, and you will be named a wizard if you heal Kanzar. But, if you cause him any more pain, you will be killed here, in the chair, where you sit."

"Level-four wizard!" Roland yelled in response.

Again sounds of confusion and disbelief broke out among the Council.

But Onius only said, "Heal him."

Roland dug deeply into the wound and then closed it up, layer by layer, fusing organs back together and bringing the flesh back to new. Soon he removed his hand from the wound, leaving only a small scar on Kanzar's side.

"I leave this scar for you to remember me by."

Roland then lifted his head up. Once again, he sat in the chair in the middle of the Wizard Council. The chairs were now strewn across the balcony and floor of the testing room. Some wizards looked sick or ready to faint.

Kanzar pulled himself up off the floor and lifted his cloak. There, on his right side, sat a thin scar.

The High Wizard's eyes blazed with a deadly look, and Roland knew he needed to be careful around the man.

"Congratulations, Roland Tyre," Kanzar said, forcing the words out, barely holding on to a modicum of control. "You are the newest level-four wizard. As is our rule, let nothing that happened in here today be spoken of outside of these walls. You are dismissed."

Roland headed toward the door and, with one hand on the handle, turned back to his older mentor, Onius Neeland. Roland was now one level higher than his mentor—well, *former mentor*—and he knew that, one day soon, he would be a level-five wizard—the most powerful wizard of all.

CHAPTER EIGHTEEN

Erryl stood in the circle with the other guardians in Celestar once again. He had dreaded the daily ritual because he was becoming bored of it. But a part of him still delighted in it because he could be part of the awesome power of the Orb. One by one, the guardians took turns placing their hands on the Orb and feeding it their own life source. Each time, the Orb glowed brighter for a brief moment.

In the last week, the Orb had once again grown larger. It was now the size of a man. Erryl thought back to the day when the Orb had spoken to his mind. He remembered its command to find someone, but he didn't know whom or how. He had always felt anxious to leave Celestar and see the world around him. But, could he really leave when it came down to it? How would he survive?

It was now his turn, and he placed his hand on the Orb, as he always had. Instantly, he sensed his own life source being drained out of him, feeding the Orb. He knew what they did here was a great service and a sacrifice for all of Alaris. But he wondered if the rest of the people in the land even realized where the barrier got its power from. It was a thankless job, but Erryl felt a sense of personal pride in knowing he was a part of protecting their land.

As he had done for the past week, he tried now to listen to

the Orb again—but it stayed silent. No other directions came to him. He frowned but kept his hand on the Orb until his turn was finished.

Pulling his hand away, Erryl closed his eyes and let the next guardian take her turn. Time seemed to stretch forward endlessly as they stood there around the Orb, basking in its power. Then Erryl felt a lurching in the power, and someone screamed and fell out of the circle. He opened his eyes and saw his mother on the other side of the ring of guardians, sprawled out on the marble floor. Forgetting their protocol, he broke the circle as both of his hands left the chain of guardians.

"No," yelled one of the protectors from outside of the circle. "Guardians, close ranks now."

The Orb flared suddenly, growing thinner and brighter for a moment, almost as if it had sensed their apprehension. Erryl turned toward it and thought he saw a faint outline of a creature inside the Orb—a creature with wings. As soon as he had seen it, though, it faded away, and other guardians filled in where Erryl and his mother had left the circle.

He wondered if anyone else had seen what he had. But he pushed thoughts of the Orb out of his mind and fell to the floor beside his mother. He put his hand to her cheek and held back his own tears.

"Mother, Mother, are you all right?"

His mother's eyes flickered open, and she smiled ever so slightly. "Erryl." Her lips parted.

Soon his father stood over him. He had not broken the chain. How could he have not? His wife lay on the floor.

His father shook his head. "It is her time. You must get

back into the circle, Erryl. Do not forget your duties."

"My duties?" Erryl couldn't believe that his father could be so callous.

"We all face it, Son. She has done all that was expected from her, but now she is too weak. The guardians cannot be weak. Someone else must take her place now."

Erryl felt anger rise within him, a feeling he found foreign compared to his peaceful life as a guardian. Then he noticed how hard his father was clenching his neighbors' hands on either side, his knuckles white. He studied his father's face. The glow from the Orb reflected lightly off a tear rolling down his cheek.

"But she is your wife," Erryl said.

"I know, Erryl." His father let out a small sob. "That is what makes remembering my duty so much harder."

His mother groaned one last time, and then her eyes closed. A protector came over and moved Erryl aside, picking up his mother in his arms.

"Behold the guardian," the protector said. "She has given her life source in the service of the Orb. She has sacrificed all to fulfill her duty. May her sacrifice be remembered always."

The older members of the circle repeated, "May her sacrifice be remembered always."

The words felt uncomfortably rote and stiff to Erryl. He had been allowed into this circle, with the true Orb of Life, only a few months ago, since he turned fourteen. This was the first time he had personally seen this happen. Now he knew what happened to guardians who disappeared from Celestar.

The Orb of Life glowed brighter as the protector placed

the body on the floor next to the pedestal. Tendrils of light came out and wrapped themselves around her small, frail, tender body. A small cry escaped Erryl's lips. He closed his eyes to fight back tears.

When he opened them again, his mother had vanished and the light of the Orb returned to normal. Another protector guided him back to the circle. He grabbed the others' hands again and stood numbly as the guardians finished their session.

By the time they had finished the ritual, Erryl was more exhausted than normal. So he passed by the diner, where they fed the guardians, and went directly to his small home. The rooms didn't seem as bright and inviting as they usually did.

He passed by the sitting room and noticed that a book his mother was reading earlier that day was sitting out. His eyes welled up with tears again. He walked over, gently picked it up, and put it back in the bookcase without even reading the title.

Numbly, he continued on to his own private room and lay down on the soft bed without removing his white guardian's robe or his soft leather shoes. He grabbed a lightweight silk blanket and pulled it up over himself, for comfort more than for warmth, then closed his eyes and fell into an immediate, deep sleep.

Hours later, Erryl woke up to the dark night. Still grieving for his mother and trying to understand the sacrifice she had so willingly given, he became determined to find out more about the Orb. Something wasn't right. It shouldn't be growing so big.

Being only fourteen years old, he couldn't boast much in the way of life experience, but he was a curious boy.

Questions filtered constantly through his young mind: Why would guardians not be allowed to leave Celestar? Why did guardians of the Orb die? And, were the protectors protecting the guardians, or were they *guarding* them? These questions now reached a crescendo in his thinking.

Tonight, he decided, he was going in search of some answers. He got up from his bed and listened at the door. All was quiet. Then Erryl did something he had never done before. He changed into dark clothes, pulled a dark hood over his short hair, then snuck out of his room and into the night.

This close to the barrier, the air always held a glow. Overhead, the stars shone down in a moonless night. The glow from the barrier and the stars was enough light to help Erryl make his way through the streets of the housing complexes. His destination was the Orb.

Growing up in Celestar, he had been well educated. The guardians, apparently, worked better when they were intelligent. Erryl's learning had brought an increased hunger to learn more—more about the guardians, the Orb, Alaris, and their place in the broader world.

He knew there were more kingdoms around them. Mahli and the other smaller territories to the north, Elvyn to the east, Solshi to the west, and Quentis and Tillimot to the south. He had been taught about all of them.

Peering around the streets and buildings, he once again got the feeling that the guardians were being guarded and held in rather than protected.

The guardians existed to feed the Orb as it protected Alaris. The Orb, however, had always been small, about the size of a large pumpkin. But it had grown in recent months and now even more so in the past few weeks – now the height of a man and almost as wide as it was tall.

Erryl heard the sound of footsteps and slid behind a large column on the front of one of the housing centers, his heart beating wildly. A lone protector walked by without even noticing him. The man seemed to be focused on getting somewhere, so Erryl wondered where. Why would a protector go somewhere with such purpose at this time of night? He followed.

Soon he noticed another protector, coming from the opposite direction, then another. It was becoming harder to hide, so he slowed down and stayed farther back in the shadows. He wiped his wet forehead with the back of his hand and took a deep breath. They were heading into the Orb building.

Among the protectors, Erryl saw Geran, the protector of his sector.

A group of at least twenty protectors entered the small hall next to the room housing the Orb. No one stood guard at the door. There was no need. Nothing bad or dangerous ever happened in Celestar.

Erryl slid in through the door behind the small group and then hid behind some packing crates in the far corner of the room. His heart pounded, and he wiped sweat off his face once again. He scrunched down as small as he could, pulled his hood over his face even farther, and then peered out from the shadows of the crates to where the men stood.

A man Erryl had seen only once stood up in front of the

group. He was the head protector or *governor of Celestar*, as he liked to be called. Naylor Ellian was his name, a tall man with shoulder-length hair and a deep voice. Something in the Governor's gaze intimidated Erryl, and he tried to make himself even smaller. The man seemed to stare at Erryl's hiding spot for a moment.

"Protectors, I have asked you here this night for an important purpose." Governor Ellian paused for effect. "As many of you know, the barrier has been failing. I have received a missive from the Citadel that we are to do nothing about it. In fact, I have been commanded to *reduce* the number of guardians at each session with the Orb. High Wizard Kanzar Centari wants the barrier to fall."

Erryl gasped, but it wasn't heard over the instant murmurings of the protectors.

"Let the barrier fail? How could that be?"

"It has been here for almost one hundred fifty years, protecting Alaris from others."

"What would the guardians do if it fell? They have no other purpose."

Governor Ellian took back his control of the meeting. "Soon the Citadel will send battle wizards here to help protect us. They will ensure our safety and the safety of all the citizens of Celestar. Being at the corner of the barrier, we might be in a dangerous situation."

"Why would he want the barrier to fall?" Geran asked.

The Governor held the eyes of Geran, one of his oldest protectors. "It is time to be part of the world again, Geran. Surely you long to travel and see what else is around us?"

Erryl agreed with the Governor's reasoning. He would like to see the world around him, as long as he was sure they would be protected. He figured that the Wizard Council at the Citadel had things in hand and would know how to handle this.

As if reading Erryl's mind, Governor Ellian continued, "The Citadel has control of the situation. When the barrier falls, Alaris should be in position to take full advantage of the situation, and each of you will be called upon to support Kanzar in his plans. I, for one, have pledged my allegiance to the High Wizard of the Citadel."

Erryl thought it strange that the governor had pledged his support to the High Wizard, when he knew a Chief Judge ruled the land. Celestar had always been ruled through the Citadel, and many, though not all, of the protectors were low-level wizards. But Erryl found it alarming that he didn't even mention the Chief Judge.

The men nodded at the Governor's words, and, after a few more instructions, the meeting disbanded. Before leaving the room, the Governor motioned Geran over to himself, and, with a few small whispers, they left the room together.

Erryl followed behind the two and soon found that they were headed toward the Orb. Before even entering the room, Erryl felt the Orb's power pulsing through him, affecting everything he did and thought.

He had been in this room hundreds of times over the last few months, but each time he was amazed at its brightness. Even at night, the room glowed with unearthly power. A great glass dome stood overhead, and, in the center of the room, the Orb itself sat on a carpet of red.

Erryl watched the two men approach the Orb; its size now dwarfed both of them. As it had grown bigger, the white coloring had become more translucent and iridescent. He could almost make out the shape of something inside the Orb, but not quite. The Governor reached out his hand cautiously toward it.

"Governor," Geran said. "You know we cannot touch it."

The ruler of Celestar held his hand in midair. "Why is that, Geran? Why can't anyone but guardians touch it? Not even wizards are allowed, apparently. Have you ever wondered about that?"

Erryl stayed still, watching them from behind a far column. There were no shadows to hide behind in this room, but he hoped the wide column would conceal his presence. He hadn't known that wizards were not allowed to touch the Orb. That was something interesting to think about. Some of the protectors were wizards.

"No one knows." Geran had a thoughtful look on his face. "I suppose it goes back to its creation. Wizards weren't trusted much after the war. We were sent here to protect it, but only the guardians can touch it and feed its power."

"But, can you imagine the kind of power it contains inside it now? It is ten times the size it once was. Aren't you curious?" The Governor's eyes glowed with enthusiasm.

"No," Geran said.

"Don't you wonder why the Orb is growing? What kind of power could we have at our disposal if we could harness it?" The Governor's eyes grew fervent, and he reached his hand closer to the Orb, his fingers turning white with the reflection.

Geran reached his own hand out to pull Governor Ellian's back. But, with a flash of his hand, the Governor caught Geran's hand instead.

"What are you doing?" Geran turned his head.

"What if you touch it first? Then we will know if anything has changed." The look in the Governor's eyes turned hard.

"What are you talking about?" Geran struggled to pull away from the governor, but the man's grip held him firmly.

"I received another instruction from the High Wizard," the Governor said. "He wanted me to test the Orb…see if we could harness the power." The Governor moved Geran's hand closer to the Orb. "I can't very well test it myself, can I? Not if it would kill me."

Erryl gasped as he realized what was happening. The sound of this echoed in the room, and the Governor turned around, his eyes scanning the area. Finding nothing, he turned back to the Orb.

Geran brought his other hand out, beginning to form a small spell of fire against his leader. Erryl stood frozen in place. The flame grew larger, but before Geran could release the magic, the Governor pushed Geran's other hand toward the Orb and held it against the bright surface.

Governor Ellian brought his hand back from Geran's and took a step away from the Orb. Geran shrieked in agony as his hand burst into flames and fire shot up his arm. A white light burst from the Orb—not unlike when Erryl's mother had died—and consumed Geran instantly. In moments, nothing was left of the man, and the light folded back into the Orb.

The Governor raised his eyebrows and mumbled under his

breath, "I guess wizards still can't touch it." With that, he walked out of the room without looking back around him.

Erryl stood still for a moment, reeling in confusion. Tears filled his eyes as he thought about poor Geran. He didn't deserve to die. What kind of man was the High Wizard to order such a thing? Erryl found himself feeling not very fond of wizards at all—or their plan of letting the barrier fall.

Glancing in quick motions around the room, he approached the Orb himself. He had touched it numerous times before, as part of the ceremony, but could he touch it now? *Should he touch it now?* was probably a better question. His thoughts turned back to what had happened to Geran. But he was a wizard; Erryl definitely was not.

Why was the barrier failing? he wondered. Would the Orb talk to him again and give him clearer instructions? He took a step closer and felt warmth from the Orb. He felt comforted in its presence. Stepping within an arm's length from it, he took a deep breath.

He would help the Orb, he decided. Someone had to do it. And he might be the only one who stood in a position to do so. Reaching his hand tentatively out, he saw tendrils of light reach out toward him. He closed his eyes and pushed his hand forward the rest of the way to the Orb. It was smooth against his skin, almost glass-like, but more porous. He realized that he wasn't being consumed or killed. He took a deep breath and was thankful for that.

Suddenly, into his mind came thoughts and a vision.

Within the blackness of his closed eyes, he saw a picture of a boy. The young man was not much older than himself. His skin was dark, unlike Erryl's, and his hair was short and curly. He wore glasses over his brown eyes. The figure walked toward Erryl. An older man, with lighter skin and a bushy beard, walked on the boy's left side. They appeared tired and lost. As the young man came closer, Erryl could see an intelligent intention in his face—but the sadness in his dark eyes almost overwhelmed Erryl.

Find him, and bring him to me, a voice said to Erryl's mind, echoing the sentiments told to him the first time the Orb had spoken to him. Erryl jerked his head back but somehow was able to keep his hand on the Orb.

"But how?" he whispered out loud. He would do what the Orb wanted, but he needed some direction.

I need him. Alaris needs him. He is the one, the voice continued, deep and clear.

The vision then widened, and Erryl could see the area surrounding the two men much better. They walked in a lightly wooded area next to a large outcropping of rock. To their left, a small stream wound away behind them in a crooked path.

Find him for me. The voice began to fade. *Bring him to me, Erryl.*

Erryl opened his eyes, and the room dimmed. He removed his hand from the Orb and gazed around in awe and wonder. The Orb had spoken his name. How could that be?

Who was the young man he had to find? How was he going to find him? These and other questions flooded his mind, but one thing remained certain—Erryl would find him. If it was important to the Orb and to Alaris, then, as a guardian, it was his duty.

CHAPTER NINETEEN

Bakari rode slumped over Adi's neck, the horse taking it easy with her tired rider. Kharlia walked beside them, lost in her own thoughts. It had been only a day since their encounter with the bandits. Bak's energy was slowly returning. He lifted his head and breathed in the fragrance of the forest. The rich soil, pine needles, and the Dunn River all combined into a scent that he was not used to yet, although it was quite pleasant.

"Kharlia?" he called out. When she turned to him and smiled, his heart leapt with joy. "Why do you stay with me?"

"What?" Kharlia's eyebrows furrowed.

"This might get more dangerous the farther we go. You don't need to do this." Bakari looked down at her from the back of the horse.

Her lips tightened, and her eyes flashed. One hand held the reins of the horse; the other one was on her hip.

Bakari didn't like that look and tried to smile at her to diffuse her anger. He started to apologize but didn't get very far with his words.

"Bak, we've been over this before. This is not just your fight. I know what I am getting myself into, and I choose to be here on this adventure with you."

Bakari laughed. It felt good. He wasn't laughing at her, in a mocking way, but the fierceness of her loyalty to him and to their mission made him happy. She tried not to smile but soon broke into a giggle with him.

Kharlia pushed her hair behind one ear and began walking again. "Don't think you're all that special, Bakari. I'm still mad you would ask me that again."

Bakari couldn't keep a wide grin from his lips. "I promise to never ask that again. My brain isn't fully awake yet."

"Humph" was all Kharlia said, but her smile matched Bakari's. After a few moments, she asked, "Does doing magic always make wizards tired?"

Bakari thought back through all he had studied on the subject over the years. He sifted out and pulled together the information and thought about her question.

"Bakari," Kharlia prodded, "I'm not asking for a dissertation, just your opinion."

"Sorry," Bakari mumbled, then spoke louder as he said, "Personally, the only times I've been tired after using magic were the two times I communicated with animals. My normal scholarly studies don't cause too much strain. However, many wizards feel a period of fatigue or hunger after performing complex spells or magic. The energy that the body expends during moments of magic needs to be replaced by either sleep or food. However, in the specific case of Roland, the counselor apprentice from Cassian, he tells me that he never tires and thinks he has more power than the rest of us."

"That's one long opinion." Kharlia laughed to not upset Bakari.

"Well, I am used to studying and not quite as used to

talking to a pretty girl," he said back. He didn't know why he had said that. Maybe he was still weak and not thinking properly. Maybe he should just stay quiet, until he could gather his thoughts better.

"Bakari, I think you're blushing."

"No, I'm not. How can you tell, anyway?"

"Your ears get darker, and your cheeks flush a deeper brown."

Not wanting to talk more on that subject, Bakari changed it. "Do you want to ride with me for a while? We need to move faster, and, at some point, I think we will need to cross the Dunn as we move farther north."

Bakari sat up straighter and reached his hand down to Kharlia, pulling her up behind him. He smiled again and breathed in her sweet scent.

No sooner had she hopped onto the horse than a ruckus ensued on the other side of a nearby thicket. The horse whinnied and stopped and wouldn't go any farther. A deep-voiced yelling also ensued. Two wild boars, about the size of a dog, ran out onto the path in front of Bakari and Kharlia. Then the animals took off down the path in front of them.

Soon a large man with bushy hair and a beard ran out of the bushes to their left and continued running toward the boars. In his hand, he held two long sticks with a net stretched between them. As he neared the boars, he threw the net high into the air, and it landed on one of the boars, trapping it inside. The other one escaped back off into the bushes.

Bakari and Kharlia trotted a few steps closer to the man and then stopped to watch the rest of his activity. He pulled out a long knife and, with a steady hand, cut across the neck of the wild boar, as if to be careful to not cause the animal any prolonged pain. He then proceeded to take the net off. Only after all this did he turn around and look at the two of them.

He did a double take and rubbed his hands over his full beard. "Well, my, my. Don't see a lot of young people out in these parts, all alone. You kids lost?"

Bakari felt Kharlia stiffen behind him. But he didn't know what to make of this wild man and stayed silent.

The man walked closer to them and stuck out his hand. "I mean you no harm. Name's Harley, it is. Harley Habersham. I know it's a mouthful, so most folks call me Har or Harley."

Bakari smiled at the friendly stranger. "My name is Bakari. And this is Kharlia."

They shook hands.

As Bakari looked over at the boar, they all clearly heard his stomach rumble.

"Sounds like you're hungry, Bakari. You two on the run from something?"

Bakari didn't answer, feeling nervous about that line of questioning. Harley appeared to accept his silence, so he tried to settle his nerves.

"No matter what your business is, seems like you could use a good meal. All bony you are. We need to put some more meat on those bones so you can be strong for your girl here."

Bakari blushed and started to say that she wasn't *his girl*, but Kharlia punched her small fist into his back and laughed.

"Thank you, Sir. A good meal sounds great," Kharlia said graciously.

"No need to call me *Sir* here, Missy. Har or Harley will do, like I said. My cabin's not too far away from here. My wife and boy are there. Hopefully, a nice pot of something is waiting for us to eat. I'm starving." The big man patted his stomach. "This here wild boar will need to be cured for a while before she's ready for eatin'."

Harley packed up his boar and slung it over his broad shoulders. Then Bakari and Kharlia followed him to his home, a small, two-room cabin made of pine logs. A clearing in the front housed a vegetable garden, and a small stream, leading to the Dunn River, flowed around the back.

Soon they were all seated around a table, Harley bringing in a few extra crates for the newcomers to sit on. Bakari noticed that the child Harley had mentioned did not come sit with them, so Bakari guessed it must be only an infant, probably sleeping somewhere.

They ate a nice thick stew, fresh bread, and turnip greens. It felt nice to be full again. In the last few days of their journey, they had relied on Kharlia's foresting skills and Bakari's book knowledge for finding edible plants, neither of which had filled them up much.

After eating, Harley turned to Bakari. "So, Son, what do you do in life that brings you up this direction?"

Bakari fidgeted nervously with his feet, but Kharlia stepped in. "Bak is a scholar, and I am a village healer. He's helping me find herbs growing up in this area."

Harley's wife, Sarah, brightened up. "A healer? Harley, did you hear that?"

Harley nodded his head and then spoke. "Our son is sick

with a fever, and we don't know what to do. He keeps getting weaker and sleeps most of the day. Could you—I mean—*would* you be willin' to look at him?"

Kharlia's eyes lit up. Within moments, she had grabbed her pack headed off into the other room with Sarah.

Once they had left, Harley resumed speaking to Bakari. "How far north are you headed?"

Bakari didn't know this man and wasn't a good conversationalist, but he felt he could trust him. "As far as we can get—all the way to the barrier."

Harley's eyes widened. "Strange happenings up there, on the other side of the river. You better stay farther south."

"Happenings like what?" Bakari's desire for knowledge pushed him forward.

"People live up there that no one hardly ever sees. A strange place that used to be on Elvyn lands but got stuck this side of the barrier." Harley's eyes shifted around in his nervousness. "You just don't want to go there, Bakari. The closer you get to the corner of the barrier—people see things they don't want to talk about."

Bakari received the impression to push the man further. His wizard powers told him this man knew more than he let on. "What things have you seen, Harley?"

Harley got up and walked to the fire, where the pot of stew had been cooked. He poked around in it a few times. It was warm enough to not need the fire for warmth. He turned back around and stroked his beard.

"You seem like a nice kid, Bak—can I call you Bak?"

Bakari nodded.

"I don't know what you two are running from," Harley continued. "Oh, you do seem the scholarly type, and I hope with all my might your girl is a healer, but you don't belong out here."

Bakari opened his mouth to answer.

"Stay away from the barrier. There are sightings of odd animals around it and rumors of seeing *people* on the other side."

"Harley," Bakari said, looking him in the eyes. "I need to hear and understand what you know. Have you seen a city around there?"

Harley stood up and almost knocked over a small table. "What do you know about a city? Who are you really?" The man paced the small room nervously.

Bakari decided to level with him. "I am a scholar wizard. The Chief Judge is in trouble. I serve him. We heard that the barrier is failing, and I need to find out why."

"And, why did you ask about a city?"

Bakari brought up in his mind the map they had seen at the library in River Bend. He had memorized every last detail. "*Celestar.* Does that mean anything to you?" He had purposefully not answered the man's question.

Harley fell back in his seat and stayed silent for a minute.

Bakari needed to find out, so he pushed forward. "I need you to bring us there, Harley. You know where it is, don't you?"

Harley only nodded his head, at first, then his eyes glazed over. "Bright lights, gleaming spires, and people that never leave or come. I haven't seen it myself, boy, but I trust those who have. I have been close enough to see its lights reflecting in the night sky. Something mighty strange, to have a city no one knows about, tucked away at the corner of the barrier."

"That is why I need to go there."

Kharlia and Sarah emerged from the bedroom. Harley's wife held their young son, probably not more than two years old.

"Harley, she did it! She is a healer indeed." Tears streaked down Sarah's face. "His fever broke."

Harley moved next to his wife and put his arm around her.

The large man looked at Kharlia and then Bakari. "How can I repay you?" he asked before thinking through what the answer might be.

Bakari gave him a toothy grin, and Harley knew then what the price would be.

"Fine," the woodsman said. "But only as far as the large outcropping of rock. I'll point the way from there. I'm not going all the way to that city. We'll all gather supplies today and leave at first light. With horses, it will be about five days of traveling."

CHAPTER TWENTY

Alli needed to expend some energy. She was fidgety from sitting around the Citadel and watching the power plays between the wizards and the Chief Judge. This morning, she walked to the practice yard and proceeded to stretch and work her body. Wearing tight leather pants and snug leather armor over a thin shirt, she soon worked up a sweat.

She picked up a staff and twirled it faster and faster around her head and then her body. Becoming one with the weapon, she removed all distractions from her mind. She swung the staff out with one hand and brought it back with the other. She jumped over the staff, released some of her powers, and somersaulted back to the ground. Faster and faster she turned, until she became a blur to any curious onlookers.

The young apprentice was oblivious to the growing crowd until she stopped moving and opened her eyes. She flushed from the attention more than from the exertion of the workout. The crowd applauded, and an older man walked up to her.

"My girl," he began. "That was one of the most beautiful routines I have ever seen. You must be quite something to behold during an actual battle."

Alli gave a short bow of her head in deference to the man. "Thank you, Wizard. I just needed to blow off some steam. I'm bored."

"Bored!" The elderly wizard laughed. "Well, you brought some excitement to the gathering for sure. I am Battle Wizard Geoffrey." He extended his right hand.

The man stood at least a foot taller than Alli, with shortly cropped, silver hair. His older years were upon him, but he was still fit and trim, with muscle definition showing through his attire. "Would you like to take on some real challenges? I would love to show you around the battle wizard training grounds."

Alli's eyes lit up, and a smile crossed her young face. She pushed a strand of hair out of her eyes. "Lead the way."

Geoffrey laughed and led her on a short walk away from the onlookers. Entering the official training grounds of the battle wizards, Alli was awed. Before, when living at the Citadel, she had only been allowed to practice among the other apprentices. But now, glancing around, she saw full-fledged wizards using swords, staffs, bows, knives, and—some—only their wizarding powers.

"High Wizard Kanzar wants us ready at all times," Geoffrey said as he motioned around the practice yard. "You must know of the Chief Judge's words the other day. He intends not to relinquish his position. There could be a battle soon."

Alli frowned up at the larger man. "Why should he relinquish his legally obtained position?"

"Ahh. I forgot that you serve in Cassian," Geoffrey said with a twinkle in his eye.

Alli was positive the man *hadn't* forgotten where she came from. He was one of Kanzar's men for sure and was trying to lure her into wanting to be in their good graces. Taking in the wonders of the yard, she was surely tempted. But her loyalty lay with the Chief Judge and her mentor, Gorn. Though, since arriving at the Citadel, Gorn had been more subdued than normal and she hadn't seen much of him.

A young wizard, in his late twenties, came walking up to the two. "Who is this young girl, Battlemaster?"

Battlemaster? Alli didn't realize she was speaking to the highest ranking battle wizard in the land. Her face betrayed her emotions, and the newcomer laughed.

"Just showing a promising young apprentice what she has access to, if she wants to become a full wizard," Geoffrey said.

Alli heard the bribe running through his words. If she agreed to be on their side and to fight against the Chief Judge, they would allow her to test to be a full wizard. Was that the bargain Roland had made to be named a wizard? She had heard that he passed the test the previous day but hadn't spoken personally to him yet. It was unlike him, not to come and gloat.

"Is she any good?" asked the young wizard with a smile, and his eyes lingered on Alli's tightly clad body. "She looks the part…but kind of small."

Alli glared at the arrogant young man. Were all young men so bad? She thought of Bakari. At least he seemed to hold a good head on his shoulders—though it usually was stuck in a book.

"I assure you I can hold my own." She flashed him a cutesy smile. "Want to go for a bout?"

The young wizard looked at the Battlemaster, who motioned that he agreed to the demonstration. So the two headed off toward a small practice area to choose their weapons. All were blunted with tied-up rags, but the force of a hit would still sting.

"My name is Maddox," the young wizard said as he tied back his dark hair.

"Alli," she replied.

With these introductions out of the way, the two grabbed swords. Alli took a defensive posture, at first, in order to study the movements of her opponent; Maddox came driving in with no thought. Alli easily sidestepped him and swung her sword around, slapping him on his rear end.

Maddox blushed and came at her harder. Alli stuck her sword out, blocking his. Back and forth they went, neither yielding much to the other. Sweat streamed down Maddox's face as he pushed himself harder.

Alli had studied his moves long enough. The man fought well, but arrogance had him not paying enough attention. He didn't seem to realize that Alli had hardly moved as she parried or dodged each blow.

"Getting tired?" the man said as he puffed out air in an attempt to distract her.

Alli smiled innocently and then stopped moving. This sudden change made Maddox overreach, and he moved past her. Alli then jumped up into the air and flipped over the young wizard, appearing once again in front of him. The move stunned the young man, and Alli smacked him hard with the sword once again.

"Staff!" Maddox yelled, and someone threw him a long, black staff. He swung it hard at Alli's legs. She jumped over it and came down behind him, swatting him on the back. He turned swiftly around and began wildly swinging the staff around him.

With each of his moves, Alli stepped to the staff's rhythm. She became a blur around Maddox, anticipating every move and reaching her sword in to swat him on every part of his body.

During one jump, Alli sensed movement behind her and ducked as another man intruded on their fight. With an eye full of annoyance, she glanced at the Battlemaster, who only smiled in return.

So, that is how it was going to be. They were going to test her now. Two against one: Maddox with the staff, the other with a sword.

Alli struck out at both, somersaulting through the air. While in midair, she pulled two knives out of her boots and threw them at both opponents. The blunt handles smacked each of them hard on the chest. Landing beside a tree in the yard, she felt grateful for a brief respite in the shade as the other two regrouped.

Two more of the Battlemaster's men came out to fight against her. Four against one. She put on her best grin. Now she could blank her mind from everything around her and do what she did best.

She ran straight up the trunk of the tree and flipped back over their heads, knocking two of them down on the way. The other two advanced with swords. She brought out a second sword from a scabbard on her own back and stood with one in each hand. The thrill of battle settled familiarly upon her. It was what she had been born to do.

With moves resembling the grace of a dance more than the crudeness of battle, she flew around, under, and over the four men, scoring hits over and over again. Tiring of not being able to touch Alli, one of the wizards brought forth a ball of fire and threw it at Alli.

The crowd gasped and then watched the Battlemaster. His face showed no emotion.

Alli brought forth her own power and, with a rush of wind, blew the fireball away. It exploded at the feet of one of the other men and knocked him out of the fight. If this was how they were going to play, she would show them what she was made of.

Dropping one of the swords, she brought forth a stray bolt of lightning from her right hand. It shot around the practice yard. The crowd groaned as they thought she had missed. But the bolt took on speed and power as it circled the yard, going faster and faster, until it became a blur of fire that could hardly be seen.

Her opponents froze, mesmerized by the control and finesse of her spell. Then, without warning, the lightning shot inward and circled the feet of the three remaining men. They brought forth air and fire of their own, but it was no match for Alli's strength. She tied their hands with cords of air and then, using the bolt of lightning, dug a hole in the ground beneath their feet. The men dropped three feet into the hole.

"Alli," a voice said to her from the sidelines. "That is enough."

It was Gorn, his face set firm, but his eyes sparkling with

pride.

With a flourish of her hand, she extinguished the circling bolt of lightning and walked toward the Battlemaster. On her way there, the men screamed for her to untie their hands. Without even turning around, she flipped her hand in a circle, and they were free.

Gorn walked over and joined her in front of the Battlemaster. He gave a slight bow to the man but did not appear happy.

Alli looked up at Geoffrey, wet her lips with her tongue, and pushed her hair out of her face. "My loyalty cannot be bought with bribes."

Battlemaster Geoffrey appeared taken aback and, for the first time, lost his composure. "Gorn, you should have more control over your apprentice."

Standing toe to toe with the man, Gorn controlled his anger by a thread. "You put her up to this, Geoffrey. Pitting four battle wizards against one apprentice is not our usual practice. And, allowing them to use magic directly against her is against all the rules. You are lucky she didn't kill them all. I would say she had plenty of control."

The crowd grew quiet, not used to having their Battlemaster's honor put on the line. Then one loud clap began in the crowd. Alli scanned the crowd and finally saw the smirk on Roland Tyre's face. This time, she joined him in his smile.

"Quite a display today," Roland said to Geoffrey. "I'm sure your intentions were noble, Battlemaster, and you were only interested in testing the young girl's strength."

The Battlemaster gave a slight bow of his head toward

Roland. Alli covered a gasp by placing a hand over her mouth. The man had actually acquiesced to Roland's authority. What had happened during his testing?

"I think we are done for today." Roland took command. "Kanzar would like to speak to Gorn and his apprentice." Roland motioned for the two of them to follow him out of the crowd.

After they were out of earshot from the group, Alli put her hand on Roland's arm to stop him.

"Why did the Battlemaster bow to you?"

Roland beamed. "I am a wizard now, Alli. I passed their test."

Alli continued with her question. "But, surely, a level-four wizard would not bow to a level one wizard."

"No. You are right." Roland winked at her and started walking again. "But a level-four wizard would bow as an equal to another level-four wizard."

"What?" Alli couldn't believe her ears. Roland, a level-four wizard? That was unheard of. What had happened in that test? "You?" she said out loud.

"Yes, me. Level-four wizard Roland Tyre." He bowed with a flourish. "At your service."

"Oh, great," Alli moaned. "And I thought your head was big before."

Roland laughed. "Hurry up. We really do need to see Kanzar."

"Can I at least get a drink first?" Alli asked innocently. "I did just beat four battle wizards."

"Yes. I guess you deserve that," Roland said, and both he

and Gorn laughed.

After freshening up, they entered Kanzar's office. Onius stood next to the self-proclaimed High Wizard. Alli noticed a new look from Kanzar while he watched Roland. She couldn't quite place whether it was fear, hatred, envy, or pride—or a mixture of all four.

Onius spoke first, getting right to the point, "Gorn and Alli, we are sending you on a special mission."

Alli wondered if word of her battle had already reached Kanzar's and Onius's ears. *Most likely.*

"The barrier is failing," Onius continued. "And we need your help."

"Have you found out how to strengthen it?" Gorn asked.

"Oh, no, my good wizard," spoke Kanzar for the first time, his voice deep and his eyes dark. "You misunderstand us. We need your help with making it fail. Have you ever heard of Celestar?"

"Wait." Alli couldn't hold her words in. "You mean you want the barrier to fail? Why?" She turned to Roland—he seemed as clueless as she. Gorn held his mouth tight and shook his head at her in a way that said not to question Kanzar. Onius held his face neutral. Only Kanzar appeared pleased with her outburst.

"My dear apprentice," Kanzar said, looking down at her. "Don't worry yourself about the workings of the Citadel."

His condescension sent bristles down her spine, but he was the leader of the Citadel. Maybe there was something she didn't know.

Kanzar continued, focusing his attention on Gorn. "The

barrier has been a hindrance to us for too long. Now that it is failing, we will take full advantage of the situation and put Alaris back as the rightful leader of the southern countries - as we used to be."

Onius pulled out a map and pointed to the northeast corner of Alaris—a small unmarked spot, east of the Dunn River, that used to be on Elvyn land but now stood on the Alaris side of the barrier. "This is where Celestar is," Onius said. "The barrier will fail first here— and this is where you need to be, Gorn."

"Who is in Celestar that needs our protection so badly?" Gorn asked.

Kanzar laughed. "You are not going to protect them but to guard them and to make sure they never leave the city. I will send additional troops to finish the job."

Gorn blinked in surprise and held his jaw tight but said nothing more.

A few more instructions were given, and then Alli and Gorn were dismissed.

CHAPTER TWENTY ONE

Erryl walked south for two days. Two scary, difficult, exhilarating days. Leaving Celestar had been the hardest thing he had ever done. Dreaming of the outside world was one thing; actually going out into it was another. Slipping out of the city the night after the Orb had spoken to him wasn't as difficult as he had thought. The guards at the gates were not used to anyone escaping the city. They were half asleep as Erryl climbed over the city wall and disappeared into the night air.

He had slept that night underneath one of the largest pine trees he had ever seen. The soft bed of needles and fresh forest scent provided him enough comfort, and the exertions of the day made his body weary enough to fall asleep.

The next morning, Erryl had hefted his small pack up over his shoulder, its contents lighter than when he had first left. He had filled it with a small assortment of food that now dwindled alarmingly low. His feet hurt, and he began to get discouraged.

The vision had been clear but also quite short. Something inside him continued to urge him on now, farther south. All of a sudden, a shimmer of light flared up, off to his left. Curiosity grabbed him once again, and he went to investigate. Pushing himself through a knee-high brush of ferns and small plants, Erryl wound his way through the enormous trees.

Coming around one such tree, he found himself only a few

steps from the barrier. He stopped with an abrupt halt, almost tripping over himself. Furrowing his eyebrows, he studied it up and down and along its length. It truly amazed him. He didn't know how it worked, but he did know that his own life source, given to the Orb, was part of what had kept it intact.

The barrier blinked and then shimmered brighter, and Erryl took a step back. His heart raced—first, with fear, then with wonder. He couldn't believe what he saw. He was actually *seeing through* the barrier.

Hearing the sounds of a struggle, he peered past the barrier. In the thick forest of trees, a group of people had appeared. With long hair and builds similar to the ones he saw through the barrier a week before, they fought among each other. Some had blond hair; others brown or black. All stood slender and tall.

He knew he should be afraid, but his legs wouldn't move. His eyes were drawn to one of those people, tied to a tree with ropes holding her hands behind her. She looked up at him with astonishment. The woman was easily the most beautiful person he had ever seen—long blonde hair, fair skin, pale lips, and light blue eyes that locked onto his. He was mesmerized.

Erryl took a hesitant step forward. A flash of light blinked directly in front of him and blinded him for a moment. When he opened his eyes back up the barrier was back in place.

All Erryl could think of was the woman he had seen. She shouldn't be tied up like that. He didn't understand what was going on. Who were they? Why were they fighting?

Erryl sat down on the ground for a moment to think. He pulled out a waterskin and took a long drink, thinking about what was happening. The sounds of the forest around him—the birds chirping, a squirrel chasing another squirrel through the trees, and a slight breeze rustling the pines and cedars—these all calmed his mind.

Getting up, he took a few minutes to walk along the barrier, waiting for something to happen. He didn't need to wait long.

The barrier hummed, flaring bright again. And, once more, he saw through it to the other side. He focused again on the woman tied to the wide and tall tree. She was seated on the ground in a small clearing and turned once again as if to grab his attention. She flipped her long hair out of her face, and Erryl jumped with surprise.

Her ears! "She's an elf," he said out loud. He had read about Elvyn, the kingdom directly east of Alaris. Their people lived mostly in the Elvyn Forest, in dwellings built up high in its humongous trees. He had been taught that they were aggressive and that he should be careful.

The elf woman moved her head back and forth, trying to get his attention again. She mouthed something to him, a pleading to come and untie her. Erryl surveyed the scene around him. Four men moved through the trees a dozen yards away, on the other side of the woman. They yelled and fought with swords. Then another dozen men came running back, closer to where the woman was tied up. Erryl heard a loud wail and a roar that grew louder behind them.

The woman craned her head to look to her side, and Erryl saw another figure tied up against a tree. He was a well-toned man, his dark hair hanging past his shoulders. And he had a dangerous but disciplined air about him.

Erryl was afraid now. He could get hurt. But the woman needed his assistance. And so, in spite of what he had been taught about other kingdoms, he took a step forward, tentatively, his curiosity and need to help winning out.

He reached his hands forward to where the barrier should have been, and his hands passed through. Shock registered across the woman's face as well as the tied-up man's. Erryl quickened his pace and reached the spot right behind the tree where the beautiful elf woman had been tied up.

"Look!" One of the other men, a few trees away, had yelled out to the others. "The barrier is down, and there's a boy here." Three men moved forward, pulling their swords out. At the same time, new screams of terror rang out from behind these attackers, and they turned back around.

Another ten men or so came running closer to Erryl, with a larger, fat elf in the lead. That made over twenty of these strangers, now getting closer to Erryl and the woman tied to the tree. The loud roaring and wailing Erryl had heard earlier grew louder, solidifying into a large beast that came crashing through the underbrush and knocking down small trees behind the men. The creature was dark brown, twice as big as a wolf— with even larger fangs—and ran on all fours, though his front legs were slightly smaller than his back legs.

The elf woman spoke something to Erryl that he couldn't understand. She looked at him impatiently, then changed to his tongue as she repeated it again, "Please, cut my ropes."

Erryl stood still, in shock, as the beast tore through two of the running men and quickly closed the hundred-foot gap between them. A loud growl from the creature's throat kept Erryl frozen in place.

"Get hold of yourself, boy, and help us," the man yelled.

Erryl regained his senses, pulled out a knife, and cut the ropes off the woman. As soon as she was free, she raced to the elf man's side and untied him. Standing up in a swift, fluid motion, the elf man rubbed his wrists, then glanced around for a weapon.

"I still can't use my magic," the elf woman told him.

Erryl stood there, dumbfounded, and tried to understand what was happening. One thing he did understand, though, was the mad beast moving toward them.

The elf man nodded at the woman's words and moved silently behind one of the guards, who was paying more attention to the beast than to his apparent prisoners. Hitting him on the back of his head, the elf man grabbed the man's sword and then turned to fight the other guard who stood close by.

More men raced into the camp.

The woman screamed toward the approaching group. "You must find another animal to feed it, or it will kill us all."

"Get the prisoners," the larger elf man yelled. He seemed to be in charge of the group, but most were more concerned about the beast than about recapturing their prisoners.

The barrier began to shimmer and hum once again.

"Breelyn!" shouted the elf man to the woman Erryl had untied. "Go." He pointed to the barrier.

Breelyn? Erryl thought to himself. *What a pretty name.*

She shook her head. "No, Alair, I will not leave you. I will stay and help fight."

"No," Alair reiterated, his voice curt but still sympathetic. "That is not your duty. You must protect the kingdom, and I must protect you." Alair turned to fight off one of the other men. "Now, take the boy and go!"

The beast howled once again and starting running faster, heading right toward Erryl and Breelyn. Alair shouted at the beast, and it turned his way, looking momentarily confused. Breelyn seemed to understand what Alair had just done for them, and tears came to her eyes. Breelyn reached over, gripped Erryl's hand, and leaped toward where the barrier flashed once again.

Peering over his shoulder, Erryl saw Alair, leading the beast away, but the other men turned and headed toward them, swords out, weaving in and out of the trees. Alair yelled as the beast got closer. Racing around a tree, he threw a branch in the beast's face.

"Hurry," Breelyn encouraged Erryl.

He ran as fast as his legs could carry him. His chest burned and his legs ached. Once they had crossed into the area where he had come through the barrier from, Breelyn stopped, and Erryl almost tripped, his body carrying him forward still.

The barrier shimmered again as one of the pursuing men brought up his bow and quickly nocked an arrow. He sent it flying at the pair of escapees as the barrier began to solidify.

"Alair!" Breelyn wailed one last time. "Thank you!" Then the barrier solidified once again, and the two of them were separated from the rest of that madness.

Then Erryl cried out and fell down. The arrow had made it

through before the barrier closed and had grazed his upper arm, drawing blood. It stung horribly.

The elf woman stepped over to him. She was taller than he had first thought, standing just as tall as he. She brought her hand to his arm and held it there for a minute. Erryl stood still, feeling her warm hand on his arm. He had never been this close to a woman before—besides his mother or the other guardians.

Gritting her teeth, Breelyn let out a breath of air. "I forgot that my magic is still blocked." She reached down and tore a small piece of cloth off of her tunic. She held his arm and wrapped it around snuggly, stopping the trickle of blood. "That will have to do for now. It's not bad."

"What was that thing?" Erryl's heart pounded with fear.

"A barrier beast," Breelyn said. "Animals close to the barrier grow crazed, and magic doesn't work on them." She turned around and stared at the barrier. "Physical force hardly does either. I hope Alair is all right."

Erryl stared at the strange woman with confusion, her back still to him. "Who are you?"

Breelyn turned around, and her smile grew wider. "I am Breelyn Mier, one of King Arrowyn's protectors."

His eyebrows furrowed as he tried to piece things together. "You are an elf?" He stepped nervously, leaning on one leg and then the other.

Putting her hand on his shoulder, Breelyn said, "Yes, I am from Elvyn, the first to cross the barrier in one hundred fifty years. And what is your name, young man?"

Erryl couldn't believe he was talking to an elf and tried to gather his wits together. He stood taller and tried to appear important. "I am Erryl Close, guardian of the Orb, from the city of Celestar."

Breelyn smiled, and Erryl relaxed somewhat. Her face lit up the forest around them with her beauty.

"What are you doing out here?" she asked.

Erryl glanced down, and his cheeks turned pink. He took a moment to prepare to answer. "Things are not right in Celestar, and the Orb told me to find a young man, about my age, and bring him back to Celestar."

Breelyn's eyes sparkled when he mentioned the Orb. But his task had come rushing out. He had felt he could trust the elf for some reason. Looking back up at her, he continued.

"He and another man are somewhere near a large outcrop and a small stream. That's all I know. I've been searching for two days."

"And the Dragon Orb told you this?"

Erryl almost jumped, surprise surely written all over his face. "What do you mean, *Dragon Orb*?"

"When you said *Orb*, I thought…" Breelyn stumbled for words. "I thought you were a guardian of *the* Orb?"

"I am." Erryl took a deep breath before he continued, "But I didn't realize it was a *Dragon Orb*—What does that even mean?"

"A Dragon Orb is…" Breelyn looked around the forest and seemed to be choosing her words with deliberate care. Turning back to Erryl, she got his undivided attention. "A Dragon Orb is a dragon egg."

"An egg?" Erryl sat down on the ground and tried to put things together in his mind. "It spoke to me. The Orb's been growing…Does that mean…?" He didn't need to say the next words. He was smart enough to know that an egg meant an animal and a dragon egg meant a dragon. Was that who had spoken to his mind?

Erryl put his hand to his head to stop the dizziness, but it didn't help. Breelyn tried to calm Erryl, but he didn't know if he could be calm ever again. This was too much.

She sighed. "Let's start over and tell each other what we know about the Orb and the barrier. I think we're both here for the same purpose."

"You do?" he asked.

"Yes. To protect us when the barrier falls."

"The barrier is falling?" Erryl put his face into his hands once again. His entire world, everything he knew, seemed to be crashing down on him.

Breelyn glanced wistfully back at where the barrier now stood. "I don't know how long we have before it comes down again. The men chasing me didn't want me to know about the barrier's weakness. I'm not sure what they are planning. But, if it comes down again, we'd better be far away from here."

Breelyn motioned for Erryl to stand up and start walking again. "Lead the way, Erryl. I am stuck on this side of the barrier for a reason. I think the reason must be to help you find this man whom the Dragon Orb seeks."

CHAPTER TWENTY TWO

Chief Judge Daymian Khouri stood in his guest rooms in the Citadel and gazed out of a window facing south. Even though he hadn't been too fond of being in the Citadel for the last four days, it had given him time to recuperate more. He felt stronger now from surviving the two attempts on his life.

Daymian took a moment to relish the scenery before him. He loved Alaris, in all its natural beauty, from the mountains in the North to the desert in the South, from the Elvyn Forest in the East, to the meadowlands and farms covering the middle and western portions of the kingdom.

Currently, the late-summer grass was browning outside of the Citadel. He spotted cattle being moved around to newer spots to feed. A few wagons were coming up the farm roads between Whalen and the Citadel, bringing goods to the wizards and others who lived here.

Willing himself to look farther south, he obviously was not able to see to Cassian, but he thought constantly about what could be happening there. Kanzar was behind the uprising of the King-men, and he feared for his city as well as all of Alaris. Two of the newly appointed judges, including Mericus, had gone to Cassian to supposedly help maintain peace; however, Daymian doubted their visit consisted of understanding and niceties. More likely, they had been sowing the seeds of rebellion and distrust – under the direction of Kanzar.

Battle Wizard Gorn and his young apprentice, Alli, had just left Daymian's rooms, informing the Chief Judge of a secret mission for Kanzar, the details of which they were not at liberty to share. They had explained only that they would be leaving soon.

One by one, his friends and leaders were deserting him. Bakari had left. Onius seemed to be spending a lot of time with Kanzar. And now, Gorn and Alli would be gone. That only left Roland, and the new young wizard worried Daymian almost more than the rest.

Wizards nodded their heads to Roland in deference now, and he was amassing quite a following of other younger wizards and apprentices in the Citadel. Daymian wondered why Kanzar had let that happen. Usually, Kanzar was not one to give up shares of any of his power, but he might be finally making a mistake in ignoring the new young wizard's growing powers.

A knock came at the door, and Daymian strode toward it with a scowl still on his face. No attendants had been afforded him at the Citadel, another sign of Kanzar's power play. Speaking of Roland—in walked Onius and Roland before even being invited in. Both wore flowing wizard's robes, though Onius's blue one hung on his thinning frame, while Roland's red attire fit him well and actually made him appear regal.

"Onius." The Chief Judge nodded to the counselor. "Something on your mind?"

Motioning toward a grouping of chairs by the window, Onius led the way. When all three were seated, Daymian waited for Onius to speak first. Watching Roland, Daymian marveled that the young man had finally learned to control his tongue. Roland actually sat in patience until Onius spoke.

Onius cleared his throat. "Daymian," he began. The Chief Judge noticed the lack of title given to his name. "We've known each other long, and I would like to think I have served you well."

The Chief Judge nodded his head in the affirmative. "I hold no complaints."

"Throughout the history of Alaris and the western lands, there were times when regimes and kingdoms came under fire and even toppled and changed hands. Most of these times, many lives were lost, and the kingdoms were set back in their prosperity. It took them years or decades to recover; some never did." Onius stopped to wet his lips.

The Chief Judge motioned for Roland to pour them some drinks. Roland appeared surprised at the request but sat the closest, so he did as Daymian bid.

Onius took a drink and continued. "We, us in this room, are now in a unique position to stop a bloody war and to limit the damage and carnage that will come."

Daymian lifted his eyebrows but still let the wizard continue.

Onius leaned closer to Daymian. "Daymian, I am asking you, not as a representative of the Wizard Council or even as your counselor, but as a friend, to step down from the judgeship and allow a king to rule Alaris."

The Chief Judge's throat went dry. He opened his mouth, but Onius continued. "I know all of your arguments, so let's not rehash those. The people want a king, and the time has come to grant their wishes. Will you step down?"

Silence hung in the air. Daymian personally didn't have anything against having a king per se—a good king, at least—but he had many problems with the way this coup was unfolding.

A few birds squawked at each other outside on the balcony. Daymian put them from his mind and thought deeply, then stood up. Resting his hand on the back of his chair, he scrutinized Onius's former apprentice. "Roland, you are being uncharacteristically quiet."

Roland turned his eyes up with a start. "Sir?"

"I have never known you to be one without opinions to share." The Chief Judge walked around behind the young wizard's chair, standing behind his back. "I heard that you passed the wizard test and are now a level-four wizard."

Daymian gauged Onius's reaction to this, and it was as he had anticipated. His former counselor's lips were held tight.

Roland moved his head to look up toward the Chief Judge, his eyes smiling but his lips even. "I am not at liberty to discuss the happenings at the test. But, yes, I am recognized as a level-four wizard."

"One of the mightiest in the land," Daymian commended.

Onius sat, his arms folded and face stern. "What does Roland's wizard status have to do with your answer, Daymian? I am not here to play games. I need answers now. I am not the only one with ideas of how to get you to step down."

It was Daymian's turn to get angry now. "Roland, stand up!"

Roland complied with the order before even thinking.

"Whom do you recognize as the leader of this land? Whom do you serve?" the Chief Judge asked.

Roland's eyes grew wide, and his cheeks reddened. He took a long moment to think.

Onius growled. "Roland knows to whom his allegiance is owed. He is a wizard!" The old wizard stared hard at Roland and waited for him to answer.

Roland turned back to the Chief Judge. "Do you want me to be honest, Sir?"

"Of course, Roland," the Chief Judge said, losing a little of his steam. "That would be refreshing. I have had enough dishonesty lately." He gave an obvious glance toward Onius.

"My allegiance at this moment is to myself," Roland admitted.

Onius gasped.

"At least there is one honest wizard." Daymian smiled.

Roland then continued, "However, Kanzar is an extremely volatile and dangerous man, Chief Judge, and I would recommend thinking long and hard about what to do and where to take your stand."

Turning to Onius, the Chief Judge finally got around to his answer. "And that is why I cannot step down, Onius. I can't let Kanzar Centari be king of Alaris. I, too, know all the arguments for and against a king or even the judge system—believe me. I have been defending the system for years. I also know the war and carnage and damage that can come through a split in the government. But, as long as I am still breathing, I promise you that Kanzar Centari will not become the rightful king of Alaris."

Onius fell back down into his stuffed chair, all his anger and defiance gone. He motioned with his hand for Daymian and Roland to sit down once more. They complied and sat in silence with their drinks.

The sun lowered in the sky and sent rays of light into the room, sparkling off of chandeliers and glass lamps. A few faraway voices from in the practice yards floated through the air.

"What if there is another way?" Onius spoke softly. "What if there was someone other than Kanzar to be king? A way of compromise. A way to keep the country from bloodshed. Would you listen to that?"

Roland looked wide-eyed at Onius. "But, who? How?" He leaned forward farther and added, "Kanzar's arm reaches throughout the kingdom."

The Chief Judge looked intently at Onius. "I *would* listen to that, Onius. But, who do you have in mind?"

Onius leaned forward, and Roland and the Chief Judge followed suit. What they were about to discuss could be dangerous for all three. As Onius opened his mouth to speak, a loud knock came at the door. All three jerked upward in their seats at the sound. And Onius glared at the Chief Judge.

"I am not expecting anyone," Daymian said as he moved to answer the door.

A contingent of guards stood in the doorway, the chief of whom stepped forward into the door's opening. "The High Wizard requests your presence, Sir."

Daymian wasn't happy at being disrupted. "I would be pleased to meet with him later, after the evening meal. I am meeting with other company at the moment."

The guard looked into the room, and his face drained of color. Speaking to the two wizards in the room, he stammered, "I am sorry to interrupt, Sirs, but the High Wizard was adamant about bringing the Chief Judge to him immediately."

Onius nodded his head, appearing relieved that they had not finished their conversation. Daymian wondered what the old wizards were up to. It looked as if politics in the Citadel among the wizards had as many problems as his own government. None of them could be trusted fully, it seemed.

"Sir?" the guard asked. "We need to go."

"Yes, yes," Daymian said. "I am sure you do. I understand how Kanzar can be to those that don't obey his every wish and whim."

The guards all eyed each other gravely. Kanzar's reputation was one more reason Daymian could not hand over the country to him. He hoped Onius did have a better idea and could be trusted, but that discussion would need to wait until later.

With Daymian in front, six guards behind him, and Onius and Roland in the rear, the group made a strange-looking procession as they walked toward the High Wizard's chambers.

Two additional guards, in starched uniforms, stood at attention outside Kanzar's rooms. After informing the High Wizard that the Chief Judge had arrived, they led the procession into the room.

Once again, Daymian was overwhelmed by the opulence with which Kanzar surrounded himself. Today, his wife, Alana, a strong and formidable battle wizard, stood with him. Kanzar seemed surprised to see Onius and Roland in attendance with the Chief Judge.

"Onius, I hadn't invited you to this meeting," Kanzar said.

Onius took a step forward. "Your summons interrupted our meeting with the Chief Judge. We decided to come along to see what was so urgent."

Kanzar's face clouded over. His wife looked no less stern.

Then Roland stepped out from behind the group and gave a short nod. "Kanzar."

Kanzar's face was barely civil as he glared at the newest wizard.

"I hope our presence does not interfere with your discussion," Roland stated. "I am sure we all want to settle our differences as peacefully as we can."

The Chief Judge was again surprised at how in control young Roland acted and was even more shocked at how the great Kanzar Centari seemed to be slightly cowed in Roland's presence.

Roland winked at Kanzar, and the man took three strong steps and ended up in front of the newly raised wizard.

"Don't toy with me, young man." Spittle flew from Kanzar's lips. "Your presence here will be tolerated only if you are silent."

Roland held Kanzar's gaze and didn't turn away. The Chief Judge enjoyed Roland's display of his newly elevated station as wizard and let a slight grin roll over his lips. The wizard test must be quite rigorous, indeed, to change the dynamics of the Citadel in such a short time.

Kanzar turned back to the Chief Judge. "Daymian, your

presence is needed back in Cassian, to help settle down the citizens there. My wife, along with a battalion of my soldiers, will escort you and your remaining men back to Cassian."

This surprised Daymian. "There were not any problems before I left. Maybe your newly appointed judges are not up to the task of governing."

Kanzar waved his hand in the air. "Don't concern yourself about them. They will be fine."

His apparently carefree attitude infuriated the Chief Judge. "I *will* concern myself about them, Kanzar. They may be *fine*, but what about the people? I am still Chief Judge, and, as such, the other judges fall under my responsibility, no matter how they were appointed."

Kanzar's eyes narrowed. "Watch your tongue, Daymian. I am losing my patience with your stubbornness in maintaining your position. Many would like a change in the land."

"Many, *you* have led in rising up against the true, legal government," the Chief Judge said, raising his voice. "I will reiterate for you: I am not stepping down as long as those in rebellion to this land's government use unlawful tactics and coercion to gain power."

Alana stepped forward a few steps, hand on her staff. Kanzar waved her back.

Kanzar then laughed and sent fire along the ground, encircling the Chief Judge. "I am not intimidated by you, Daymian. You are a pathetic leader and deaf to the cries of our people. The barrier will soon fall, and Alaris needs to be a strong kingdom with a strong leader—a king that can stand at her head and make Alaris a leader once again among the western lands." Kanzar turned as if he was speaking to each person in the room. His fists were clenched, and his eyes blazed with fanaticism.

"Too long have the elves held power; too long have Mahli and the territories kept us from the northern kingdoms; too long have Tillimot and Quentis and Solshi held us to our borders. They are all weak and will once again bow to the might of Alaris and her wizard king."

With those words, Kanzar brought his fire up in a circle around the Chief Judge. Daymian held his hand up to shade his face from the heat. His black pants became hot, and sweat began dripping from his forehead.

"Kanzar, enough!" bellowed Roland, and, with a flick of his wrist, he extinguished the flames.

In two inhumanly long leaps, Alana reached Roland and brought her hand out to strike him. In a flash, Roland moved to the side, caught her wrist, and bent it backward. A howl escaped her lips.

Kanzar stared on in disbelief.

"Roland, stop," Onius ordered.

The Chief Judge stood in surprise. Roland's abilities were more than any of them had guessed.

Roland pushed Alana away in front of him but kept a defiant eye on Kanzar. "You, of all people, should have control over yourself. How do you propose to govern a land—which is what you are proposing, isn't it?—if you can't even control your temper in your own room?"

Kanzar stood still, looking livid, hands clenched to his sides, a murderous intent on his face.

"If you want my loyalty, you have to earn it. Loyalty is not blind," Roland continued. Behind him, Alana inched forward, but before she could do anything, Roland rolled his hand in the air and brought forth a gust of air that bound her to the floor. "You see my power. You didn't believe me when I told you." Roland's face almost glowed now. "Daymian Khouri is still the legal Chief Judge of this land, but I propose a solution: We let the people decide. If they vote to keep it the same, then Daymian maintains his position and authority. If the people vote for a king, then the Chief Judge will step down and a peaceful transition will occur."

Daymian stepped forward. "I agree to this, but only if a suitable king is found that the people agree with."

Kanzar ground his teeth at Roland. "When did you become such a shrewd negotiator?"

"Onius taught me all I know," Roland said, lightening the tense mood. "Blame it on him."

Kanzar growled, "Agreed."

Roland winked. "See, that wasn't so hard. What would you all do without me?"

The Chief Judge smiled, Onius barked a laugh, and Kanzar's and Alana's eyes sent darts toward the young, pompous wizard.

"You are a dangerous boy, Roland," Kanzar said. "I'd watch my step if I were you."

"*Boy?*" Roland tensed. "A boy that might save this country from plunging into civil war."

Kanzar threw his glass on the floor, and it shattered into a hundred pieces. "Get out of my office. Now." Kanzar pointed his finger at Roland.

Daymian maintained his decorum and gave a short bow to the group. "I will take your leave now to make preparations for my departure from the Citadel. I will not need Alana or your men to escort me. I will be fine." He turned and left through the doorway with the rest of the group. After a few steps down the hall, Roland raced up to his side.

"I will provide a group to escort you," Roland said.

They walked a few steps farther, out of earshot of the room. Onius had turned the other way, down another hallway.

"Why this sudden concern for my interests, Roland?" the Chief Judge asked. "You always thought me boring and dull."

Roland's face reddened. "How...?"

The Chief Judge slapped him on the back. "Roland, you really are too powerful for your own good. You are still so young and, in many ways, naive. I have been dealing with men wanting power for decades, and, in a few moments, you subdued some who hold the greatest power in the land. Make sure you are not getting in too deep. Choose your side, and make sure of your convictions and what you want. Remember what we talked about before."

"I told you the truth, Sir. Right now, I am the only one I trust. I'm on my own side."

"That might be a lonely side," Daymian said.

Roland sighed. "It might be. But my goal is to become the most powerful wizard. I don't care so much for politics."

"You did well enough in there."

"Gut reactions and years of training." He laughed, then seemed to turn serious. "You asked why I am helping you. You are a good man, Sir, and good, honest men seem to be in short supply these days. Kanzar certainly isn't one, and I am not sure what game Onius is playing these days either. I probably do trust Onius still, but I am being cautious in that regard. Bakari is a good man and, possibly, the only one I am sure of that I can trust, but we don't know where he is. I don't care one way or the other if we have a king, but I am helping you because it is the right thing to do—right now."

"Well, then I thank you for your help, Roland. And may you continue to make good choices in the future."

"I will send some hand-picked men to you, but you should leave soon. I don't trust Kanzar to keep his word," Roland said. "Leave tonight before Alana and her men are ready."

The Chief Judge began to walk away, when Roland called him back again.

"Have you heard from Bak at all?"

Daymian shook his head. "No, I haven't, Roland. I hope he is safe and doing well."

"Me, too," Roland said, turning down another hallway in the Citadel. "I do miss teasing that kid sometimes."

CHAPTER TWENTY THREE

Alli and Gorn had ridden hard for two days. In a few hours, they would come to the Dunn River with, hopefully, a place to cross. Little of note had happened so far, and Gorn had stayed unusually quiet. His face was stern, and his forehead carried new wrinkles under his graying hairline. Alli had been patient and had tried not to interrupt his thoughts, but her young, inquisitive mind could stand it no longer.

"Gorn. What is going through your mind?" Alli said. "Your face is battle ready, but there is no danger around us."

He glanced her way and said nothing for a moment. Then he let out a great sigh, as if he'd finally resolved something in his mind. "Not all battles are external, my young apprentice. Some are fought within us."

"You are unusually poetic today." Alli laughed, her short hair bouncing around to the steady gallop of her brown horse.

Gorn's deep blue eyes pierced her sparkling green ones as he kept an even pace with her, though his horse was quite a bit larger. "How do you stay so happy and optimistic in these times, Alli? You saw what it was like at the Citadel. War is brewing, and I'm afraid we are being thrust into its center."

"Didn't you teach me in battle to only focus on what I can control? I can control how I feel and how I react to what's going on around me. I choose to be happy."

Now it was Gorn's turn to laugh. And laugh he did. So much so that he had to slow down. "Let's stop to eat," he said after he got control of himself. "There is a nice shady spot by a stream over there. The horses are thirsty, and I am hungry."

Alli was caught up in his mirth. "When are you *not* hungry, Gorn? The day I see you not hungry, I will know something is wrong."

They let the horses wander close by, drinking their fill from the stream and eating some creek-side grass, while the two of them sat on a small patch of ground around an aspen tree, one of the few mixed in with the evergreens, which grew more thickly the farther north and east they traveled. A squirrel ran out in front of them, and soon another chased behind. It was hard to imagine the turmoil facing Alaris at that moment.

"Alli," Gorn began, "I must tell you some things. You are correct that I fight a battle. My insides are in turmoil. I had to decide where my loyalties lay in what is coming. This is a dangerous time for Alaris."

Alli looked at him intently but didn't offer any comments. Biting into a piece of dried pork, she decided to hear her mentor out before making any judgments. Gorn brought the waterskin to his lips and drank his fill before continuing.

"Among the wizards at the Citadel, there has been talk for years, even decades, of reinstating a king in Alaris. Many of us didn't care one way or the other, but some—including Kanzar and, later, some of those following him—became very pointed on the manner. I'm still not entirely sure where Onius stands on the issue. There is no love lost between him and Kanzar, but…" Gorn trailed off, as if trying to find the right words.

"What?" Alli prompted.

"I'm not sure. I have always respected and trusted Onius. I hope he keeps his head on his shoulders, but I'm sure things have been hard for him also. All those who supported Kanzar knew they needed to wait until the time was right. Then the barrier started showing signs of weakness a few years ago."

"A few years ago?" Alli was surprised by how long it had been happening.

"Yes. Kept in strict secrecy, with only a few full wizards knowing about it. There are places where the barrier disappears for moments. And the entire barrier is weaker—thinner, in a way."

Alli lay back on the grass and stared up. Through the branches of the aspen tree she could glimpse patches of white clouds floating across the blue sky. "How does this relate to your internal battle?"

"I fear I have been dishonest and have deceived you, the Chief Judge, and others. I have been out fighting the Kingmen, but all along, I have suspected that Kanzar stood behind it. When you take the wizard test, Alli, you pledge a strong allegiance to the Citadel, the wizards, and even their leader, over and above all else."

"*I* wouldn't know," Alli mumbled softly, still sore at not being able to take the test before they had left the Citadel.

Gorn ignored her comment and continued. "Now, Kanzar has sent us to where the Orb is: the power behind the barrier. I had hoped our assignment would be to make sure it stayed safe and that the barrier could become strong once again. But

Kanzar intends for it to fail. That is a hard thing for me to support. So, I suppose, before we arrive, we will need to decide whose side we are on."

"Whose side?" Alli jumped up. "Gorn, we have been the Chief Judge's battle wizards—well, *I'm* not a wizard, but you know what I mean. These King-men are disrupting the proper channels of authority and killing innocent people. If Kanzar is truly behind that, then we fight against him."

Gorn smiled and tore off a chunk of bread from a small loaf. After chewing, he motioned for Alli to sit back down. She reluctantly did so.

"Now you see my quandary. I swore in the past to uphold the wizard leadership of the Citadel. I also pledged to protect the reign of the judges and uphold the law. In the past, I did both without any personal conflict. But now they *are* in conflict, and Kanzar's reach is vast."

Alli nodded her head. "Is Kanzar setting himself up to be king?"

"Yes, and now I see how dangerous that is. He has become incredibly strong in my absence and, until recently, had total control over the Citadel."

"What happened recently?"

"Your friend Roland happened," Gorn said matter-of-factly, standing back up and calling the horses back to them.

Alli laughed and shook her head. "That arrogant fool. What did he do?"

Before answering, Gorn motioned for them to mount and start riding again.

"I was not there for the testing—something happened

there, though. Roland might be arrogant, but I would suppose from what I have seen that he is probably the only wizard right now who can control Kanzar and thwart his dreams of becoming king."

Alli kicked her horse gently to speed up its gallop. "That does sound bad."

Their conversation dwindled over the next few hours as they rode hard and fast toward the river. Alli tried to think of what her place was in all of this. It frustrated her still that Roland had been tested and she hadn't. After performing in the practice yard the other day, she knew more than ever how powerful she really was. If taking the wizard test meant swearing loyalty to Kanzar, though, she couldn't do that. The man was more arrogant and foolish than Roland. Thinking of Roland usually turned her cheeks pink, and she rode faster so Gorn wouldn't see her face flush.

Soon they arrived at a small village, next to the Dunn River. It was abnormally quiet, and Alli instantly put up her guard. No children ran in the streets and she saw few adults out and about. Those they did see kept their eyes lowered and continued on their way.

There was still enough daylight left to continue their travels, and, although a stay at an inn sounded nice, Alli knew they had to continue on. Riding up to the river, they found the river barge station and dismounted there. A man sat in a small hut next to the river. He was old but had the strength of one who still used his muscles every day.

"Are you the barge master?" Gorn asked.

The man would not meet their eyes, and he paused before

answering in the affirmative.

"We need to cross the river," Gorn stated.

The man nodded. "Two gold pieces, for you and your horses."

Gorn's eyebrows lifted. "Kind of steep, isn't that?"

"Times are hard. Our village flooded earlier this year, and we have to work hard to build it back. Materials are not cheap this far north."

Gorn grudgingly agreed to this price. After bartering in a nearby inn for some food, they brought their horses down to the river's edge.

The barge master brought the horses onto the barge first and then motioned for them to board. He untied the thick ropes, holding the barge to the shore, and grabbed a long, thick carved branch in his calloused hands. Across from them, on the other side of the Dunn River, sat a similar landing.

"I am sorry," the barge master whispered to the two.

"Sorry?" Gorn questioned.

The man glanced around nervously once again and then, instead of jumping on with them, used the thick stick to push them swiftly out into the middle of the river, without him on the barge with them. The current began to pull the barge downriver, in the opposite way from their destination.

"What?" Why?" Alli yelled at the man, who was already getting smaller and smaller on the shore.

Out of the town and behind the trees on the shore emerged a group of men. Many nocked their bows while approaching the two.

"Mercenaries!" spat Gorn. "That's why the town was so

quiet. They had already taken this village and recognized us."

"Kanzar's King-men," Alli said.

Gorn agreed. "His reach is long. Somehow, he told them about us. I'm afraid Kanzar may have changed his mind about our mission."

The men on the shore began shooting arrows before the two could react, and one hit Gorn in the thigh.

Alli raised her hands up and threw a bolt of lightning in their direction. It blasted into the ground, and half a dozen men went flying into the air. Her greatest strength was hand-to-hand combat, so she ground her teeth in frustration. They were too far away for that.

More arrows flew toward them. The horses, spooked by the arrows, moved around on the barge too quickly, and they both ended up on the same side of the barge. The weight difference was too much, and the barge started to lean to one side.

"Alli, move to the other side." Gorn moved with her. The arrow still stuck out of his thigh, and he groaned in pain. Reaching down, he broke its shaft off at the skin so it wouldn't get in his way.

"You need to get the tip out," Alli screamed at him.

"Later." Gorn brought his hands up and conjured a strengthening wind that he threw at the shore. It knocked down another dozen men.

Alli followed his attack by pushing up the dirt in front of them. But the distance soon became too great for her power to have much force. The barge still rocked back and forth and leaned closer to shore. Then Alli had a thought. She moved to the back of the barge and pushed air at the water behind them, which pushed them closer to the shoreline. The remaining men ran down the shoreline to reach them.

As the men shot off another barrage of arrows, Alli tried to stop them, but her focus needed to be on getting the barge to the shore. If they floated too far south, it would take them even longer to reach Celestar. They couldn't afford that delay. And the only way for her to utilize her full skills and finish this off was to be on the shore fighting the men.

One of those arrows hit her horse in the side, and it reared up on its hind legs, rocking the barge again so violently that the other horse began to slip off. Gorn reached toward his falling battle horse, grabbing the reins to try to stabilize him. But his hands got stuck, and, as the horse fell into the murky water, Gorn fell with him.

"Gorn!" Alli jumped to the edge of the barge to help him.

They were now within a few feet of the bank, and the horse could stand. Gorn hung to the side of the horse and was being dragged through the water.

"Let go of the reins," Alli yelled again, but Gorn did not answer.

Another arrow flew over her head, and she turned to see six men within fifty feet of her. She ground her teeth and went into battle mode. Gorn could take care of himself for a few more moments.

Pushing herself, Alli jumped the last ten feet from the barge to the shore. Leaping again—almost flying through the air—she landed in front of the six men. Four had arrows focused on her, while two others drew swords.

"You should have brought more men with you," she said and then ran straight toward them. This tactic surprised them, and only two of them got off shots with their bows before Alli had reached them. With grace and ease, she spun around and dodged the arrows.

Grabbing the bows from two of the men, one with each hand, she plunged them over the heads of two other men and pulled hard, causing the string of the bows to cut into the back of their necks. They fell to the ground, moaning. The two men she had taken the bows from turned back to her with knives in their hands now.

Alli pushed out both of her palms, and air flew into the two men's hands, throwing their knives out of their reaches. Then, before they knew what had happened, Alli ran up the side of a nearby tree, twisting back around behind them, and knocked both of them out with the blades of her knives on their necks.

A loud neigh bellowed behind her, and Alli turned to see her horse still struggling on the barge. Gorn's horse stood on the shore now, with Gorn still hanging from the reins. He wasn't moving.

Sensing, rather than hearing, the other two men behind her, Alli jumped into the air, her feet reaching the height of a man, and spun around, kicking one man in the head, pushing him into the other man. Both men fell to the ground, but the second one drew a small knife from a sheath at his side and threw it, end over end, at her. The close range made the knife difficult to dodge, and, even though Alli moved like a flash of light, it grazed her forearm, bringing a sting of pain.

The man sat there and glared at her in disbelief. Then he began to stand up. But Alli rushed him hard and, with a kick to his head, sent him crashing back against a hard pine tree.

With all six men down, she now turned her attention to Gorn, rushing to his side. She cut the cords holding his hands to the horse. His gray hair lay plastered to his large face, and his eyes remained closed. She turned him on his side and began to pound on his back, trying to force the murky water out of his lungs.

"Gorn. No!" she screamed. "This can't happen. Wake up, Gorn." Tears streamed down her face.

After her repeated pounding, Gorn finally coughed out a lungful of water and took a deep breath. Then his eyes fluttered open for a moment.

"Alli," he whispered feebly before his eyes closed once more.

Alli sucked in some air and wiped her eyes. At least he wasn't dead. But, looking at the arrow stub in his thigh, Alli realized that he wasn't going to recover soon either.

As she stood up, a group of townspeople came near. They stood tentatively a few yards away from her.

"Are there any more?" she asked them, referring to the mercenaries.

"No," one of the men said. "You two took care of them all. I can't believe it."

"Are you a wizard, Miss?" asked a teenage boy.

Alli forced a mirthless laugh. "No. Only an apprentice."

The boy's eyes opened wider surveying the damage she had wrought.

"My friend here is one, though." Alli pointed to Gorn. "He's hurt. Can you help me take him back to your town?"

The barge master stepped forward. "I am sorry, Miss. I really am. You see, they would keep my family unless I followed their orders."

Alli smiled sadly. "I understand." Her voice held compassion for the man. "You can make up for it by helping me with Gorn."

The man seemed relieved that the wizard apprentice wasn't going to retaliate on him. He gladly agreed to help, motioning two teenage boys forward to help him. They took Gorn back to the small village and into one of the homes and put him on a straw bed.

A woman identifying herself as the village herb woman, came to help. Seeing the arrow stub, with its tip stuck inside still, the woman grimaced. "It needs to come out now."

"I will do it," Alli said, a determined look on her dirty face.

The herb woman nodded and poured a numbing concoction on Gorn's thigh, then cut a line around the stub for the arrowhead. Alli grasped the stub hard. In one swift pull, she removed the arrow.

Gorn groaned, and his eyes fluttered for a moment but stayed closed. Blood poured from the wound, mixed with water from the river. Between applying herbs and attaching bandages, they eventually got the wound to stop bleeding and then covered it.

The herb woman left, saying she would be back later that night. Alli sat next to Gorn. She smoothed the gray strands of hair off of his forehead. She didn't know what she would do without him. He was a strict mentor, but a fair one nonetheless. Alli had left her family five years ago and had only seen them periodically since then. So Gorn had become a father to her, this past year, as they had traveled around Alaris, enforcing peace for the Chief Judge.

Alli sat on the wooden floor and leaned her head back against the bed. *Another battle completed.* How many would she fight in her life? How many could she fight, without it changing who she was inside?

She closed her eyes and fell asleep.

CHAPTER TWENTY FOUR

Bakari stood on a jagged cliff overlooking the Dunn River. The late-summer sky held a promise of cooler weather as they traveled farther north, and the thickening evergreens of the Elvyn Forest offered much-needed shade.

A beautiful gray hawk floated in the air above him. For a minute Bakari was lost in his thoughts of how nice it would be to soar over the river and the trees. It would be so much easier and quicker than the route they were taking. His legs hurt from all the riding, and he didn't look forward to crossing the river.

Before the barrier existed, the land on the far side of the Dunn River had belonged to the elves. For some reason, the barrier had not followed the border of the river exactly, leaving some formerly Elvyn lands as part of present-day Alaris.

Below this jagged cliff was the narrowest part of the river, but it would require them to cross between two canyon walls, about forty feet above the river. Bakari took his mind away from his daydream of flying and continued to calculate the best way to cross the ravine, determining wind speed, rope strength, and altitude. Then he brought up similar situations in his mind, events he had read about, and used them to calculate their best advantages.

Kharlia stood with Harley next to the horses. As Bakari looked at her, he couldn't help smiling. Her resilience to her changing life amazed him. And the girl had an insatiable desire to learn about things and to help in any way possible.

She must have felt him looking because she turned toward him, then smiled and waved. Bakari's heart lifted, and butterflies grew in his stomach. Her penetrating, dark brown eyes found his, and he could not suppress a silly grin.

Harley had mentioned that he usually crossed the river farther north of here, on a small barge, but he had heard of some trouble there recently with mercenaries, and so they had decided it would be safer to cross farther south. They had brought ropes and hooks with them and would use them to tie off to trees on either side of the ravine.

Bakari walked back to the others. "I figured out what trees will be the best and determined the length of the rope."

"We will have to leave the horses here, then," Harley said. "The end of the trail for me is only another day farther. Hopefully, the horses will still be here when I get back. I will take care of Adi for you."

Bakari felt saddened at the news that he would need to leave his faithful horse. He reached over and gave Adi a hug and rubbed her nose for a moment. She had carried him a long way from Cassian. Digging some gold out of his pack, he held it out for Harley. "If they are not here when you return, you can buy new ones. We couldn't have gone this far without you."

Harley snorted, running his fingers through his long beard. "I don't need your money, Bak. Not a lot of use for it out here. What Kharlia gave us—healing our son—is payment enough. And I'm not so sure about you needing me so much, anyways.

You do seem fairly capable, from what I've seen."

Bakari moved his head down in embarrassment. "I'm just a scholar, Harley."

Harley laughed. "That's like saying the Dunn River is *just a stream*. Mark my words, young wizard; you are destined for far greater things than being a scholar."

"I agree." Kharlia reached over and put her hand on Bakari's forearm. Warmth spread throughout his body, and he didn't say anything for a moment.

"Bakari?" Harley asked. "Are you ready?"

Bakari shook himself out of his thoughts. "Sure."

"Oh, young love." Harley smiled at the two of them. "Such long ago days for me. Come on, now, let's get this over with. I don't like heights, and I hope you got it all figured out right. Not the place I would choose to die."

The three walked to a place where a strong, straight cedar tree stood next to the edge of the cliff. Bakari tied one end of a rope around the tree, then coiled the middle up and tied a grappling hook onto the other end.

"Looks kind of short to me," Harley mumbled. "How are you going to throw that thing across and hit your target there?" He pointed at a tree on the other side.

Bakari chuckled, and, with secret amusement flashing in his dark eyes, he threw the rope up into the air. At the same time, he brought his hands up and guided the rope by magic across the ravine.

"Well, I'll be..." Harley stared in astonishment. "You wizards do have a way of making things easier, don't you?"

Bakari continued to direct the rope to the other side and

around the tree. "Magic's a gift, Harley. I don't take it for granted. But it does come in handy sometimes."

The rope, now attached to the other side, held tight. Bakari got out the other hook and hung it over the rope. "Now we can grab the hook and slide across."

Harley rolled his eyes and patted his stomach at the same time. "Will it hold me?"

"Of course it will, Harley," Kharlia said, putting her pack onto her back. "Bakari knows what he's doing."

Bakari hoped Kharlia was right. Every time he drew on his extensive, but unused knowledge, Bakari felt nervous. What if he had miscalculated something? What if he remembered something wrong? It was a lot of pressure to always know everything.

Sometimes he wished he could rely on someone else's experience to guide him. But, lately, his adventures were so new that no one else was there to teach him. He wondered what Roland would do in these situations. Bakari laughed inside and smiled. The poor man wouldn't always be able to get by on his arrogance and good looks.

"What's so funny, Bakari?" Kharlia asked.

"Oh, nothing. Let's go." Bakari grabbed his own pack and looked at the other two travelers. "Harley first, then Kharlia, and I will come last."

Harley got his pack onto his back and grabbed the hook. The line sagged considerably. "Are you sure this is goin' to hold me, young wizard?"

"Yes. I'm sure. It needs to sag a bit since it's going slightly downhill. It will carry you down fast. As soon as you clear the cliff on the other side, drop off the line and roll. You should be fine before the hook hits the tree."

"Should be?" Harley arched his eyebrows.

With that, Bakari gave him a shove, and off he went, sailing high over the river. A loud whooping noise came from Harley's mouth, but, in a matter of moments, their guide hit the other side, rolled, and landed safely.

Bakari used his magic to pull the hook back. Next, he got Kharlia ready. He stood in front of her, standing a few inches taller than she. Without much notice, she leaned up on tiptoe and kissed him gently on the lips. Then she let go of him and swung down the line.

Bakari stood there with a silly grin on his face. His heart almost burst with giddiness. He brought his finger to his lips and held it there for a moment, relishing the memory and wondering at his luck in having met her.

"Bak. Bakari!"

Hearing his name, he looked back across the ravine. Kharlia had yelled his name from the other side. How had she gotten there so quickly? He shook his head to clear the fog of love from his brain.

Pulling his pack on he grabbed his bow with his left hand. Reaching up for the hook with his other hand, he heard Kharlia scream. Bakari looked back over and saw a medium-sized, but fierce-looking creature loping up the hill behind Kharlia and Harley, leaving their backs to the ravine with its forty-foot drop.

The creature resembled a cougar but with coarser fur, a spiked tail, and larger fangs. It paced back and forth in front of the two, coming closer with every turn. Bakari wondered if his sliding over on the line would distract the beast, scare it off, or make it attack his friends sooner. He reached out and tried to push air at the animal. Nothing happened. Bakari was too far away to try fire and wasn't very good at it anyway. Then he tried shooting an arrow, but it just bounced off the creature's rough hide.

Taking a deep breath, he reached out toward the creature's mind. He knew what to look for and how to do it better now. But, in this case, he met with a formidable barrier. Evil pushed back at him, forcing him to stagger backward.

The animal must be hungry. Maybe he could find something for it to eat. Pushing his senses outward, away from the creature, he tried to find something else close by. It was more difficult, being farther away on the other side of the river.

Finally, he sensed a deer on the other side but couldn't see where it was. He lifted his bow, pulled out an arrow, and tried to shoot it toward where he felt the deer was hiding. It landed in a thicket, and he thought he heard a noise. So did the cougar. It growled and turned away for a moment. Then, turning back toward Bak's friends, the cougar took a step closer to them with another vicious snarl.

"I think you only made it mad!" shouted Harley. "Don't you have any more tricks up those wizard sleeves?"

Bakari couldn't stay here and watch his friends die. So he grabbed the hook in his right hand and swung down the line toward his friends.

The cougar turned its attention away from Kharlia. At that same moment, the deer ran out of the thicket, and the cougar turned toward it. Seeing the deer as an easier target, it pounced.

Bakari knew, though, they were just putting off that fate. The cougar would be back, and then they wouldn't be able to travel safely. Before hitting the other side, he once again reached his mind out to the animals.

First, he felt the mind of the deer, a simple brain with only one thought at the moment—to get away from the cougar. Bakari only had to nudge the deer away from them, and it turned in that direction.

Bakari hit the ground on the other side and rolled. The cougar took his attention off the deer for a moment and considered this new option. Bakari gathered his powers, gritted his teeth, and brought himself once again to the border of the evil creature's mind. This time, he tried to push only one single thought deeply into the cougar's mind. *Deer.* It worked. The cougar turned and took three giant leaps toward the deer. The deer, however, moved closer to Kharlia in its effort to run away.

"Kharlia, move!" Bakari sprinted toward her.

The cougar turned also and took a giant leap toward the fleeing deer, missing Kharlia by mere inches.

"Bak!" Kharlia screamed.

Harley tried to reach over and help her, but she stumbled and fell. Then the cougar looked between the fleeing deer and Kharlia, lying on the ground, and turned back to the girl.

Scooting backward on the ground, using her hands and feet to move away from the crazed beast, Kharlia screamed.

The cougar let out a low and menacing growl and stalked closer to Kharlia.

Bakari, ten feet away, tried to grab the creature's mind again. Once again, it pushed back against Bakari's mind. In the corner of Bakari's vision, he watched Harley move backward, farther away from the creature. Reaching down, the woodsman grabbed a long stick. Bakari understood.

Harley moved in closer to the beast, the stick held out in front of him. The creature turned its head toward the large man and growled again. This distraction afforded Kharlia time to stand up. However, the beast still stood too close to allow her to escape. She paused, frozen in fear, tears streaming down her face, mere feet from the ravine.

Bakari continued to push against the cougar's mind, distracting it. Its coarse fur standing up on end, the cougar snarled at the young wizard. Harley moved in closer, and the cougar took a few steps toward the man and away from Kharlia. Then Harley hurled the stick like a javelin.

"Kharlia, run!" Bakari yelled.

As Kharlia took a step, the beast moved away from Harley's javelin throw, its spiked tail whipping around and catching Kharlia's leg. Kharlia screamed, then tripped and fell down, with one leg falling over the edge of the cliff.

"Bak, don't let him kill me! Please, Bak, do something."

Tears clouded over Bakari's vision. This was all his fault. He screamed and ran straight toward the creature, not knowing what else to do. He hoped the distraction would allow Kharlia enough time to stand back up. However, the creature stood its ground in front of its fallen prey, reaching its paw out and swatting Bakari back.

Once again, Bakari summoned fire and air and anything he

could think of, to push the creature back, but none of the magic worked—it just slid around the creature.

Kharlia tried to bring her leg back onto solid ground and brought herself up onto her hands and knees, with her feet still dangling off the side. The cougar turned, mere feet away, opened its mouth and growled. Fangs dripped with saliva as the creature took another step closer.

"Bak! Bak!" Kharlia screamed hysterical. "You can't let it eat me. You can't!"

"Kharlia!" Bakari screamed in fear. "I don't know what to do." Bakari tried to move through his mind to find a solution, but he couldn't concentrate with Kharlia kneeling so close to the edge of the ravine's cliff.

The cougar now took one last step toward Kharlia, his hungry and vicious face only a short distance from her. She swung her knees back over the cliff's face, now only hanging on with her hands, forty feet above the roaring Dunn River.

"Kharlia, what are you doing?" Bakari shrieked.

She just looked at him. "I won't let him eat me!" And she let go from the top of the ravine. "I love you, Bak."

"Noooooo!" Bakari screamed.

Harley ran to the edge of the cliff with another stick and swatted the creature away with a blood-curdling scream. The cougar roared and moved closer to the two men, ignoring the stick in Harley's hand.

Bakari snapped. He turned to the beast and dug deep into its mind, pushing aside any blocks the cougar had put up. Bakari didn't care. He pulled all the magic he could into himself and grabbed hold of the creature's mind. He felt the filth of its evil and didn't care. He let the creature's basic instincts wash over him as he became one with its mind. Bakari grabbed the center of that mind and tore it apart. The creature howled in agony and jumped toward Bakari. But Harley used the stick to swat it back, and the creature turned toward the older man. Then it howled and rolled on the ground.

Bakari stood over it, his face twisted with rage and revenge as he ripped the creature's mind from it, piece by piece. He let the pressure build up inside the cougar's head, pushing all the power he'd amassed into the animal. The cougar's skull shattered, showering bone and blood over Bakari. He left the cougar's body lying on the edge of the cliff.

Bakari felt something touch his shoulder, and he turned and pushed his mind into the new threat.

"Bakari, no!" shouted Harley. "It's me. It's me. Bak!"

A hand squeezed harder on his shoulder, then something big and thick hit him across the jaw, and he fell to the ground, all his magic withdrawing, leaving a sudden void.

Bakari lay on the ground, breathing hard as he tried to remember who and where he was. *Kharlia!*

"No. No. No." How could she be gone? "Kharlia. Kharlia."

Harley put an arm around Bakari and helped him sit up. Then he wrapped his burly arms around the boy, and Bakari wept until there were no tears left.

Leaving Bakari alone on the ground for a moment, Harley moved over to the fallen cougar. He pushed it toward the edge of the cliff.

"No, Harley. I couldn't stand knowing the beast was down

there, with her.''

Harley turned a grave look to the young wizard. "I'm so sorry."

Bakari only nodded. After a few more moments, he rose weakly and walked to the cliff's edge. Harley came over next to him and put his arm around him. Black dots swarmed his vision and he held on to keep from fainting.

"She was a brave girl," Harley said, "and a fighter. Maybe she's still alive."

"Maybe," Bakari whispered, grabbing a hold of that thin thread of hope. He reached out with his mind to see if he could sense her. But he could not. He didn't expect himself to; it wasn't a skill he was overly powerful in. "Harley, I need a few minutes alone."

Harley nodded, tears in his eyes. "I understand." The man walked away, back toward the trees.

Bakari knelt on the cliff's edge and stared down at the roaring river. In a matter of weeks, Kharlia had changed his life. He knew they were both young, but he loved her.

He continued to gaze down. If she had landed in the water, she might have survived. He would go after her. *Yes.* That's what he would do. They would hike south until they were able to get down to the river's edge, and then he would follow it until he found her, one way or the other.

He sat still for a moment, deep in thought. Then another thought intruded upon his grief.

Come to me, the voice pleaded. *Come to me.*

Bakari lifted his head and scanned the area. He had definitely heard something. He closed his eyes and moved his mind deeper. He felt a presence, strong but distinct.

Come to me. Alaris needs you, the deep, quiet voice said again. *Come to Celestar.*

"No," Bakari said out loud. "I need to find Kharlia." How could he leave her and go to Celestar?

He knew what he was doing was important. The Chief Judge had counted on him. Bak might be the only one who could discover the secret of the barrier and help to avert war. But, what about Kharlia?

Bakari, I need you, the voice spoke again. This time, it spoke with such longing that Bakari sank to the ground. The call was so tender, yet compelling, and he felt an instant connection to the speaker.

Harley came back over to Bakari. "Bak, we need to move. There may be more of these creatures around." He shivered. "And one is enough for me to ever meet."

Bakari stood up slowly, painfully, like an old man. He glanced south, down the river, once again and groaned.

"If you want to go after her, Son, I will go with you," Harley said. "But you have to know the Dunn flows fast, and it will take weeks or months to fully follow it. And there's no guarantee we will find anything one way or the other."

A lump formed in Bakari's throat. He knew what Harley said was true. With the books he had studied, he knew full well the lay of the land, the dangers that existed, and the slight chance of finding her.

He could hardly tear his sight from the river, but he finally did. "Something calls me to Celestar, Harley. Something that needs me – though it pains me to say - maybe even more than I need to find Kharlia. Something that would help all of Alaris."

Harley only nodded. Picking up their packs and weapons, the two men walked away from the edge of the ravine and back into the trees. At the edge of the trees, Bakari turned his head back longingly one more time.

"Kharlia," he whispered so softly that he barely heard it himself, "I will find you again."

CHAPTER TWENTY FIVE

Gorn had stayed asleep for the entire previous day. Alli had hardly left his side. Today he had been awake for most of the afternoon, but he could not regain his strength.

"You need to eat, Gorn," Alli told him for the third time in the last hour.

"I don't feel like eating. I just want to sleep," Gorn mumbled and tried to close his eyes.

Alli leaned over him with a piece of cheese and stuck it between his lips. His eyes popped open in surprise, and he glared at her. Alli had never known Gorn not to be hungry. She knew his wound still ached from the arrow and he must have taken quite a bit of river water into his stomach, but it had been almost two days since her mentor had eaten anything substantial. So she glared back at him until he took a bite out of the block of cheese.

"There, are you happy now?" Gorn asked.

Alli touched her hand lightly to his arm. "I want you to get better, Gorn."

This tenderness was not lost on Gorn. He took a deep breath and let out a long sigh. "You must go on without me. I am not going to heal quickly enough, and we need to find out what is going on in Celestar."

"I can't leave you here." A few tears came to her eyes, and

she brushed them away, hopefully before he saw them.

Gorn reached his hand to hers. "You must, Alli. This is much bigger than you and I. I will be behind you shortly. This is what wizards do. They do hard things sometimes."

"But I am not a wizard yet, am I?" Alli said with a slight grin, though her eyes still held tears.

Gorn started laughing, but then his laugh turned into a cough. "You are more wizard than many of us are. Don't let the title stop you from doing what needs to be done."

The herb woman walked back into the room. "I see he is eating something."

Gorn rolled his eyes. "Why is everyone so worried about me eating?"

"Gorn," Alli said. "This is Mags. She is going to take care of you when I leave."

"So, I see you already decided to leave me?" Gorn said with a pout, followed by a twinkle in his eye.

Alli's eyes filled with tears again. "Don't make this harder than it is."

Mags leaned over Gorn. Her hair was gray and her skin a little wrinkled, but her eyes sparkled, blue and bright. She brought a bowl of soup up near him.

"Now, sit up, and I will feed you," she said with compassionate authority.

"I can feed myself," Gorn muttered, but he sat up as she had said.

"I wish I could heal like Roland," Alli said.

"You possess plenty of other skills that young man doesn't, Alli. Don't worry about me. I see that Mags will make sure I get better." He smiled at the older woman, and she actually blushed at the old wizard.

Alli rolled her eyes. "You will know he's better when he doesn't stop eating and he's not so cranky."

Gorn grunted, took the spoon from Mags, and shoved the soup into his mouth as if to tell Alli he would be fine. After a few bites, he reiterated, "I will see you shortly. Don't do anything drastic until I get there."

"Me?" Alli said with a wide-eyed innocence. "They won't even know I'm there."

Gorn chuckled, spitting out a portion of his soup, and the two ladies joined in with the laughter.

Alli reached down and hugged her mentor, not letting him go for a full minute. Brushing the tears from her eyes, she said her final good-byes to Gorn and Mags, then headed toward the river. The barge master said he would take her across that afternoon.

Later, as Alli stepped onto the barge again with her horse, memories of what had happened earlier haunted her for a few moments. When the barge master got on with her and pushed off, she felt much better. Soon they hit the shore on the other side.

Waving good-bye to the barge master, she turned her horse and continued to head northeast. It should only be a day or two until she reached Celestar.

* * *

The Chief Judge and his party had traveled two days out from the Citadel—having left secretly in the middle of the night—when a rider approached his group on the road, coming north from Cassian. Daymian traveled with six of his original men and three of Roland's hand-picked men: one, a wizard in his thirties; another, a young teenage apprentice; and the final man, a large, muscled guard who hardly left Daymian's side.

As the rider came closer, Gilan, Daymian's guard, stepped out in front of the Chief Judge, the rest of his guards forming a circle around him. Wren, the wizard, stopped the man on horseback with a wave of his hand.

"Where are you coming from so quickly?" Wren asked the rider.

"Cassian, Sir." The rider bowed his head slightly, apparently recognizing Wren as a wizard from the Citadel by the small insignia on his breast. The man dismounted.

Daymian stepped out from behind his guards. "What news do you have from the capital?"

The man clearly did not recognize the Chief Judge. He looked to the wizard for a confirmation to proceed. Wren nodded.

"The city is quiet enough, Sir, but on lockdown. No one may enter or leave without the judges permission. Most people are staying indoors."

"What about the Chief Judge?" Daymian asked, trying to gauge what was being said about himself.

The rider was handed a waterskin, and he took a few swallows gratefully before continuing. "They say he abandoned his post."

Daymian bristled at the comment but kept an even face. "And his family?"

"They are being held within the palace walls. No one has

seen them for a week." The rider spoke in a nervous tone.

Daymian frowned and felt a tug on his heart. His family needed him.

"How did you get in and out?" Gilan asked suspiciously.

The rider took a few steps back, the reins of his horse in his hands. The burly guard *was* a fearsome sight to stand close to. "I am to bring a message to the High Wizard."

"What is that message?" Wren asked.

"That's for the High Wizard's ears only, Sir. You understand." The man put his foot into the stirrup and added, "I must ride with haste."

Before the man began riding again, the apprentice wizard, Tam, put his hand forward, and the horse and rider hit a block of air and instantly stopped. The Chief Judge was surprised at such boldness from Tam in front of the wizard.

Wren glared at the young apprentice. "What is the meaning of this?"

"We need the information being passed on to Kanzar," Tam stated.

"We are not here to interfere with the High Wizard's plans, only to bring the Chief Judge to safety." Wren's jaw held tight as he pulled Tam away from the rider.

"Wizard Roland Tyre told me to keep my eyes open and to report back on any evidence of Kanzar's plans."

At the mention of Roland's name, Wren clenched his jaw even harder. Daymian still marveled at the quick influence Roland had achieved among the wizards' ranks.

"Fine. Just read his missive. No killing."

The rider still sat on his horse, watching the wizard and his apprentice argue. His eyes widened as he now seemed to realize that Daymian was the Chief Judge. Clearly, he knew his life was being determined, and he let out a long-concealed breath when Wren mentioned not killing anyone.

Tam dug through the rider's bag and produced a rolled-up scroll. Wren took it from him and handed it to the Chief Judge.

Daymian considered the scroll for a moment. He knew the information inside would be helpful, but their way of getting it was not lawful. Laws and rules existed against intercepting someone's letters and missives.

Then Gilan walked up next to Daymian. "Sir, we need to hurry. We are in difficult times. Sometimes rules have to bend. Kanzar would not hesitate to do this, and he would kill the rider along with reading this message."

"I know that." Daymian gave a thoughtful glance at his guard. "But I am not like Kanzar. Nevertheless, you are correct in that we need the information."

Looking up and down the road, to make sure of no other imminent interruptions by travelers, Daymian noticed a stirring up of dust from behind. It would be quite a while before its source reached them, but it did push him along quicker, and he broke the seal on the scroll. As he did so, he felt his stomach broil. By disobeying the law, he, the Chief Judge, had chosen a dangerous road for Alaris.

His eyes went wide and then filled with anger as he scanned the script. The same note was sent by pigeon also, so Daymian was sure Kanzar would still get the information. It appeared that the two newly appointed judges ruled Cassian and had imposed martial law. Some dissenters had been made examples of, with beatings and a few hangings.

He finished and rolled the scroll up again. The rest of the group looked at him expectantly. He gave the scroll back to the rider and sent him on his way with a look of apology for what he had endured at their hands. He even offered him a small purse of silver to ease the man's burden.

After the rider was far enough away, Daymian motioned the others to mount and start riding. His six guards took up the front with Gilan riding next in front of Daymian, the wizard, and apprentice.

In a few moments, he shared the missive with the rest of the group. "The only good out of it seems to be that the people are not being easily convinced of my leaving them all alone. They are good people and are holding out for my support."

His men took in the information. Then Tam said, "But they won't be able to hold out forever. We need to establish a base and pull in those who are loyal to you. That is why we are going to Orr."

"To Orr?" questioned Wren. "We are to taking him to Cassian. A vote will be held there between having a king or keeping the judge system."

"I also question your choice of Orr, young man," the Chief Judge said. "My family could be in trouble."

"Wizard Roland thought that, since you are from Orr and you have much family there, Orr would be a good place to base your operations." Tam glanced back over his shoulder at the two of them.

"Roland Tyre, again." Wren sighed. "For a new wizard, he sure is making himself an entangled piece of this puzzle."

The Chief Judge actually smiled. "He sure is. Maybe that boy learned something as my counselor apprentice after all."

"If we are going to Orr, Sir," Tam said, "we will need to skirt around Cassian and head straight there. The quicker the people know where you are and that you did not desert them, the better." His excitement made Daymian smile. The young were always seeking adventure.

"I appreciate your thoughts and excitement on the matter, but we need to get my family out first," Daymian said.

Gilan turned around from up front. "I hoped you would say that, Sir. I'm itching for a good brawl." The group laughed and began to plan how to rescue his family. Daymian knew his city, its passageways, and its secrets better than anyone. A plan was beginning to form in his mind.

CHAPTER TWENTY SIX

Erryl stood next to Breelyn on the banks of a small stream. He turned to her and asked, "How old are you?"

"Haven't they taught you that you're not supposed to ask about a girl's age, Erryl?" Breelyn laughed, and her voice floated like music in the warm afternoon air.

Erryl blushed and mumbled, "Sorry."

Breelyn put a hand on his shoulder. "I am joking. You shouldn't be so serious. Anyway, since you did ask, I am almost thirty summers old."

"That's twice as old as I am," Erryl said.

"But not old for an elf. Those farther away from the barrier can live over one hundred twenty years. King Arrowyn Soliel was a small boy when the barrier went up, and he is still alive." Her eyebrows furrowed, and her mouth dropped to a frown when she had mentioned her king.

"Are you all right, Breelyn?"

"Yes, but our king is quite old and not doing well. I am one of his protectors and am anxious to see him again."

"What does a protector do?" Erryl asked as they began to walk once again.

"A protector protects the king. My assignment was to walk along the barrier and make sure it was still intact. We had heard rumors of breaches." Breelyn directed him farther into the forest, following a game trail.

"Like today? Is the barrier failing, then?"

"Yes, like today. I'm not sure what is happening. I was going to visit the watcher and governor in Silla—one of our cities by the border. It is their job to watch and report back to us. We hadn't heard anything in a while. And then Alair and I were attacked."

"Will they attack us also?"

Breelyn appeared surprised at the question. "I don't know why they would. Frankly, I don't know why they attacked us in the first place. They are supposed to be guarding the border in case Alaris attacks again."

"Alaris...*attack*?" Erryl was confused. "Why would *we* attack? We put up the barrier to protect us from having others attack us."

"No, Erryl," Breelyn said. "You've been taught incorrectly. Alaris attacked us, and now that it is failing, we have to be ready."

"Maybe *you* were taught incorrectly," Erryl said in defense, protecting his own kingdom.

Breelyn didn't answer back. She only gazed up into the enormous trees and stopped for a moment. Erryl stood behind her and wondered what she was looking at.

"I miss my home." Breelyn sighed.

"Where is your home?" Erryl decided they wouldn't get anywhere arguing over who was taught right. He wanted to find out more about these people.

"Lor'l. It is a grand tree city—the capital of Elvyn. It lies east of here, by the coast."

Erryl's eyes lit up. "The *coast?* You mean the sea, with water and everything?"

"Yes, the Blue Sea," Breelyn said. "But, Erryl, we need to find the man in your vision. We'll have plenty of time to answer all your questions later."

Erryl was amazed at how much Breelyn knew about the world. He knew he needed to focus on finding the man the Orb wanted, but that was hard with someone like Breelyn next to him. He kept stealing glances at her as she walked with assurance through the forest. After walking a short time in silence, he couldn't stay quiet any longer. "How did you learn to do magic?"

She motioned for Erryl to follow her through the trees. They continued to search for the large outcropping of rock he had seen in the Orb's vision. That is where he would find the man the Orb wanted.

"Erryl, you told me how you felt when you touched the Orb."

"It's wonderful. Full of light, peace, and understanding."

"Well, that's how magic feels to a degree. The power has always been with me, so it's hard to explain how I use it. My magic is second nature to me, a life force flowing through me and making the elements of the earth and forest more clear. I command the elements—or, rather," she said sheepishly, "I *ask* the elements to do something for me—and they obey."

Erryl thought for a moment. "So, magic is not anything mysterious or secret; it's only a deeper understanding of how the elements around us work. Everyone has different abilities. My father is a great artist and draws pictures of Celestar and of the Orb, and another guardian runs fast and jumps higher than anyone else. And you and the other wizards have the ability to control the finer elements around us."

"And you, Erryl," Breelyn said, pausing as she hacked away at a thorny bush in front of them, "have an amazing curiosity, driving you to figure things out in ways that are simple to you but are much more difficult to others."

Erryl beamed at her praise. He loved seeing her eyes sparkle.

"What you said, about magic and my ability to control the elements, is the best definition I have ever heard, even from learned elves." Breelyn continued her praise. "You are quite an intelligent young man."

"Well, I've been going to school every day since I was three," Erryl said. "We were taught that our life source would be stronger for the Orb if we were learned. But we didn't go out of the buildings much. Most everything I know is from a book."

Breelyn didn't answer him, and he stopped asking her questions for the time being. He found the silence difficult, but he could tell she was concentrating on their surroundings.

For a while longer, they traveled in silence, until Erryl stopped short and said, "In my vision, a stream flowed on my left. I think it was this stream. We need to cross to the other side and stay close to it." He closed his eyes for a moment, reliving the vision.

Soon the trees thinned closer to the stream, and then the stream split into two forks.

"Now we don't know which way to go." Erryl furrowed

his brow in concentration.

"You stay here, and I will scout ahead," Breelyn said, motioning with her hand. "And don't wander off." Breelyn walked behind a tree and then downstream from where Erryl stood.

He heard a sound and looked down in front of him. *A little green frog!* Erryl had read about frogs but had never seen one in real life. He stepped closer, but the frog jumped away.

"Come here, little frog." Erryl squatted down on his haunches and moved his hand toward the amazing creature. Once again, it hopped out of his reach, and he gritted his teeth in frustration.

Standing back up, he searched for the elusive creature. Soon, up jumped the frog, and Erryl laughed in delight. The frog jumped across the mud next to the stream and then took a detour to the side. The grass and mud turned swampy, but Erryl waded in, mud covering his feet.

"Erryl," Breelyn called to him. But he stayed focused on the frog.

"Just a minute. I've almost caught this thing."

He turned away for a brief second to look in her direction. When he turned back, the frog was nowhere to be found. Erryl stood quietly and listened intently. A loud croak signaled the frog's location, and Erryl ran forward about ten steps. When he tried to stop, his feet proceeded to slide on the marshy grass, and he tripped over a tree root and rolled down a small hill.

"Erryl!" Breelyn yelled as she ran the short distance to the young man. Erryl felt his face blushing bright red as he looked up at Breelyn. He was lying on his back, covered with mud, but he held up his hand to show her.

"You caught it." Breelyn giggled.

The frog squiggled in his hand, and, finally, Erryl let it go, watching it hop away along the marshy ground.

"But now you are filthy." Breelyn shook her head.

Erryl frowned, sat up, and turned around, his back facing Breelyn. He wasn't mad; he just needed to compose himself. He sat and gazed out at their surroundings for a moment. A brief familiarity overtook his senses.

"I'm sorry, Erryl." She approached him slowly.

"I'm not mad, Breelyn. Look!" Erryl pointed straight ahead. Down a small hill from them, then back up the other side, was a path to where a huge outcrop of rock sat. The stream they had followed wound around the left side.

"That's it. That's the rock from my vision."

Breelyn helped Erryl up from the ground. He was covered in mud, his white tunic hardly recognizable now. On the way to the outcrop of rock, they found a deeper part of the stream, and Erryl cleaned himself off as best he could. But then he was soaking wet.

"This is fun," he said out loud. "They should let us out of the buildings more often." He ran ahead along a short, flat stretch of ground.

Soon Breelyn was running beside him and, in a few long strides, overtook him. Not wanting to be outdone, he laughed and sped up. They both laughed out loud, their voices echoing off of the high rock wall looming ever larger in front of them.

Breelyn raced back out in front again, but then the trail dipped slightly, and two men stood in front of them. She stopped and put her arm out to halt Erryl's motion. He skidded to a quick stop beside her.

The two men did not appear happy, and Erryl recognized them as two of the protectors from Celestar. They wore loose robes and pants, not fitted for this forest terrain. A sword hilt sat on the hip of the shorter man, which he now put his hand on.

"Erryl Close," the other man said. His eyes were dark, both in color and with anger. "We have been searching for you."

Erryl stepped back a step, but Breelyn stepped forward.

"And who might you be?"

The taller man held an air of danger. He bowed his head slightly at Breelyn. "We are here for Erryl. He ran away from an important duty. We are protectors of the guardians."

The two men walked closer, and Breelyn stood her ground. "I am a protector from Elvyn." She pushed her long hair back behind her ears to prove the point.

The two men hesitated. They, as Erryl, had never met an elf before.

"Then you will come with us also. I'm sure Governor Ellian and, eventually, Kanzar will want to speak to you." The shorter man moved in closer and pulled his sword out of its scabbard.

"Don't hurt her," Erryl said. "She is helping me."

The taller man seemed confused. "Helping you with what?"

"The Orb told me to find someone…to bring him back to Celestar." Erryl hoped he looked serious, but he knew it would be difficult for them to take him seriously in his wet and dirty clothes.

"Enough games, Erryl. You have a vivid imagination. Both of you are coming back with us." The taller man came directly in front of Erryl and Breelyn. He reached to grab Breelyn's arm but soon discovered her standing behind him, holding his hands behind his back.

"How did you...?" the taller man yelled.

The shorter man lifted his sword and sliced it down toward Breelyn. She brought one hand up in the air and directed the sword to fly out of the man's hand. He glared at her and went to retrieve the weapon. Using her magic, she pulled a root up out of the ground and tripped the man.

The man she was holding used this opportunity to break out of her hands. He brought up his hand now and pushed a spell toward her. Sparks flew from his fingers, and Breelyn barely dodged them. However, when she did, she entangled herself with Erryl's leg and fell to the ground.

The man took advantage of this opening and kicked her leg hard as he picked up a rock with his magic and flung it at her.

"Noooo!" Erryl yelled and jumped in the way, taking the brunt of the force. The stone hit him squarely in the shoulder and took him down hard to the ground.

Breelyn jumped up and rushed to Erryl's side. She leaned over Erryl. He couldn't move his arm, and tears filled his eyes.

"Stand up slowly, elf." The taller wizard protector of Celestar had retrieved the sword the other man had dropped and now held it at Breelyn's back. "Governor Ellian wanted the boy, but he didn't say anything about an elf. If you are killed or disappear, he will be none the wiser."

"No, but we will know," a new voice said from behind them all. Standing on a lower shelf of the outcrop of rock was a thick man with a bushy beard. Standing next to him, a thin, ebony-skinned youth with glasses glared at the two men.

"That's him!" Erryl said, forcing his voice to remain steady. "That's the man from the vision."

The two newcomers walked closer. They looked tired and dirty, but determined.

"What vision?" the young man asked, clearly in charge of the two. His eyes held a determined gaze, wrapped in sorrow.

"The Orb sent young Erryl to find you," Breelyn answered. "These men here decided to try and take us back before we could."

The young man arched his eyebrows at the two men. "I am Wizard Bakari, and this is Harley Habersham. You will let these people go, and we will all go and see the Orb together."

The taller wizard continued holding the sword.

Then Harley, the old man with Bakari, took a step forward, a long walking stick in his hands. "Put the sword down. That is no way to be treating a beautiful young lady." Harley bowed his head at Breelyn.

The man hesitated, and Breelyn flipped her hand to the side. The sword flew from his hand into the air, sticking deep into a nearby patch of mud.

Erryl rose up and held his arm, still grimacing. He walked closer to Bakari and stared closely at him. He had never seen someone with skin darker than his own, though this man was certainly the man from his vision.

Breelyn smiled. "Erryl is from Celestar and is a guardian of the Orb."

With this mention of the Orb, Bakari stepped closer. "We are searching for the Orb. I think it's the key to the barrier's failing, but you say you saw a vision of me?"

Erryl remembered himself. "The Orb asked me to find you and bring you to it."

"It has also called to me," Bakari stated. He turned to Breelyn. "And you, you are an elf woman. I recognize your kind from my studies. By your coloring, I would say you are from Lor'l or thereabouts."

"This one knows a lot, Miss. I would listen to him if I were you." Harley stepped up to Breelyn but spoke to Bakari. "This is as far as I go."

Bakari turned to Harley. "Harley, how can we, I mean *I*, repay you?" Tears had gathered in the corners of his eyes.

Harley stroked his beard then put a hand on Bakari's shoulder. "No need for any repayment. Kharlia healed my boy. That was enough."

At the mention of this third person, Breelyn asked, "Is there someone else with you?"

Bakari glanced at Harley before turning back to Breelyn. "Kharlia," he said with a thick voice. "A vicious beast attacked us by the river, and she went over the edge."

Erryl felt Bakari's sadness, and it almost overwhelmed his own senses. The pain of losing his own mother was still fresh in his mind.

"I'm so sorry." Breelyn gave her condolences with tears in

her own eyes. "Duty is sometimes hard to bear."

Bakari only nodded and turned back to shake Harley's hand. "Good luck, Harley. We will never forget your kindness. Alaris will need good men in the days to come, I fear. You may be needed again someday."

"All you need to do is ask, my boy." Harley wiped a hand across his eyes. "I have seen some amazing things on this trip. You are strong. I am sure to hear of great things from you in the future."

Then Harley turned around and headed back the way he and Bakari had come.

Breelyn called Erryl over and placed a hand on his hurt arm. A white glow surrounded the injured place for a moment, and then, when she removed her hand, he was healed.

"Thank you." Erryl grinned at her. He flexed his arm. It worked as good as new.

Bakari raised his brows. "You are a wizard, too?"

"I am Breelyn Mier, one of King Soliel's protectors. We call ourselves mages, but it's essentially the same. My power comes from the earth, and that is how I can heal," Breelyn said matter-of-factly as she waved for the four men to follower her.

The two protectors from Celestar gave wary looks at Breelyn, but she grinned sweetly at them and then turned instead to Bakari.

"So, what do you know about the Orb, Wizard Bakari?"

CHAPTER TWENTY SEVEN

Anyone looking around the Citadel could tell they were preparing for a battle. Weapons were being forged, uniforms cleaned, and horseshoes repaired. Groups of mercenaries filled the fields between Whalen and the Citadel. The tension that only comes on the eve of war filled the air.

Roland did not believe in this war, but he needed to be careful. His newly found status, as a ranking wizard, was being tested on all sides. Helping the Chief Judge was already pushing things, but Daymian Khouri was a good man and didn't deserve what Kanzar had planned for him. So Roland had instructed his men to take the Chief Judge to Orr rather than Cassian. It would keep Daymian farther away from Kanzar and, hopefully, give all of them time to stop Kanzar's aggression.

Roland stood on a small balcony on the second floor of the practice facility, overlooking the practice yard. The cool air signaled autumn, and the trees around the outside of the practice yard were showcasing their yellows and reds.

Apprentices and wizards alike where honing their skills in the small arena. When they noticed him watching, many pushed themselves forward, trying to gain favor in his eyes. Rumors had flown around the Citadel about his standing and status. The story became more wonderful with each telling. Roland himself did nothing to dispel these rumors.

Roland felt a hand on his shoulder. He knew it was Onius. He'd felt the man coming nearer for the last thirty seconds.

"Making quite a stir these days, aren't you?" Onius chuckled softly. "I must admit, when I allowed you to be tested, I didn't foresee such chaos."

"Have you foreseen who is going to get killed in this war, Onius?" Roland said without turning around. "What Kanzar is doing is wrong, yet you still stand at his right side, his apparent second-in-command."

Onius took a step around Roland and stood at the railing next to him. "The Citadel's politics are not simple, Roland. You don't understand the decades Kanzar's plans have been in motion. They can't be brought down in a day."

Roland grunted and turned his attention back toward the practice yard. "But now," he gestured with his hand, "how do you justify this? How can you say war is good for Alaris?"

A loud noise erupted from the ground below, and Roland noticed a few apprentices holding some older wizards at bay with spells of fire.

"You shouldn't encourage them so." Onius frowned over at Roland.

"Why? I think I prove that apprentices these days can be as powerful as full wizards."

Onius held his mouth tight. "But not as disciplined."

Roland laughed out loud and turned away from the practice yard to face his former mentor. "Onius, when did wizards have to become old to be respected? It seems to me it is the *disciplined* wizards who are now betraying their country. When did your group become so stodgy and boring? I'm sure you must have been my age once."

Onius did smile at that and reached his hand over to pat Roland on the shoulder. "You might be on to something." He took a deep breath and let it out in a long sigh. "Maybe we have lost something through the years. Who knows, Roland? Maybe you will be in charge of all of this someday," he said as he spread his hands wide to encompass the Citadel's great structure.

"I'm counting on it," Roland said with a laugh.

"And when you are, I hope you meet an arrogant, whining, know-it-all apprentice," Onius said with an even wider smile. "It will serve you right."

They both laughed together. Then Onius seemed to grow serious once again. "The Council decided you will stay here when we march south. Most of these apprentices will also stay behind, with a few of the older council members."

"To watch over me?" Roland raised his eyebrows.

"Yes, to watch over you, Roland. Kanzar not only doesn't trust you, but I think he may actually fear you. He wants you left here, with the apprentices, to take care of the Citadel."

Roland protested, but Onius ignored him and then moved forward again. "I will concede the power you possess, but you and the apprentices do need more training and discipline to be prepared to fight in a battle. The battle wizards need to know that their men can be counted on to obey direct orders without asking questions."

Roland thought for a brief moment. "That would be hard for me sometimes."

"Don't I know?" Onius smiled fondly at his old student.

"There will be plenty to do here to keep up the Citadel."

"So, the newest wizard is being relegated to a caretaker and babysitter?" Roland slapped his hand on the wooden railing. "And Kanzar doesn't even have the gall to tell me this directly?"

"The High Wizard is concerned with more things than your welfare," Onius said.

"So he sends his messenger to come to me? What is your role in all of this, Onius?" His former mentor was infuriating sometimes. He played politics at its highest—deceit, secrets, and double crosses. What was Onius really after?

The fighting below stopped, and a few apprentices turned toward Roland. He took a moment to wave and to congratulate the men.

"Kanzar does not intend to hold a fair vote, I am sure you are aware," Roland said at last.

"Leave Kanzar to me," Onius said darkly. "I will do what must be done."

Roland stood up straight, in front of Onius. "And I will also do what needs to be done, Onius. I hope we find ourselves on the same side of this conflict."

Onius slapped his hand on the railing. "And what side is that, young wizard?"

Roland brushed his bangs out of his eyes and winked at Onius. "My side, of course." Roland turned with a flourish, his red robes swirling around his fit frame.

Onius grunted and turned to descend to the lower level.

A plan began to form in Roland's mind. Being left virtually unchecked in the Citadel might be a good thing for him. He would train the apprentices to be loyal to the Citadel and what it stood for, not to Kanzar and his machinations.

Roland walked back inside the west wing of the Citadel. He felt powerful but somewhat lonely. He didn't have Bak around to tease or Alli around to flirt with. He wanted to find someone else his own age to spend some time with. With those thoughts, he decided to find a recently met member of the Citadel cleaning staff. He still remembered her wide brown eyes and pouty lips.

"What was her name again?" he said to himself.

* * *

Chief Judge Daymian Khouri led his small group around the back side of the Cassian walls. He hoped most of his enemies' eyes would be on the front gates, where he and his guards were surely expected by now. Instead, they left their horses at a small stable behind a nearby inn, with a man loyal to the Chief Judge. Then Daymian stayed hidden, as much as possible, on the way into the city; his face was well known in Cassian.

Huddling behind a grove of trees, Daymian whispered to the group, "There is a secret door through the back wall that leads into an old barn in the back of the castle estates. And the cover of darkness will soon be upon us."

Being careful that others were not about, they moved toward the wall. Daymian moved his hand down a portion of it until he found a small crack. Fitting a knife inside the crack, he popped a secret lever, and a portion of the wall swung outward, revealing the inside of the old wooden barn.

Motioning his guards as well as Gilan, Wren, and Tam inside, he closed the wall behind them. They moved to the front of the broken-down barn, peering through broken slats to survey the grounds in front of them. The new stable and barn stood to their right, the vegetable gardens to their left. Early fall herbs, lettuces, cabbages, and turnip greens sprouted up in neat rows.

In the distance stood the castle itself. Four stories high, with balconies and parapets on the top floor. Daymian imagined that his wife and two children were being held as high up as possible. It would be easier for the usurpers to guard them that way.

He ground his teeth in frustration. All seemed quiet inside the castle grounds. Too quiet for his tastes. He surveyed the group of men with him and knew he needed to tread carefully for his plan to work.

"I will sneak inside and find out where your family is being held," Wren offered with a smile. "I will send for you when it is safe."

Daymian nodded his head. "Just hurry. The longer we wait, the more chances of us getting caught." Without Wren noticing, Daymian pulled Tam aside and whispered into his ear. The brown-haired apprentice stood a few inches shorter than himself.

"I'll go with you," Tam informed Wren as he prepared to leave the barn.

"That's not necessary." Wren began to look nervous.

"Who will you send back to get us?" Daymian asked,

pretending innocence in the change of plans.

A loud creak ensued in the back of the barn, and many of the men jumped. They all looked around nervously.

"Just the settling of an old barn," Daymian assured them.

Wren agreed to take Tam with him, and they left, crawling under a broken-down door. Daymian watched them skirt the garden and then move into the orchards, where more trees would hide them on their approach. He figured he had a half hour and no more.

Turning to his six guards, he nodded to them, and they marched to the back of the barn. Gilan followed them with interest. Three guards moved old bales of hay and then pulled up a secret door in the ground.

Gilan moved over and peered down inside, then back at the Chief Judge with a question in his eyes.

"I never did trust Kanzar," Daymian said. He then nodded to two of his men, and they lowered themselves down into the hole and disappeared. A torch was lit, and then they scurried down an underground tunnel. The remaining guards lowered the door back down and restacked the bales of hay.

Daymian turned toward the rest of the guards and Gilan. "Now we wait."

Gilan looked confused. "Wait for what, Sir?"

"Waiting for Wren to send for me." The Chief Judge moved back over to the front of the barn and peered out of the old slats once again. The night had grown darker. Daymian gazed at the silhouettes of the apple orchard, with the rising parapets of the castle behind them. Torches and lamps were being lit in the castle, giving an eerie glow to the early evening air.

It had been a fast ride from the Citadel, and Daymian's body was tired and sore, though he knew that this night would be much longer still and it would be some time before the needed rest would come. Stroking his short beard with his right hand, he thought about how much he loved his kingdom. Was he doing the right thing by standing up to Kanzar? Daymian knew that, before it was over, good men would lose their lives.

King-men! Oh, he should have done something more about them earlier. They had slowly but surely destabilized Alaris. Daymian had tried to be patient and lenient, had tried to let men speak their minds—but, if he had known from the first that Kanzar was behind it, Daymian would have moved to stop Kanzar earlier.

Daymian ground his teeth in frustration, thinking next about his counselor, Onius. That man had seemed to be playing both sides in some secret agenda only known to himself. The man had stood as his counselor for years and had given service to the Chief Judges before Daymian. What had Onius been about to tell Daymian before being summoned to Kanzar's office the other day? Did Onius actually have a plan for getting out of all of this while averting war? If he did, Daymian would listen.

"Sir!" One of the guards motioned through the old barn walls. "The apprentice, Tam, comes."

Approaching the barn, Tam came forward and greeted the Chief Judge. His face was hard to read, but Daymian could guess what had happened.

The Chief Judge turned to Gilan. "You said you were

itching for a fight. How are you feeling now?"

The large guard rubbed his hand over his shaved head and then flexed his arms out in front of him, cracking his knuckles. "I thought you would never ask."

Motioning for Tam to move forward, Daymian, Gilan, and the four remaining guards followed him into the night. Tam moved nervously and continued looking around them for trouble. But in short order they approached the steps to the castle.

Daymian peered up at the gray stone walls of the capital of Alaris and felt a small lump form in his throat. He wondered if he would ever return. Tonight, the battle for the future of Alaris would begin.

The doors opened, and Wren stood there, torchlight silhouetting him from behind. He was not pleased at seeing the small contingent. "I didn't think we were bringing everyone."

Daymian strode purposefully up the steps, his face devoid of emotion. "This is my home. I will bring in whomever I will, Wren." He pushed Wren aside and entered the foyer. His boots clicked loudly on the granite floors. Circular columns stood before him, rising to two stories above this floor. Colorful tapestries hung around the entryway, depicting scenes from around Alaris. Lamps were lit, high on the stone walls, illuminating the area, with shadows only appearing in the far recesses of the entryway.

All was as it should be—except for the twenty or so armed men standing in a semicircle to greet them. At the forefront stood Mericus, the wizard and newly appointed judge of western Alaris. He was dressed in black from head to toe, his leather pants tucked inside knee-high boots and an ornate sword hanging at his hip.

"Mericus," Daymian said. "You are far away from your western lands. What will Westridge do in your absence?"

"Westridge is not my concern right now, Daymian. I've been asked to relieve you of your duties, pending a vote on the matter."

"You know Kanzar will not allow a vote," voiced Daymian. "He means to be king and rule this land despite what the people want."

Mericus waved a hand in the air. "That is also no concern of mine right now. For now, you will be held prisoner with your family." He motioned his men forward to take Daymian and his group.

Before the men could take a step forward, Daymian raised his voice as loudly as he could and shouted, "Attack!"

Surprise spread across the faces of Mericus and his men. Through side doors, down the stairs, and from hidden panels in the walls emerged a hundred men. Daymian's chest swelled with pride as his battalion, dressed in red for battle, attacked with their swords drawn high.

It took a moment for Mericus and his men to figure out what was happening. The wizard judge gave a stern look to Wren, who seemed surprised by the attack also.

"Traitor," spat Tam as he slammed his fist into Wren. The man fell to the ground, panting for breath.

Daymian took a step forward. "You were Kanzar's man from the first, Wren."

"Where did these men come from?" the traitor asked

"A good leader always plans for contingencies," Daymian said.

Wren brought up his hand, to gather his magic, but Tam kicked Wren in the head, knocking him out before turning his attention to the rest of the fight.

To his right, Daymian heard a low growl. It was from Gilan, who ran full speed into the group of Mericus's men. He punched, kicked, and then sliced with his sword in every direction possible. Muscles bulging, he fought undeterred in his relentless attack.

Mericus shot out fireballs at the attacking battalion, though Daymian noticed that these were not killing strikes. He guessed he should take consolation in the fact that his men might live. They cleared a space for Daymian, leading him up the stairs. Meeting his other two guards—the ones who had left through the tunnels earlier—at the top of the stairs, he asked them about his family.

"All is secure, Sir," they informed him.

Daymian entered their rooms, and Mara, his wife, threw herself at him. Tears fell from her eyes. He hugged her fiercely and kissed her forehead. Then his young daughter and son came up and grabbed his legs and waist.

"We need to leave now, Sir," one of his guards said. "I don't know how long we can hold them off."

Daymian nodded, gathered up his family, and moved out into the hallway. To their right stepped the man who had previously been appointed general under the new judges. Standing next to him was the other judge Kanzar had appointed from the north. Daymian never did get the man's name. At this point, it didn't matter.

Two of his guards stood between Daymian's family and the two men. So Daymian moved in the opposite direction, down the hall, pulling his family along. As the two men attacked his guards, the fighting became fiercer, and one of the guards fell. The other one held on, fighting against the two men. He tried to give time for the Chief Judge to get away.

Suddenly, up the stairs Gilan ran, his bulky frame taking two steps at a time. He crashed into the two attackers.

"Go!" he yelled to Daymian.

Daymian moved quickly as he pulled his family into another room. Behind a bookshelf inside stood a secret passage. They entered it and pulled the shelf closed behind them. Running through darkened passageways, he led his family through a maze of rough-cut hallways and stairs, descending below the level of the castle's floors. Soon they emerged into a wide tunnel. Other men waited there for them, ready to usher them to the exit.

Coming to a wooden ladder, several guards moved ahead of them. Then Daymian pushed his family up, one by one, into the back of the old barn. Soon a contingent of men came up the ladder behind them.

They left the barn through the hidden gate in the wall and proceeded to where their horses were being held. Daymian and Mara each pulled up one of their children to ride with them and, with about fifty men, fled into the night.

Behind Daymian, the sounds of battle still emerged from the castle. A few bolts of fire lit the night sky. Daymian clenched his teeth. Mericus must still be fighting. He slowed and took a last, longing look at his beloved city.

One of his men, an officer, came back to him. "You must leave, Sir. The men know the sacrifice they have made. You can't go back."

"I know, but that doesn't make it any easier." Daymian turned his horse back straight, held on to his son with his left arm, and galloped out of the city.

"This isn't over yet!" he yelled out to his remaining men. "To Orr!"

CHAPTER TWENTY EIGHT

Coming up over a small rise, Bakari marveled at seeing Celestar for the first time. Its gleaming white domes and spires stood out in sharp contrast to the green woods surrounding it. He could see the barrier, off in the distance, shimmering brightly. He took a few steps toward it, but Breelyn put her hand on his arm and motioned him back toward the city.

"There will be time to study it later," the elf protector said.

Bakari scrunched up his face. "I know. It's just so exciting to be here, near it." Stepping up to the gates, they were met by a small group of guards. They stood in front of the approaching group as if to stop them. The two men from Celestar accompanying Bakari and his group stepped out in front of Breelyn and Erryl.

One of them glanced back at the small group and motioned with his arm as he said, "We brought back Erryl Close, the escaped guardian, but some others have insisted on coming along with him."

Breelyn looked at Bakari, and he nodded to her. She would take the lead for now. "I am Breelyn Mier, protector for King Arrowyn Soliel, king of Elvyn. I have come through the barrier."

The guards stumbled over themselves. Turning to one

another, they began arguing about what to do. They too had never seen an elf before. Not only that, but she had breached the barrier.

Breelyn continued. "We would like to speak with your governor. I am sure we can sort things out."

Erryl turned a worried look at Breelyn. He had spoken to her and Bakari about what the governor had done to Geran, his old sector protector. So they knew the man was dangerous.

One of the guards stepped forward. "Who else is in your party?" He eyed Bakari suspiciously. "You seem to be a long way from home—wherever that may be."

Bakari ignored the insult. He was used to standing out in a crowd. "I am Bakari, the scholar wizard sent here, under the direction of the Chief Judge, to learn about the barrier. I would like to see the Orb."

One of the guards mumbled, "Another young wizard. Governor Ellian will not be happy."

"Another?" Bakari asked, wondering what other wizard had made the trip here quicker than he had.

"A girl," the man said. "Feisty little thing. Hardly seems old enough to be out on her own."

Bakari smiled for the first time in days. By the description, he hoped it would be Alli. It would be nice to see a familiar face in all of this.

The two men with them grabbed Erryl's arms. Then the taller one spoke.

"Well, for certain, we will bring in our escaped guardian. He needs to return to his duties."

Erryl tried to pull his arms away, but the men held fast.

Breelyn touched the shoulder of both men, and they immediately dropped their hold on the young man. The gate guards kept looking at Breelyn nervously.

She smiled sweetly and stepped closer. "We will not be kept waiting. Please lead us directly to your governor." She motioned for the others to join her and walked straight through the gates. The guards scrambled to stay ahead of her.

Bakari observed everything here with interest, filing his surroundings away in his mind for future use. The buildings were clean and white, flanking wide streets and walking paths. The few people walking about wore the same clothes, albeit more clean, that Erryl wore: loose-fitting white tunics and pants. Ahead of them loomed a smooth white building. Four spires reached heavenward, one on each corner, with a large dome of glass in the middle. Bakari felt power radiating from the building.

Erryl pointed. "That is where the Orb is. You can feel its power, can't you?"

Bakari and Breelyn both nodded. But Bakari felt more than power. Distant echoes of the voice he had heard on the cliffs of the river now came back to him.

Their group was escorted around the side of the building and through a smaller door. Entering the large building, Bakari glanced around. Smooth walls, clean tile floors, and high ceilings met his gaze. They were led to a set of double doors at the end of the hallway. The guard put his hand on the door, but Breelyn pushed him back with authority and moved in ahead of them. Bakari had to almost run to catch up with Breelyn's long strides.

Ahead of them, on a chair of significant size—not quite a throne—sat an older man with dark hair and a goatee. Jewels hung around his neck, and silk robes covered his strong frame. A girl stood in front of him, her back to the approaching group.

Upon noticing their arrival, the man rose from his chair. "What is the meaning of this? Who let these people in?" A scowl covered his face, and his hand went to the pommel of a sword at his side.

Bakari walked forward with Breelyn at his side. They stopped a few feet behind the girl, who had yet to turn around.

"I am Breelyn Mier, protector of Elvyn," she said, introducing herself for the second time that day.

The governor's eyes went wide, and he reached his other hand toward the arm of the chair, to steady himself. "So, the barrier is down?"

"Not fully," Breelyn informed him. "It was a momentary lapse that allowed me through. Your brave guardian, Erryl Close, saved my life, and I have come to see he is rewarded."

Erryl stepped out from behind the group. His clothes were still dirty, and he felt afraid of the governor, but he stood his ground bravely.

Before the governor could say anything else, Bakari spoke. "And I am Bakari, scholar wizard. I have traveled here to learn more about the barrier and the Orb. There is trouble brewing in the land, and it will become even more likely if the barrier falls."

With mention of his name, the young girl had turned around. She smiled now at Bakari, and he felt relieved to find a friend here.

The governor still stood. "I see you know Wizard Allison Stenos, here?" the man said with a sneer.

Wizard, huh? Bakari wondered if she had indeed passed the wizard test or was only masquerading as one. A look, warning him to be careful, crossed her face, and Bakari knew he needed to find out more before he proceeded. Knowledge of the situation was always preferable to actions made without any information.

"We appreciate your hospitality, Governor," Bakari said. He motioned at Breelyn with his eyes to follow his lead. She caught on. This was not a man to threaten but to stroke his ego. "I can see you run a good, clean city here. We are pleased to see it so spotless and taken care of. You are to be commended."

The governor visibly relaxed and sat back down. "Of course. Of course. I thank you. We always try to please the Citadel. How is Kanzar doing, anyway?"

If Governor Ellian was in league with Kanzar, this was a dangerous place indeed.

"I grew up in the Citadel as an orphan, Sir, but have been stationed in Cassian. I have not had the pleasure of seeing our wizard leader recently." It was hard for Bakari to act the counselor. This was a job far more suited for Roland.

"Good Governor." As Breelyn spoke, the room fell silent. Her radiance, even after traveling, amazed Bakari. Her presence itself was a breath of fresh air, her voice light and musical. "I bring you tidings from King Arrowyn Soliel. You are the first leader in Alaris we have met in one hundred fifty years. We look forward to working with such esteemed leadership."

"Where are my manners?" the governor said, apparently impressed with Breelyn's greeting. "I am Governor Naylor Ellian of Celestar, and I welcome our Elvyn neighbor to our esteemed city. I will prepare proper rooms for you at once, and perhaps later you will join me for a meal."

They all agreed, and the travelers were escorted out. The guards moved to take Erryl back to his rooms. The guardian looked at Breelyn for support, and she nodded to him that it would be all right.

Bakari found himself next to Alli as they left the building and walked toward a smaller one. "A wizard now?"

She gave him a pout. "No, not yet, but Gorn was hurt on the way here, and I needed to improvise. They don't know the difference anyways. I'm stronger than any of their weak wizard guardians."

"And the governor?" Bakari asked.

"He is a dangerous wizard in his own right, and he tightly controls the people here. He is up to something. I arrived this morning. What is this Orb you spoke about?"

"As far as I can tell, the Orb controls the barrier. Breelyn thinks it's an ancient dragon's egg," Bakari said.

The group entered the building and was escorted to separate rooms, to clean up and rest. The room Bakari entered was small but serviceable. He was not used to much more. It held a comfortable bed, a washbasin, a pair of chairs, and a small wooden table. The table held an assortment of fruits and breads.

Grabbing a slice of melon, he sat on the edge of the bed.

He slipped off his boots and laid his head back. The comforter felt cool to the touch.

Closing his eyes, Bakari tried to remember everything that had occurred in the last two weeks since leaving River Bend. His chest constricted; the pain of losing Kharlia was too fresh. He turned his mind to the others. He hoped the Chief Judge was safe at the Citadel and worried how Roland was getting along. He wondered if his friend was behaving himself.

Right before full slumber would have grasped Bakari, he felt a call come to his mind. A presence filled his mind and heart: similar to what he had felt earlier, but now more clear and immense. It was magic...but on a level he hadn't felt before.

A soft, but intense, deep male voice called to him, *Come to me*. It whispered this to his soul. The voice's pleading dug deep into his breast, but he was too exhausted. He surrendered to a deep sleep.

* * *

Later that evening, Bakari woke up and went to eat with Breelyn, Alli, and the governor of Celestar. They finished eating a nice meal of braised chicken, sweet breads, and fresh vegetables. It felt good to eat a solid meal again. Throughout the meal, the governor steered the conversation away from any talk of the Orb.

From what Bakari had sifted from his conversations with others that afternoon, Celestar had been founded at the time of the barrier's creation. A group of wizards and other men built the city. They had been the first guardians. The governor of Celestar took his orders from the wizards, and, in turn, the Citadel provided everything that the city needed.

Come to me, a voice spoke into Bakari's mind during the silence of dessert.

He sat up straight with a start. He had forgotten about the call he'd heard while falling asleep earlier. He closed his eyes and reached out, much like he did whenever he merged his mind with an animal's.

The voice became clear, sharp, and powerful as it said, *I need you.*

Who are you? He knew a being of extreme intelligence conversed with him but as yet didn't know who it was. Was it another wizard, calling to him?

Where are you? Bakari thought.

I am the Orb. This message came to him loud and clear. *I am the Dragon Orb. Come to me now!* These thoughts burst through his mind.

Bakari opened his eyes to find everyone staring at him. He took off his glasses and rubbed his temples. His head hurt.

"Bakari?" Alli turned to him. Her green eyes held his with concern. "You've been in a trance for a quarter of an hour."

Bakari leapt to his feet. "The Orb calls to me. I must go now," he announced to the group.

The governor started, spilling a glass of wine to the marble floor and making a shattering sound that brought servants running to the room. Ignoring the cleanup around him, the governor lifted his hand toward Bakari.

"That is not allowed," he said in a steady voice. "You must

not interrupt the guardians."

Without anything else being said, a group of protectors appeared at the two doorways into the room.

Bakari sighed. *Why must everything be so difficult?*

Alli stood. Her face was filled with resolve. "If Wizard Bakari asks to see the Orb, he will see the Orb."

The protectors moved closer. Breelyn stayed seated, watching the exchange, almost with a look of excitement in her eyes.

Alli stepped toward the closest protector. He threw up a shield in anticipation of her kick. However, in one fluid motion, Alli took two steps and jumped up and over the man, her feet running sideways on the wall, landing with a flourish behind him. Her short hair swayed silently against her chin. Then she hit the man from behind, knocking him down. This brought a flurry of activity in the room as the remaining protectors rushed the young girl.

Two of them were, apparently, wizards. One summoned a ball of fire, while the other one tried to push Alli's feet out from under her with a rush of air. Alli dodged both as she sidestepped the fireball and it hit a wall behind her instead. She leapt high into the air, flipping end over end, and arrived in front of the wizard who had tried to knock her down.

He brought out a sword, and Alli smiled. The young battle apprentice was now in her element. Two knives suddenly flashed in her hands as she knocked the sword away. Back and forth she parried with the blades, pushing the attacking wizard farther back into a corner, her hands a blur of activity.

Two other men approached behind her. One moved with

strong arms to grab her from behind. Without leaving the wizard any opportunity, she reached down and back through her legs. Grabbing one attacker by the ankles, she pulled him down and under her. Jumping on his chest once he was on the floor in front of her, she twisted around and pushed the other man down with a large puff of air from her hands. Bakari stood watching with his mouth open. Seeing the grace of Alli's movements was like watching a beautiful dance.

Breelyn sat with a look of mesmerized appreciation on her face also. "She fights like a battle-trained elf. Her battle dance is beautiful."

Scanning the room in a glance, Bakari saw the back side of the governor's cloak disappear behind a back door. Bakari ran toward it, but it shut before he got there.

"Bakari!" Breelyn pointed to an open door. "Go to the Orb. We will take care of this."

Bakari knew where to go. The building holding the Orb rose up high in the middle of the city. He ran as fast as he could through the paved streets, the scent of flowers filling the air. The early autumn evening had turned cool, but twilight still glowed in the deep blue sky.

As he bolted through the front doors, Bakari met a wave of power that almost brought him to his knees.

Following the source of power, he entered a door and stopped. A group of similarly dressed guardians stood around an immense white Orb. At least ten feet tall, the Orb sat on a golden pedestal on top of a bright red carpet. The room—surrounded by tall white columns holding up a clear, glass-domed ceiling—sparkled with power. Lamplight from around the room reflected off of the iridescent Orb.

Bakari saw that Erryl stood in the circle. The group held hands and, one by one, in turn, reached their hands to the Orb. As they did, the Orb brightened in power, almost showing a shape inside it. Bakari stood for a moment, hidden behind a column, trying to take in what he saw.

On the other side of the room, the governor burst forth and grabbed a guardian out of the circle. The neighboring guardians murmured and immediately closed ranks, and each grabbed the other person's hand. Then the governor did this again. The Orb seemed to dim in power.

Another protector in the room, watching the guardians, approached the governor. "Sir, what are you doing?"

The governor turned on the man. "This is too much power. The Orb is getting too much power."

"I don't understand," the protector said. "This is what the guardians are supposed to do."

"Not anymore." He pushed the protector out of the way and reached for another guardian. "The guardians' job is done. The barrier must come down."

The protector came back to the governor. "You are not in your right mind, Sir. Please, step away."

Governor Ellian then brought forth power from his hands and, with a flash of firelight, took the man down.

Come to me! The voice reverberated in Bakari's mind once again, only this time much stronger. Bakari stepped out of his hiding place and approached the guardians and the Orb.

The governor turned to Bakari and laughed. "Ahhh, Wizard, you do not know the rules of the Orb, do you? Only guardians can touch it. They feed it with their life source. This is how it has been for one hundred fifty years. A wizard can't touch it."

Bakari hesitated.

Erryl turned to them, still holding hands with his neighboring guardians. "It is true, Bakari."

The others in the room gasped and turned their heads toward their governor.

The Orb visibly grew before them once again. Bakari walked up to it.

"Bakari, are you sure?" Erryl asked.

Bakari hoped he was sure. He went deep into his mind, finding an immense place of power, and then searched the presence of the Orb. It was alive. A living creature breathed inside it. The other guardians stepped away, leaving Bakari alone in front of the Orb.

Bakari reached his hand onto the Orb, and it flashed brightly. The governor laughed out loud, maniacally. "You will die now, Wizard!"

But Bakari did not die. Instead, intelligence, power, beauty, and love filled his mind and soul. He opened his eyes, and the Orb glowed almost clear. Curled up inside the Orb sat a beautiful, bright, fierce blue dragon. Bright yellow eyes peered through narrowly opened slits. It was the most awesome sight the young wizard had ever seen in his life. His soul was touched by this ancient and wonderful creature, and he bonded instantly with it. He knew then what powered the barrier—the power of dragons.

Even though it was new to him, it was a comfortable,

ancient bonding that took place. The bonding comforted Bakari and gave him hope once again.

Oh, Kharlia! he thought. *I wish you were here to see this.*

A name exploded in his mind. "Abylar!" Bakari said, naming him out loud, and the ancient dragon seemed pleased.

"Come to me!" The sound filled the room, and this time all heard the voice of the mighty, magical creature.

Bakari pushed his hand through the dragon's orb, and the shell cracked into a hundred pieces but still held together. Taking a step back, the young wizard stood in awe of the giant dragon egg in front of him. A short silence filled the room and then was shattered by a blast of eggshell—hundreds of pieces shooting around the room at once.

The guardians ran, screaming, to a corner of the room, and the governor stood in place, barely able to control his shaking.

Stretching, the dragon burst in one final motion through the egg—his wings stretching ten feet to either side. Standing wobbly for a moment, but soon gaining his strength, the fierce blue creature, with scales across his forehead and down his back, took two large steps toward the governor.

He let out a loud wail, and blue fire erupted from the dragon's throat and consumed the governor in one breath, leaving only a pile of ashes on the floor. The others in the room shrieked and ran toward the door, but Erryl stood by Bakari's side, looking as mesmerized as Bakari himself was.

Bakari stretched his hand forward and brought his mind in contact with the beautiful, noble creature's mind once again. The dragon turned and took in Bakari's gaze, intelligence in his glowing yellow eyes. Those eyes spoke volumes to Bakari's soul, and he grabbed hold of Erryl's arm for support. The love for him, from the dragon, almost brought him to his knees.

With a great flap of his giant wings, Abylar soared upward, higher and higher, toward the dome of the room. Bakari was held in the trance and now saw through the dragon's own eyes. He flew straight toward the glass dome.

Without even stopping, Abylar crashed through the dome and flew out into the fresh evening air. Bakari's mind could see whatever the dragon saw. Looking down, he saw the entire city of Celestar, its white domes and spires growing smaller and smaller. His stomach became woozy, and he fell to the floor of the room, shattered glass and eggshell littering the tile floor around him.

I will return, Bakari, spoke the fierce voice in his head. *I must eat and gain strength. Wait for my return.*

Bakari then broke contact with the dragon's mind and slumped to the floor. Barely conscious, he saw Breelyn and Alli rush into the room.

"The barrier is down, Bakari!" were the last words he heard the elf protector say to him before he slumped to the ground.

The barrier is down, he thought as he lost consciousness. *What have I done?*

CHAPTER TWENTY NINE

In the capital city of Cassian, Onius stood in the castle office of the Chief Judge. However, Kanzar, not Daymian, now sat behind the desk. Onius tried not to look directly at the self-proclaimed leader. He felt that, if he did, Kanzar would see the duplicity in his soul.

Kanzar was speaking harshly to Mericus about letting the Chief Judge get away. His face was red, his eyes hard. "You have failed again, Mericus. First, you actually let him get to the Citadel. And now, you let him escape Cassian and go to Orr with a group of his men. When I am king, I will remember who failed me and who helped me."

Mericus glared back with hard eyes. "High Wizard, I did not fail you on purpose. These times are unpredictable. We didn't anticipate him hiding a battalion of soldiers, and he had others with him, from the Citadel, who helped. I did my best with what I had at my disposal."

"I will not hear pathetic excuses," Kanzar spat in anger, and Mericus backed away. "I want to know who from the Citadel helped him. I will have them punished for not upholding their loyalty to me." Kanzar seemed to scrutinize Onius.

Onius wasn't in the mood for Kanzar's intimidation. "It seems, Kanzar, that many who are not wizards—guards and apprentices alike—are not aligned with your goals."

Kanzar stood and threw his chair back. It crashed to the ground behind him. "All who live in the Citadel owe their allegiance to me."

Onius knew he shouldn't push, but he did anyway. "What about Roland?"

The man went crazy. Kanzar yelled and screamed. Bringing up his hands, he shot a string of red fire at one of the walls, knocking down paintings and lamps. "All will bow to me. I will be their king!"

Onius glanced at Mericus. Their leader was becoming crazed with power. Onius and Mericus had spoken about this lately and Onius hoped he could truly count on the new judge in the coming days of the conflict to fulfil his part of their plan.

"When will the last of the men be ready to fight, Mericus?" Kanzar asked, turning back to his most recently appointed judge. "Or will you botch that up also?"

"Sir," Mericus said, trying to hold his voice even, "the last of the battalions from the Citadel will be here soon. The battalion from Westridge should also be arriving with the other mercenary groups by the end of the week. Within two weeks, everything should be organized. Where will we go first?"

Kanzar sat back down, his temper smoldering. "We will finish securing Cassian, then go south, to Orr. Daymian Khouri has beaten me for the last time."

Mericus bowed briefly, caught Onius's eye, and then left the room.

"Onius," Kanzar said. "What is your game?" Kanzar moved out in front of his desk.

"I am here as your advisor, Kanzar. It is my job to point out weaknesses in your plans." Onius smiled outwardly but cringed inside. His plans would have to proceed carefully. He hoped, in the meantime, that not too many innocent people would die. "Do you want to send men back to the Citadel to check on things there?"

"No," Kanzar said. "Apprentices and a few guards are no trouble to me. That upstart boy will be cleaning rooms and training young ones; he won't have time to cause much trouble. What harm can he do?"

Onius thought about Roland and his thirst for acknowledgment and power. *What harm, indeed?* Roland was the one person who could undermine anyone's plans. He hoped the boy kept a good head on his shoulders and stayed out of Kanzar's way for now.

Kanzar continued about his plans for domination. "Write a proclamation, and let it be known that, as of this point, Daymian Khouri is considered an enemy to the newly established government of Alaris. He orchestrated an attack in the capital, and now he has escaped to form a rebel hold in Orr. All associates of his are under orders to surrender or face punishment for rebellion and sedition."

Rebellion and sedition? These words echoed in Onius head. If he was caught with his owns plans, Kanzar would hang him for those same crimes. Nodding, he excused himself.

The war has indeed begun.

CHAPTER THIRTY

The last few days had been busy around Celestar. With the death of the governor and some of the other protectors and the destruction of the Orb, the guardians—being the sheltered people they were—didn't know what to do with their lives.

The day the dragon had flown free from the Orb, the meaning of their lives had been taken away. That was the day all of Alaris had changed. For one hundred fifty years, the barrier had stood as a supposed guardian against others, when, in reality, it had protected others from Alaris's own wizards and their greed. That protection was now no more.

Bakari stood next to Erryl on a hill outside of the city. The boy was a continual source of questions and held a thirst for knowledge that Bakari had not seen outside of the ranks of scholar wizards. In turn, Bakari also had learned a lot from the boy, as well as from Breelyn. He found himself feeling slightly jealous of the knowledge the elves possessed.

Over one hundred fifty years earlier, the wizards of Alaris had been the aggressors and had tried to overrun Elvyn and the other kingdoms around Alaris. Not all wizards believed in this offensive activity, so some formed a secret alliance of wizards and other important people from among the nearby kingdoms searching for a way to stop that aggression. Their solution was the Orb—a dormant dragon's egg with the incredible means to magnify power.

Lost among the years was *how* the egg was obtained; they knew only that it came from the mountains of Mahli, to the north. These wizards formulated the plan with others to form the guardians—a group of specially chosen people, people of purity and intelligence, who would feed the orb with their life source. That power would then form a barrier around Alaris, not to keep them safe from others, as had been taught to Bakari and Erryl, but to protect the neighboring kingdoms from Alaris's assaults.

Erryl turned to Bakari now with another question. "But, why now? Why did the Orb grow so large and hatch now?"

Bakari shook his head. He had turned this same question over in his mind multiple times each day. "Maybe it was merely time for the egg to hatch." However, deep inside, Bakari somehow knew the truth—it had something to do with himself. The dragon had called to *him*.

Touching the Orb and being in contact with the mind of the dragon had been the single most wonderful feeling Bakari had ever experienced. The intelligence and power exuding from Abylar was amazing in itself, more powerful than dozens or even hundreds of wizards. The touch of the dragon's mind was different from that of a wizard—a different source of power, a higher, more encompassing power.

With only a slight rustle of the trees, a group of elves emerged from the forest, where the barrier used to be. In their lead strode a tall, strong man, with long, dark hair and with a bow slung over his back.

"Alair!" came the squealing sound of Breelyn's voice from behind Bakari and Erryl.

Breelyn came running, out of the city and down the hill, toward the elves, almost falling down. Rushing to the tall, strong man, she hugged him fiercely.

She brought the elves up toward Bakari and introduced Alair to him.

"Alair is my protector. He stayed behind the barrier to let me get safely through." She beamed up at the sturdy man with a few tears glistening in her eyes.

Bakari greeted the man warmly. Alair looked to be at least double Breelyn's age, but Bakari was learning it was most likely hard to tell age among elves.

"How did you escape?" Breelyn asked Alair.

"The attackers fled from the beast, and I ran like crazy to get away from it. When I thought I would die, these brave men," he swept his hand around to the other men, "Crylen and Iman, came to my rescue. They diverted the beast with something else to eat. The rest of the men here are from their small village, along the barrier—or along what used to be the barrier." His brows furrowed.

"I know," Breelyn said. "It's hard to think of the barrier being down permanently now."

Walking out of the city, perhaps to see what all the noise was about, came Alli and the recently arrived Gorn. The man had become worn and aged since the last time Bakari had seen him. Alli held on to his side and helped him come forward.

"I will need to go back and tell the king all that has transpired here," Breelyn said to Bakari. "I'm not sure who the men are that attacked me, but I need to stop in Silla and check with the watcher there on my way back to Lor'l."

Bakari felt strange being the one people now deferred to. Communicating with and freeing the dragon had made him the assumed leader upon the death of the governor. Bakari wasn't really comfortable with that.

The sun darkened, and all glanced up in surprise on this cloudless day. Shielding their eyes, they collectively sucked in a breath. The dragon had returned. Soaring down through the sky, the blue dragon spread his wings wide, spikes and scales of varying shades reflecting the bright sun. He had grown since leaving only a few days ago. The wind carried him without him having to flap his wings, and he lowered himself closer to the growing crowd.

Citizens and guardians of Celestar all gathered together to watch the spectacle. Abylar came to rest on a flat field, down the hill from where the gathering stood. Holding the dragon's yellow eyes in his own gaze, Bakari descended the small hill. Abylar loomed up larger in front of him, easily two dozen feet high and five times that long, counting his tail. Bakari assumed that the young creature was not nearly done growing yet.

Coming to a stop in front of the magical being, Bakari stretched forth his hand and touched the rough, scales of the dragon's hide. Abylar swung his head down and around, peering intently into Bakari's eyes.

Bakari's mind joined with the dragon's presence, a much more smooth, natural, and powerful link than he had ever experienced with other animals. Their minds completed and complemented each other. One immense magical mind.

Bakari's knowledge of the past now increased a hundredfold, and the thoughts made him sway. Abylar eased off, allowing Bakari to catch his breath.

Kneeling down on his belly, the dragon spoke again to Bakari's mind. *Mount up, Dragon Rider. We are meant to soar and fly together.*

Bakari reached both hands timidly up to the dragon's back. Then he hefted himself up on the mighty creature, using a large scale as a foothold. He found what seemed like a natural spot to sit, at the base of Abylar's neck. The flesh was softer, and his body fit perfectly.

"You are wonderful," Bakari said out loud with a laugh of glee as he grabbed hold of a large spike in front of him. The dragon stood back up and, with a flap of his jagged wings, lifted them into the air, his long tail swirling around him.

The gathered group on the hill clapped and yelled in amazement.

"A dragon rider!" Breelyn yelled. "A real dragon rider!"

Reaching out his mind to Abylar, Bakari asked if they could search for Kharlia, along the banks of the Dunn River, before settling back down. With a loud roar from the dragon and an assurance from Bakari to the others that he would return soon, Abylar flew south toward the Dunn River.

With the speed of the dragon, they soon found the spot where Kharlia had gone over the cliff. Directing the dragon to fly down lower and to follow the river south, Bakari searched carefully in the water and along the banks.

With the quick, rolling waters of the river and the thick Elvyn Forest on either side, Bakari's heart sank as he soon realized it was hardly possible to search for her from above. There were just too many places she could have exited the river. He reached his mind out and felt the normal creatures of the forest around him but nothing human at all.

With a deep pain in his stomach, he wiped tears from his eyes and directed Abylar to turn back around. Placing his hand on the dragon's neck for support, Bakari felt a calming sensation from Abylar. He would always remember Kharlia: her soft touch; her bright, intelligent smile; her enthusiasm; and, most of all, her acceptance of him.

Rest and be at peace, my young dragon rider. This deep, powerful sentiment came into Bakari's mind. The dragon felt Bakari's pain and took some of it into himself, allowing Bakari to rest and find tranquility for a few moments.

Soon they flew back above Celestar, and Bakari opened his eyes. He felt refreshed and clearheaded. He looked east and north and still couldn't believe the barrier was down. He didn't think the Chief Judge had meant for him to do that when he had sent Bakari to investigate. Brief feelings of guilt came to the young scholar, but Abylar replaced them with a new purpose.

Circling twice, the dragon landed again—closer to the gathered group. Bakari knew what he now needed to do. Reaching out, Bakari beckoned with a finger at Alli to climb up with him. "Alli, your skills are needed elsewhere."

The young apprentice wizard regarded Gorn, her mentor.

"Go ahead," the wizard urged his apprentice. "What other chance will you have to ride a dragon?"

Walking to the mighty creature, Alli put her hand to his side. "So much power," she said in a tone of reverence.

"Gorn, protect the border and the guardians," Bakari said. "Their connections to the dragon will continue to help him grow."

Breelyn walked closer to Gorn. "We will send reinforcements to help the people here, Dragon Rider. They have rendered a sacrifice that won't go unnoticed, throughout all of Elvyn. Dragons hold special mythical powers among the history of our people, and dragon riders are very rare indeed!"

Bakari blushed at the respect and admiration she showed him. He called Erryl closer to him and leaned down.

"Thank you, my friend. It was you Abylar reached out to first. Your trust and instincts allowed us to find each other. We were all meant to be a part of this. One day I will bring you to the Citadel, and we will study together."

Erryl nodded. "I would like that, Bak. I really would." He stood hesitantly for a moment, and Bakari discerned his thoughts.

"You may touch him, Erryl," Bakari said.

Erryl's mouth spread into a wide grin as he reached his hand tentatively to the blue dragon and petted his scaly skin tenderly.

"I think he likes you, Erryl," Bakari said.

Abylar purred in delight, and the crowd laughed with joy.

Lifted up into the air, Bakari waved one final time. Alli held on tightly behind him as they climbed higher. For him, though, there was no trepidation, only delight.

CHAPTER THIRTY ONE

Abylar proceeded to fly in a southwesterly direction. Alli screamed in delight behind Bakari as Abylar swooped low and then climbed back up higher in the sky. Bakari half smiled, the joy of flying tempered somewhat by thoughts of Kharlia.

The Elvyn Forest soon thinned out, and fading autumn fields, rolling hills, and valleys covered the ground below them. Far to the north, the mountains of Mahli loomed. Bakari wistfully looked in their direction.

Soon, Dragon Rider. Abylar spoke in a quiet rumble to his mind. *Soon.*

Before either wizard noticed the time, the tall spires of the Citadel came into view. A lump formed in Bakari's throat. This had been his home for almost ten years. He knew every nook and cranny of the compound. It looked almost deserted now, except for a few scattered men and women.

With a loud screech, Abylar landed in the practice yard. The few men there scrambled with a yell and went running inside. Before Bakari could dismount, a group of people came running back out, weapons and magic ready for use if needed. They were led by a few elder wizards Bakari recognized from his time in the Citadel.

"What is the meaning of this?" one of the elders asked. "Bakari, isn't it?"

"I need to speak to Wizard Kanzar or the Chief Judge," Bakari announced.

"Neither is here at this time," the wizard informed Bakari. "And I will have to ask you to dismount. We can discuss this inside."

Before Bakari had the chance to say anything else, his old friend, Roland Tyre, pushed his way through the group. "What is going on here?"

The same blond hair hung over Roland's forehead, but a new power enhanced his eyes. He came to stand beneath the great dragon and looked up in surprise.

With a broad grin and a hearty laugh, Roland took a moment to find his words. The other elder wizards seemed to want to say something, but they held their peace. Bakari found that interesting.

Bakari spoke to break the tension. "I've never seen you at a loss for words, Roland."

"Bak, Bak, Bak," Roland repeated, as if still trying to gather his thoughts. "You are full of surprises lately, aren't you? And I just thought you ran off with a pretty girl."

Pain welled up in Bakari's heart at the mention of Kharlia, and he held his lips tight.

"Where is that girl of yours, anyway?" Roland asked, obviously ignorant of the situation. "Ah, but I see you brought another beauty back with you." He focused his eyes on Alli and gave a flourishing bow. "My lady."

Bakari felt Alli stiffen behind him, and she huffed out a breath.

"Roland, have some care with your words," she scolded.

"Kharlia is not with us anymore."

Roland gazed at Bakari with uncharacteristic sympathy in his eyes.

"She fell off a cliff into the Dunn River while we were fighting a barrier beast," Bakari said with thick emotion.

Roland had the good graces to stop talking for a moment. When he finally did, it was more somber. "Bak, I am truly sorry. You two were perfect for each other."

Bakari closed his eyes for a moment and drank in his dragon's power. It was the only thing keeping him from being overwhelmed by the ache of Kharlia not being by his side. Opening his eyes again, he felt calmer.

The two elder wizards stepped forward once again and began to talk; however, Roland interrupted them and invited Bakari and Alli to dismount. Bakari noticed the deference they reluctantly gave Roland and wondered what the story there was.

"He needs to eat." Bakari motioned for Abylar to fly away. "But we don't have much time."

Bakari looked back and forth between the elder wizards and Roland, not knowing to whom he should speak about the barrier.

Roland made the choice for him. "Council members." He motioned toward a few other wizards. "You may join us if you like."

They all nodded toward Roland, and the small group walked into the Citadel. They sat down in a room, where the travelers received refreshments. While eating, Bakari and Alli told Roland and the other council members about the fall of the barrier and how the dragon had come to be.

"Where are all the other wizards?" Bakari asked as he brought Roland up to speed on his life in the last couple of weeks.

Roland frowned and looked at the other council members and then back to Bakari. "Kanzar has set himself up as king. He took most of the wizards and soldiers with him to Cassian and declared himself ruler there."

"And the Chief Judge?" Alli asked.

"In Orr."

"Orr?" Bakari questioned.

"It was the safest place for him to go. Orr is where he is from. I have received word by carrier pigeon that he arrived recently, declared Kanzar to be a rebel, and is recruiting men to his cause in Orr."

"So civil war will come, it appears." Bakari shook his head.

"It may be averted if the Chief Judge steps down," offered one of the elder wizards. "Kanzar will be relentless in his pursuit."

"The Chief Judge will not step down for Kanzar," Roland said. "But, if an alternative is found, we may yet avert an all-out war."

"I need to go to Orr to be with the Chief Judge," Alli said to Bakari. "He will need my skills."

"I agree," Bakari said.

Another elder wizard stood up. "Bakari, as a wizard yourself, you are bound to support Kanzar and the Citadel."

All in the room stiffened at the wizard's words.

Bakari stared hard at Roland. "What will you do, Roland?" Bakari asked. "Are you for Kanzar or the Chief Judge?"

Roland moved his eyes around the room, looking into the eyes of each person before returning his gaze to Bakari. "I am for myself, Bak. I always have been. I will be the most powerful wizard to have ever walked Alaris someday. Let Kanzar, Daymian, and anyone else who wants the throne fight it out on their own."

The two elder wizards who had just spoken balked at this, in deep consternation, and moved as if to leave.

"You may be dismissed," Roland said to all the other wizards in the room. "But remember, the Citadel is not taking sides in this war. Those left under my care will not fight but will gather in more apprentices from across the land."

"Who put you in charge, young man?" the eldest wizard spat. "We do not report to you. This Citadel is not in your care."

"You were there on the day of my testing," Roland said. "You know the power I have. By virtue of that power, I now declare that the Citadel is under my control and leadership." Turning back to Bakari with a wink, Roland continued, "I told you I would be great someday."

Bakari nodded. "You should be careful, Roland. You need to take things slowly. Alaris is in enough trouble with Kanzar; they don't need another tyrant." He smiled as he said this and hoped Roland would heed his advice.

Roland waved a hand in the air. "I'm not out to make trouble for anyone. I am only trying to make sure the Citadel is run properly, and I figured I was the best one to do it."

Alli rolled her eyes.

With a flourish, the other wizards dismissed themselves,

staring daggers at Roland as they left.

Bakari needed to ask him something. "Roland, why are those council members deferring to you? You couldn't have taken the test much longer than a week or two ago. Why would they follow a level-one wizard—surely not just because of your charming personality?"

"Bak! You are joking with me." Roland turned to Alli. "Has our young scholar wizard found a sense of humor?"

"Roland?" Bakari waited for his answer.

Before Roland could answer, Alli jumped in for him, saying, "It seems Roland did something in the test that warranted a higher ranking. Even Kanzar's half afraid of him, while other seasoned wizards now yield to him."

Bakari studied Roland's face.

Roland stood and performed a flourishing bow. "Meet Roland Tyre, level-four wizard."

Bakari sat with his mouth open for moment, thinking, and then exclaimed, "That's unheard of."

"I told you I *was magic*."

Bakari opened his eyes wider. "That's it, Roland. In the annals of the past Citadel leaders I have heard that phrase before. I knew I had read it somewhere. Maybe you *are* destined to run the place."

"It is a difficult burden, but I will accept it." Roland laughed. "I am the only level-four wizard here at the moment, so that burden falls on me."

"We need to leave soon," Bakari said.

Roland looked intently at Alli for a moment and then jumped up out of his seat. "Can you wait a few hours?"

"Why?" Alli asked suspiciously.

"Don't you think the Chief Judge would much more appreciate a full wizard by his side?" Roland grinned.

"What are you talking about? Who would go with us?" Alli seemed confused, and Bakari could not follow Roland's words either.

"You!" Roland clapped his hands with delight and yelled for one of the servants. "Ready the testing room, and call back those blasted wizards." Turning back to Alli, he asked, "What if you took the wizard test before you left the Citadel?"

Alli's face turned pale and then filled with joy. "But how?" she asked.

"I am the highest-ranking wizard here. It is my choice," Roland said.

When the preparations were made, Roland led Alli away to be tested. Bakari thought he noticed them standing closer together than before.

In the meantime, Bakari went to the Citadel's library to research as much as he could on Mahli. He inspected the shelves of books, running his fingers longingly along the edges. Memories of his childhood raced through his mind. He breathed out a deep sigh. Bakari hoped he could handle whatever was ahead of him. This was not what he had envisioned for his life.

Strength and comfort came to his mind from Abylar, and Bakari smiled wearily. It was still hard for him to believe that he, Bakari—shy, boring scholar wizard Bakari—was a dragon rider! It was amazing to fly on the back of Abylar. To feel the power of the great beast beneath him, the wind in his face, and their connection in his mind. His smile broadened.

But Bakari discovered that no records regarding Mahli were available from more recently than when the barrier went up. He hoped the country was even still there.

Three hours later, the two riders once again sat on the back of Abylar. Alli couldn't stop grinning. She had passed the test and now held the honor of being a level-three wizard. She glanced down at Roland more affectionately than before.

"Thank you, Roland. You have given me something I can never repay you for." Alli's eyes misted over. "If you ever need me, I will be here for you. I promise!"

This was the only time Bakari had ever seen Roland blush.

"Someday, I need you to let me ride on that dragon of yours, Bak. It's not fair for you to one-up me in something." Roland grinned and chuckled. "A dragon rider? Who would have thought?"

Abylar lifted up off the ground, flew around the Citadel twice, to the cheers of the apprentices there, and then flew directly south.

A few hours later, they passed high over Cassian. Some people began pointing up at them in wonder and fear.

Bakari wondered about Onius and hoped he wouldn't have to fight the old counselor wizard. Roland had said Onius could be trusted, but his closeness to Kanzar gave pause for thought.

* * *

The sun set as they circled high above Orr and then landed among a startled crowd in the town square. A puff of dust flew out from under the dragon as he landed, sending people running for their homes. The air here was dry, and dust seemed to cover everything. Abylar informed Bakari that he did not like it there and needed to get back to the forest and mountains.

Alli jumped off of the dragon's back with a flip in the air and ran to find the Chief Judge. Soon they emerged together with a group of men by his side, a few carrying torches in the growing darkness.

A smile stretched across the Chief Judge's light brown face. He was tired and moved slower. The last few weeks had taken a toll on him.

Bakari hopped down.

"Bakari!" The Chief Judge grasped the scholar wizard's arm. "I see you have been busy."

"I don't have long, Sir. But you instructed me to find out more about the barrier. I guess I found out more than I even hoped for. Abylar here, in egg form, was an Orb that had supplied power to the barrier. Since his birth, the barrier has been down."

That news brought concern and mumbles from the gathering crowd.

Daymian nodded his head in understanding. "You know about Kanzar?"

"Yes," Bakari said. "He named himself as leader of Alaris. Do you intend to fight him?"

"I do." Daymian spread his hands around him to the crowd. "We do. If there was another way, I would listen. But I cannot have that man be our king."

"I will see what I can do to prevent the land from being

devastated in a civil war," Bakari said. "But first, I must return to Mahli with Abylar. I need to find out more about who I am and if there are any more dragon riders. I leave you with Allison Stenos, the newest raised level three wizard, to fight by your side."

The crowd applauded, and Alli blushed with the attention, but she still couldn't wipe the silly grin off her lips.

The Chief Judge regarded Alli with delight. "Wizard now, huh? Does that make you more dangerous?"

Alli laughed. "Me? Dangerous?"

Bakari joined in with them. Laughing felt good. It gave him hope again that maybe things would be better. After giving a hug to Alli and one to the Chief Judge, he climbed back onto Abylar and readied himself.

Bakari waved once again and rose into the air on the back of his incredible blue dragon. He noticed the national flag of Alaris, flying high in Orr. He frowned as he realized Alaris was now committed to civil war. With Kanzar in Cassian, the Chief Judge in Orr, and Roland in the Citadel, the kingdom stood on a reckless course to destruction, unless something could be done. And he, to his chagrin and dismay, might be the key to it all. By virtue of his dragon.

Facing north, he prodded Abylar to fly faster. Under the light of a full moon, they raced over the land of Alaris. From the dry desert to the grassy plains, they flew—back over Cassian, Whalen, and the Citadel—and toward the looming mountains in the north. Spots of snow clung to the tops of their majestic peaks.

Excitement built in his breast as Bakari realized that soon

he would see his own people. Hopefully, they would have the answers he needed to help save Alaris and the surrounding kingdoms from pain and destruction.

"To Mahli!" he yelled triumphantly to Abylar.

With a giddiness of his own and a deep intake of breath, the dragon let out a stream of blue fire that swirled around both sides of Bakari as they flew into the Mahli Mountains and over where the barrier had stood for one hundred fifty years.

# # #

Read THE DRAGON RIDER,
book II in The Alaris Chronicles
to continue the magical adventures of
Bakari, Alli, and Roland.

Other Series By Mike Shelton

The Cremelino Prophecy

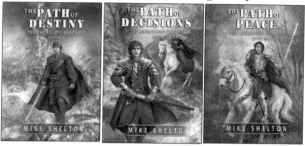

15 years before The Alaris Chronicles and a few kingdoms to the north:

A Prophecy. A Powerful Sword. A Reluctant Wizard.

Darius San Williams, son of one of King Edward's councilors, cares little for his father's politics and vows to leave the city of Anikari to protect and bring glory to the Realm.

When a new-found and ancient magic emerges within him, he and his friends Christine and Kelln are faced with decisions that could shatter or fulfill the prophecy and the lives of all those they know.

Wizards and magic have long been looked down upon in the Realm, but Darius learns that no matter where he goes, prophecy and destiny are waiting to find him.

If you love magic, sword & Sorcery, arthurian style books, and wizards read this first book in The Cremelino Prophecy to find out what destiny awaits Darius.

Sign up on Mike's website at www.MichaelSheltonBooks.com and get a copy of the prequel novella e-book to The Cremelino Prophecy, **The Blade and The Bow**.
Follow Darius and Kelln in one of their more fantastic adventures prior to The Path Of Destiny.

The TruthSeer Archives

On an island far out in the Eastern Sea join a new adventure of magic through the stones of power.

One Little lie won't hurt.

When fifteen year old Shaeleen unexpectedly becomes a TruthSeer, every lie she hears or tells causes her immense physical pain. Just as she's learning to control her new power and curb the pain, she learns a deadly truth that could thrust an entire continent into civil war. She must choose: reveal the truth and stop the pain – or sacrifice her own well-being to protect her kingdom.

The five kingdoms of Wayland have been protected by five gemstones of power for 200 years: strength, intelligence, hearing, speed, and healing. But now those stones are failing. With the help of her brother, Cole and a newfound friend, Orin, Shaeleen sets out to gather and restore the power of all the stones.

But will she succeed before the endless lies destroy her?

About the Author

Mike was born in California and has lived in multiple states from the west coast to the east coast. He cannot remember a time when he wasn't reading a book. At school, home, on vacation, at work at lunch time, and yes even a few pages in the car (at times when he just couldn't put that great book down). Though he has read all sorts of genres he has always been drawn to fantasy. It is his way of escaping to a simpler time filled with magic, wonders and heroics of young men and women.

Other than reading, Mike has always enjoyed the outdoors. From the beaches in Southern California to the warm waters of North Carolina. From the waterfalls in the Northwest to the Rocky Mountains in Utah. Mike has appreciated the beauty that God provides for us. He also enjoys hiking, discovering nature, playing a little basketball or volleyball, and most recently disc golf. He has a lovely wife who has always supported him, and three beautiful children who have been the center of his life.

Mike began writing stories in elementary school and moved on to larger novels in his early adult years. He has worked in corporate finance for most of his career. That, along with spending time with his wonderful family and obligations at church has made it difficult to find the time to truly dedicate to writing. In the last few years as his children have become older he has returned to doing what he truly enjoys – writing!

mikesheltonbooks@gmail.com
www.MichaelSheltonBooks.com
https://www.facebook.com/groups/MikeSheltonAuthor/
http://www.Twitter.com/msheltonbooks
http://www.Instagram.com/mikesheltonbooks

Printed in Great Britain
by Amazon